Prai

Monica Burns

The

Highlander's

Woman

By

Monica Burns

Copyright ©2021 by Kathi B. Scearce
ISBN 978-0-9840277-9-8
Cover Design: Maroli Design Services

Kathi B. Scearce dba Monica Burns - Maroli SP Imprints
P.O. Box 75072
North Chesterfield, VA 23236

Publishing History
Print Edition 1.0 2019 (New Cover)
Print Edition 1.1 2021 (Updated Content)

Acknowledgements

Thanks and endless gratitude to Viviana Izzo (enchantress design & promo) for her awesome help in making this cover shine and all her marketing savvy, plus reminders for this addled brain of mine, along with the occasional kick in the butt, plus the fun late-night conversations and those minion stickers on Facebook. You are truly awesome, Viviana.

Special shout out to my awesome beta reader, Kris Bloom. You are the anchor that keeps my ship from sailing south when I'm supposed to be going north, whether it's sexual tension or overall plot. Your feedback is so valued. Thank you.

Words of thanks and deep appreciation go out to Debbie Samson Fitts and Rhonda Kirby for using their eyes to do line edits for me. Ladies, you rock!

Finally, thank you to my readers in Historical Romance Addicts Too for all you do for me. I love you all ladies, thanks so much for your help in spreading the word about my books.

Author's Note

The Gaelic terms of affection included in this work are derived from different resources, including Outlander Wiki and Dwelly's Great Scots Gaelic - English dictionary.

mo leannan - sweetheart
mo ghràdh - my beloved or my love
a shùgh mo chridhe - my dearest or my darling heart
mo chridhe - my heart

Contents

Acknowledgements   v

Author's Note   vi

Chapter 1   1

Chapter 2   20

Chapter 3   41

Chapter 4   54

Chapter 5   67

Chapter 6   86

Chapter 7   103

Chapter 8   116

Chapter 9   133

Chapter 10   149

Chapter 11   164

Chapter 12   187

Chapter 13   203

Chapter 14   222

Chapter 15   238

Chapter 16   260

Redemption Preview   272

Other Titles by Monica Burns   286

Chapter 1

Late Spring 1897

Lady Patience allowed her future brother-in-law to escort her onto the dance floor. She smiled as he glanced over his shoulder at her sister, Constance, and his grandmother, the Dowager Countess of Lyndham. With an imperialistic demeanor, the elderly lady had ordered Constance to sit with her while sending her grandson away to dance with Patience.

"You mustn't worry," Patience said quietly. "My sister hasn't the slightest idea what we're up to. Your grandmother is playing her part beautifully."

"I'm beginning to regret agreeing to this deception," Lucien Blakemore, Earl of Lyndham, said with a growl. "Constance does *not* like to be manipulated."

"Do you love my sister, my lord?"

"With every fiber of my being." The intensity of emotion in his voice made Patience's heart swell with happiness for her sister.

"Then trust me," Patience said softly. "Let your grandmother work her magic, and all will be well. My sister loves you. She just needs to know that you love her as she is. You do understand what that means."

"Yes," he said with a sharp nod. "Without her gift, she wouldn't be *my* Constance. The woman I fell in love with."

"I have no doubt that when you tell her that, she'll believe you love her," Patience said reassuringly.

With a nod, the earl pulled her into his arms and twirled her out onto the dance floor with the other dancers. Over his shoulder, Patience saw her sister frown at something the dowager countess said. She laughed softly at her sister's obstinate frown.

"I like your grandmother very much, Lucien," Patience said as she smiled up at her partner. "You don't mind that I call you Lucien, do you? After all, we're practically family."

"You're quite confident about all of this," he said with a small smile.

"If I weren't, I would never have approached you with this plan in the first place." Patience laughed mischievously, and over Lucien's shoulder, she saw her sister walking out of the ballroom with Lady Lyndham. She tapped her future brother-in-law on the shoulder.

"The curtain is about to go up on the final act of our little performance. You'd best follow them now." Lucien guided her off the dance floor and carried her hand up to his lips.

"If this works, I'll be forever in your debt."

"Yes, you will, and any Rockwood will assure you I always collect on my debts," Patience said with another laugh. "Now go make my sister happy."

With a look of determination on his face, Lucien nodded, then pushed his way through the crowd and out the door Constance and the dowager had passed through. Left behind, Patience stared after him, feeling satisfied that she'd played a role in securing her sister's happiness.

She closed her eyes for a moment as she remembered her vision of Constance's future happiness. It would be a long and happy one. Of all the Rockwood siblings, Patience was the most forthcoming about her gift. If there was anything people could say about her, it was that she was as eccentric as she was impulsive. Traits that indicated she was a true Rockwood.

But it was her eccentricity that had put off suitors. The ones who *had* come calling had left as soon as they learned she had the ability to see things. Whether it was because she was different from other women or that they envisioned her gift would allow her to spy on them, she had no idea. Over time, she gave up caring and had made herself happy in her role as the spinster in the Rockwood family.

All of that had changed when Julian had entered her life less than a year ago. He'd been neither put off by her impulsive mannerisms nor her gift. The *an dara sealladh*, as Julian called it, was viewed as a gift by his countrymen. The thought of her husband made Patience's heart ache. He'd been in Scotland helping his father, the Crianlarich, for the past two months with estate business.

Despite the multiple letters they shared each week, she missed him more with each passing day. Aunt Matilda had urged her to join Julian in Scotland, but Patience knew it would only make things difficult for them both. If she'd gone, her father-in-law would have ensured her stay was as unpleasant as possible. It would have also made things more contentious between Julian and his father.

The Laird of Crianlarich had taken a dislike to her before she'd ever met him. Instead of taking a Scottish bride as his father had demanded, Julian had chosen her. Patience had been settled firmly on the shelf when Julian had entered her life. He'd pursued her relentlessly from the moment they met at a dinner party she'd accompanied Aunt Matilda to during a stay at Callendar Abbey.

It had taken him only two weeks to propose and convince her to marry him. Just like their whirlwind courtship, their wedding had been accomplished in less than a month. Although Patience was certain Fergus MacTavish loved his son, the Crianlarich was a hard man. She knew that from experience. The man had almost refused to welcome her into the castle, when Julian had taken her home to meet his father and sister after they were married.

Like his father, Julian was incredibly stubborn. He'd threatened to leave Crianlarich Castle and never return if Fergus MacTavish didn't welcome her as Julian's bride. It was the ultimate testimony of her husband's love for her. He'd chosen Patience over his father's objections, but something deep inside said the Crianlarich's vehement reservations had been because he questioned her suitability based on her age and her ability to bear a child.

A vise wrapped itself around Patience's heart. In less than a year of marriage, she'd not been able to bear a son. Perhaps Fergus MacTavish was right. Marrying her might have been the worst thing Julian could ever have done. Suddenly feeling more alone than ever before, she released a sigh. While she had no desire to go home to a cold, empty bed, she had even less of a desire to remain here.

Patience glanced around for the shortest, yet least sociable, path through the crowd to the ballroom exit. She'd taken only a few steps when a frisson brushed across the back of her neck and shoulders. It was like a cool summer breeze skimming across her skin. Confused by the sensation, she lightly touched the spot where her neck and shoulder met, then turned her head to study the dancers leaving the dance floor.

In a gentle wave of motion, the dancers parted, and her breath caught in her throat. From across the dance floor, Patience met her husband's dark gaze. Julian was here. But he hadn't sent word that he would to return to London today. Had he sensed her loneliness in her letters?

Dressed in the formal Scottish attire that had been made popular by the Queen's love of Scotland, her husband looked splendid. His strong, ruggedly beautiful male features were drawing a great deal of attention, and Patience was warmed by the knowledge that Julian belonged to her and no other woman.

He stood with his hands clasped behind his back, his gaze pinned on her as if he was a bird of prey and she was a small hare. It was a familiar, yet delicious, sensation where Julian was concerned. He was far too sure of himself to show jealousy. But if there was one thing her husband had always done well, it was to make certain other men knew she was his. It made her feel cherished and coveted.

As they studied each other across the floor, Patience drank in the fine figure he made in his formal attire. She'd always enjoyed seeing her brothers wear the Stewart colors on formal occasions, but Julian had never just worn his kilts. He made the kilt wear him. Silver buttons adorned his dark blue Prince Charlie jacket and matching waistcoat, which were a stark contrast to his crisply starched white shirt and black tie.

The formal, waist-length jacket lovingly embraced the breadth of him, while an elegant fly plaid was draped over the back of his left shoulder. It was held in place by the large silver brooch his mother had given him when he was a child. He wore the dark-red tartan of the MacTavish clan, and the sporran attached to his kilt hung just below his waist while the kilt brushed the top of his bare knees.

Black hose covered strong, muscular calves, and short tails of material known as flashes were tucked under the top of the hose to brush the sides of his legs. Patience's heart skipped a beat as she remembered how her legs had often tangled with his when they'd made love. Desire spiraled through her as she stared at her husband.

Dark hair fell carelessly across his brow, giving him the appearance of a man who cared little for what others thought of him. His sharp, angular features were those of a proud, arrogant Highlander, which his stance emphasized. In another era, he could have easily passed for a fierce, warrior Scotsman.

Excitement fluttered through her as Julian slowly made his way toward her. Mesmerized, Patience stood frozen as his gaze never left hers. Music filled the air as he stopped in front of her and offered his hand to her. He didn't say a word. Strong and masculine, his hand was fully capable of crushing hers, but it had only ever been used in tenderness with her. Obediently, she placed her hand in his.

The instant she did so, the wave of heat rolling over her made her draw in a sharp breath. Julian's gaze immediately narrowed, and a small smile twitched at the corner of his mouth. God, how she'd missed him. In silence, he pulled her into his arms and swung her out onto the dance floor.

Mere inches separated them, and Patience breathed in his crisp pine scent. It reminded her of the woods at her aunt's estate in Scotland. It was the smell of the outdoors, and it was a heady aroma. Strength radiated off of him, and she stumbled slightly. He immediately pulled her close, his arm hard and solid around her waist.

"Are you the same Lady Patience that is married tae that scoundrel Julian MacTavish?" The softly spoken question reverberated with humor, and Patience arched her eyebrows at him.

"I am indeed, sir," she said. "And what of it, might I ask?"

"I've heard he has been neglecting his wife."

"I had heard that rumor as well, sir." Patience schooled her features into a serious expression and nodded. "Do you suppose he intends to remedy that woeful situation?"

"Aye, that he does." A wicked gleam in his eye, Julian smiled. "How can he nae, when he's married tae the most beautiful woman in the room?"

"With words like that, I think MacTavish will find his wife eager for him to correct such a deplorable state of marital bliss." She laughed as she met his mischievous gaze, and his mouth curved into a sinful smile.

"And what types of pleasure do you think MacTavish's wife would enjoy the most?" Julian's brogue whispered against her skin like a wisp of heather from the highlands.

"As I recall, there is one particular pleasure she likes very much. Of course, it does require one to remove their clothes." Patience looked up at him innocently, then smiled as his eyes darkened with desire.

"You are a sassy wench, Lady Patience. I will remember that when we get home."

Julian swung her around the dance floor, and she basked in the heat of his passionate gaze. A bolt of desire sliced through her as she imagined herself entwined in his arms once they were home. Patience's body grew warm at the delightful images flowing through her mind, but in the next instant, her happiness was overwhelmed by fear and confusion.

Wheels from an overturned carriage spun wildly in the air before fire and smoke surrounded her. No matter what direction she moved, the smoke made it difficult to breathe while flames painfully seared her skin. As the fire raged around her, she tried to find a way out, but she couldn't move.

Suddenly the flames were gone, and in their place was the image of her arm and face covered with horrific scars and mottled flesh. Frightened by the terrible image, Patience gasped as a chill wrapped itself around her and the images receded into the background.

"Patience. What is it, *a shùgh mo chridhe?*" Julian's voice was rough with concern as he stared down at her. "Tell me what you see."

"What?" she whispered in a state of bewilderment.

Someplace deep inside, she noted that even with a frown of worry on his face, her husband was still devastating to the senses. As her bemusement slowly faded, she regained her focus on her surroundings. Suddenly, she realized Julian was literally carrying most of her weight as he continued to twirl her around the dance floor.

"You must put me down, Julian. Someone will think something is amiss."

"That is stating the obvious, my bonnie lass," he said in a grim voice. "But I think it better we leave the floor rather than me setting you on your feet and you tumbling tae the floor."

"Yes," she said hoarsely. "I think you're right."

With two more graceful turns, Julian maneuvered them close to one of the open doors leading out onto the terrace. As they reached the edge of the dance floor, Julian set Patience on the floor in a fluid movement that disguised the fact that he'd been carrying her throughout the dance. His arm still wrapped around her waist, he held her close so she could lean against his side. The moment they merged into the throng congregating around the dance floor, several people expressed concern for her. With a polite yet firm manner, Julian brushed their fears aside as he guided Patience toward the door leading into the dark.

Even the cool air on her face did little to make her feel better. It was far too reminiscent of the icy cold that had engulfed her as her vision had faded. With a small sound of dismay, she glanced down at her arm as she remembered the mottled skin she'd seen on her arm and face. She was no more vain than the next person when it came to being badly scarred. But it was the pain one would have to suffer for such horrible scars she had no desire to endure.

"It will soon pass, *mo leannan*," he whispered against her brow as he guided her toward the outer edges of the walled terrace that overlooked the gardens.

Patience loved hearing him call her sweetheart in Gaelic. It was a soothing sound that warmed and reassured her that she was safe with Julian at her side. With a nod, she breathed the cool air into her lungs as the weakness and disorientation that always accompanied her visions began to ebb away.

When they reached the waist-high wall that bordered the terrace, Julian slowly withdrew his support while ensuring she wouldn't collapse at his feet. Without thinking, Patience stared down at her arm once more, fully expecting to see the horrific scars she'd seen in her vision. The untouched skin made her drag in a breath of relief.

"Tell me what the *an dara sealladh* showed you, *mo leannan*." His brogue gained strength as the Gaelic rolled off his tongue. From the moment they'd met, Julian had only to speak, and she was putty in his hands. She shook her head.

"It was nothing." She dismissed his concern with a shake of her head. Despite her determination to shrug off the vision, it was difficult to completely ignore the vivid memory of her burned face and arm.

"That is nae an answer, Mrs. MacTavish." The commanding note in his voice said he would have the truth from her one way or another.

"But it is the only one I can give you, Julian. There was no rhyme or reason to it." Patience eyed him with a small amount of frustration. The dark frown of worry on his face made her soften her tone. "I saw an overturned carriage with its wheels spinning wildly in the air. Then I was surrounded by flames and smoke. You *know* my gift is sometimes nothing more than symbols representing things happening around me."

"Aye, but your aunt wrote to me that you had the same vision when you were with her last week." He paused for a moment as his large hand caressed her cheek. "She said you were left quite shaken by it."

"Aunt Matilda is far too busy meddling in the affairs of the Rockwood family and not her own personal matters," Patience said with exasperation.

"I think that is something akin tae the pot calling the kettle black, considering you are here tonight meddling in your sister's personal affairs." The amusement in his voice made her jerk in surprise.

"Who told you?" Patience exclaimed, then shook her head as she rolled her eyes. "Aunt Matilda."

"Aye," he chuckled. "She's a veritable fount of information when it comes tae the Rockwood clan. But she was right to send me word of your vision and its effect on you."

"I'm so glad you're home," Patience said softly as she brushed her fingers across his temple. "I've missed you so much."

"Nae, as much as I have missed you, *mo ghràdh*."

The Gaelic term for 'my love' filled her heart with happiness. From the moment they'd met, it had been Julian's brogue that had seduced her. He whispered more endearments as he pulled her into his arms. How she'd missed him these past two months. The nearness of him made her tremble, while the potent male scent of him filled her senses.

"You tremble, lass," he murmured with a hint of laughter in his voice as he bent his head to nibble at her earlobe. "Are you afraid of me?"

"No," she whispered as her body responded to the playful nip on her ear. "I'm only afraid you'll leave again."

"You need nae fear that, *mo ghràdh*. I've nae intention of doing so."

Julian's fingers caught her chin and tilted her head up to kiss her hard. Muscular arms held her in a tight embrace. Her hands splayed against the lapels of his jacket, the hard, solid muscles of his chest pressed into her palms and made her ache to see him undressed. The furious beat of his heart pounded against her fingertips, betraying his excitement.

His tongue slipped past her lips and mated with hers in a furious duel of heat and passion. A primitive need threatened to consume her as her body craved what she'd been denied for so long. In a wanton display of desire, she pressed her body into his and rubbed her hips against his, in a silent demand for what only he could give her.

A dark growl vibrated out of his chest as he caught her hand, and with a rough tug, dragged it down to where he was rock hard beneath his kilt. Knowing he held tight to the tradition of wearing nothing beneath his Scottish garb, her fingers grabbed the side of his tartan and scrunched it up until the plaid material fell over her wrist. With her hand beneath his kilt, she slid her palm up the inside of a sturdy thigh before her fingers wrapped around his erection in a firm grasp.

Thick and hard against her fingers, she stroked him in an upward movement until her thumb ran over the tip of him. A small droplet of wet desire clung to the swollen cap of his hard length, and she smeared it over his foreskin. The low groan rumbling in his chest indicated how much he liked what she was doing. Her hand caressed him again with a slow stroke, and another guttural sound escaped him as he thrust his hips forward against her hand.

Dark hair fragrant with a mixture of soap and bergamot brushed her cheek as he lowered his head to caress the side of her neck and shoulders with his mouth. She tightened her grip on him and slid her fingers upward with a small jerk, then back down to where his sacs were. The tips of her fingers scraped across them, and he jerked at the light caress.

Julian sucked in a sharp breath, and in the next instant, his hands were resting on her shoulders as he held her at arm's length. The desire blazing in his gaze threatened to singe her as she looked up into his dark brown eyes. His breathing harsh and rapid, Julian shook his head as if to clear it.

"Nae here, *mo ghràdh*," he ground out in a rough voice filled with desire. "I intend tae bed my wife in the privacy of our own bedroom. Because once I start, I'll nae be able tae let her out of our bed."

"Then I suggest we leave now, Mr. MacTavish, or I'll be tempted to punish my husband by dancing the night away with as many men as possible." The look of possessiveness that darkened Julian's face made her laugh. "I take it you disapprove of my alternate plan of action."

"Aye," he snapped as he pulled her back into his arms. "You are mine *mo ghràdh*, and dinnae you ever forget it."

"I won't," she said as she pulled his head down and kissed him with a gentleness that demonstrated how much she loved him. The sudden echo of a cane tapping the flagstone patio made Patience jump, and Julian reluctantly released her.

"Lady Patience?" The aristocratic notes of the dowager Countess of Lyndham's voice filtered through the air. Patience moved out of the darkness, followed by Julian.

"I'm here, my lady."

"Excellent, someone said you had come out to the terrace," the woman said as she lifted her lorgnette to inspect Patience's appearance. "You're flushed, child."

"Am I?" Patience touched her cheek with a small laugh of embarrassment.

The stately dowager countess braced both hands on the top of her cane to study Julian, who had moved to stand at Patience's side. The woman arched her eyebrows as her gaze ran up and down his tall frame. With her eyes still focused on Julian, the elderly woman's mouth twisted in a small smile of appreciation.

"*Now* I understand why your cheeks are hot with color, Lady Patience," the woman said with a distinct note of amusement in her voice. Patience could feel her cheeks grow even hotter beneath the dowager countess' amused look. With a laugh, she shook her head at the elderly woman.

"Lady Lyndham, may I present my husband, Julian MacTavish," Patience said with a distinct note of happiness in her voice. Lady Lyndham extended her hand, and Julian kissed the woman's fingers with a small flourish.

"I am honored tae at long last meet the *elusive* Dowager Countess of Lyndham." Julian's smile was designed to melt a woman's heart, and for a brief second, Patience experienced a twinge of jealousy.

"Elusive? *Ha*," the elderly woman said with an unladylike snort of laughter. "You might be able to charm all the women here, but I'm far too old for flattery, my boy."

"I cannae believe that, my lady. A woman should never tire of being told how delightful her company is, nae matter her age."

Lady Lyndham laughed again as she dismissed his flirtation with a wave of her hand, but there was a distinct look of pleasure on her face at Julian's compliment. The dowager turned toward Patience.

"My dear, might I borrow your carriage to take me home? My grandson is otherwise occupied, which is an excellent sign of his reconciliation with Constance," the dowager said with a smile. "But I have no idea how long they'll be, and I confess I am weary from all the excitement."

"Of course," Patience exclaimed as she noted the sudden look of exhaustion that had settled on the elderly woman's face. "We were actually about to leave as well."

"It would be our pleasure tae take you home, Lady Lyndham." Julian offered his arm to the woman. "Shall we?"

With a pace that matched the dowager's, Julian escorted the elderly woman back into the well-lit ballroom.

Patience's eyes fluttered open as she covered her yawn with her hand. Dawn was beginning to peek through the bedroom curtains, and she smiled with happiness. Julian was home, and all was right with her world.

"You're beautiful, *mo leannan*. I will never be able tae have enough of you." The husky words startled her, and she jerked her head in his direction.

"You're awake."

"Aye." Propped up on his elbow, Julian cradled his head in his hand as he stared down at her. "I have been for some time now."

"And you didn't wake me," she teased as she remembered how they'd spent themselves in passionate lovemaking when they'd returned home last night after seeing the Dowager Countess Lyndham home.

"No, I've been watching my wife as she slept." There was something almost reverent in his voice that tugged at her heart. Patience turned on her side and reached up to trail her fingertips across his cheeks until they came to rest on his lips.

"I hope I didn't snore," she said with a mischievous smile.

"Just a gentle roar." Julian's eyes twinkled with amusement, and with a quick shift of her body, she straddled him and pushed his shoulders into the mattress. She stared down at him in mock annoyance.

"A gentle roar? I'll have you know I do *not* snore at all."

"I'm sorry, *mo ghràdh*." He shook his head. "I dinnae lie, but it is a beautiful snore, nonetheless."

"I think perhaps I should punish you for such impertinence, Mr. MacTavish."

"And what punishment might you inflict, madam?" His eyes darkened as his deep chuckle vibrated against her palm.

Patience lowered her head to flick her tongue over his left nipple before she grabbed it with her teeth and gently abraded it. The fresh scent of evergreen mixed with the heat of his skin and brushed against her nose as she breathed in the potent male smell of him. She nipped at him again, savoring the delicious taste of him against her tongue. The action pulled a low growl out of him. His hands cupped her face, but she pulled away to move her mouth lower, to where he was already stiff and hard.

Feathering light kisses across his stomach, she blew gently on his erection before continuing to brush her mouth across his muscular hip, down to his leg. He was hot and all male against her lips. Her mouth brushed over the small birthmark on his hip that reminded her of a bird in flight. Gently, she bit down on the mauve-colored flesh, marking him as hers in much the same way nature had. Another growl rumbled out of him, and she smiled against his skin before grazing her teeth across his leg to his inner thigh.

"If this is your form of punishment, *mo leannan*, I approve."

"Do you?" she lifted her head and blew across his hard, thick length before her tongue flicked out to lightly trace its way up to the salty tip of him.

"Aye," he said hoarsely as his fingers slipped through her hair to cradle the back of her head.

She blew across his erection again before her tongue swirled around the tip of him. Repeating the action, she heard him draw in a sharp hiss of air. Slowly, she licked across the top of him as she looked up at his face. Eyes closed, he arched his hips upward slightly in a silent request for her to continue.

When she didn't move, his eyes opened, and she smiled at the frustration flashing in the dark depths. Their gazes locked, she licked the tip of him once more as she might a spoon covered with the last traces of cream. A low groan reverberated out of him.

"Should I stop?" she murmured as her tongue swirled around him once more.

"God, no." He shook his head forcefully. "But I'd rather have you astride me, lass. I want tae feel you wrapped around me—milking me the way only you can."

Ignoring his words, she swirled her tongue around the cap of his thick length before she took him completely into her mouth. The action pulled a dark cry from his throat as his lower body jerked hard in a display of pleasure. As she slid her mouth up and down over his erection, she applied pressure to the spot just behind his sacs that she'd discovered always enhanced his pleasure. Another groan of desire echoed above her head as she tightened her mouth on him. He jerked again before his hands firmly grasped her arms, and he dragged her upward to make her straddle him.

"No, *mo ghràdh*, you will have your satisfaction as well."

As he spoke, he thrust hard up into her. Pleasure streaked through her as their bodies joined, and he encouraged her to ride him hard. One strong hand curled around her hip, while his other pressed against her breast bone to force her backward until his hard, thick length hit a sensitive spot inside her. The sensation tugged a cry of pleasure from her throat. Hands braced against his hard thighs, she arched her back and worshipped his body with hers as she met his thrusts with equal force.

With each stroke of her body against his, her heart beat faster as she cried out his name as desire cascaded over her. Heat spread its way through every cell in her body until she was on fire. A familiar sensation of euphoria began to build inside her, and she increased the pace of her body rocking against his.

Small ripples of pleasure pulled at her insides as her body gripped his with increasing pressure. The faster she moved against him, the more quickly her body pulsed against his. As her spasms increased, his body continued to pound fiercely against hers until, in a fevered pitch of pleasure, her body jerked to a stop. Her cry of satisfaction echoed over them as her insides shuddered and flexed around his thick erection.

A second later, his shout of pleasure matched hers as he made one last thrust into her, then throbbed hard inside her. The intensity of their joining made her fall forward to press her forehead against hers. Harsh breaths emanated from both of them, and her heart was beating wildly in her chest.

Julian's strong hands lovingly caressed her hips before they slid up along her sides and cupped her face. With slow, tender kisses, his caresses left her, sighing as she allowed her body to settle against his. Her head pressed into the curve of his shoulder, she breathed in his unique aroma. It was reminiscent of the beautiful, harsh, and wild highlands. It emphasized the man holding her came from a long line of fiercely proud and strong Scotsmen.

"I love you, Julian," she whispered against his jaw. At her declaration, he turned his head and pressed his lips to her brow.

"And I you, *mo ghràdh*," he said with a rough edge of emotion in his voice. Nestled in his arms, Patience released a happy sigh, and a chuckle rumbled out of him. "I take it you are satisfied, Mrs. MacTavish?"

"For the moment," she said with a laugh. His hand swatted her behind, and she yelped in surprise.

"My absence has turned you into an insatiable wench." His fingers tilted her chin up so he could see her face. "But 'tis good tae know you missed me."

"I did," she whispered as she stroked a cheek rough with stubble. "Please don't leave me alone for so long if you must go to Crianlarich."

"I dinnae have a choice, Patience. My father had need of me, and I could nae shirk my duty."

Julian stared up at the ceiling, and the tension in him said her refusal to go to Crianlarich had disappointed him more than she realized. Worse, her request just now had sounded as if she didn't want him to go back to his childhood home at all. She rested her hand on his heart as she curled into his side.

"I'm sorry, my darling. I didn't mean it that way. I just missed you."

"Then next time, come with me," he said quietly. The statement made Patience stiffen.

"We both know that will make things more difficult for you." She didn't bother to elaborate that her father-in-law would do his best to make her miserable for the entire time she was at the castle.

"I know my father is a hard man, Patience. But he had thought I would marry a bride of his choosing."

"A bride who didn't have English blood."

"There's more than enough Stewart blood in you tae suit my fancy."

"And what about a bride who cannot give you a son," she choked out.

With a small jerk, she pulled away from him to roll onto her side with her back to him. The Crianlarich wanted a grandson, and she'd failed to produce another heir to the Crianlarich lineage. She wanted nothing more than to give Julian a son, but she had come to believe it would never happen. Julian's hand caressed her shoulder as he kissed the nape of her neck.

"You do your name injustice, Patience. These things take time."

"And time only proves your father right," she said with self-pity. "Marrying me might have been the worst thing you could have ever done."

"Dinnae *ever* say that again," he bit out harshly as, with a sharp tug, he forced her onto her back so he could stare down at her. The anger on his face made her eyes widen. "You're mine, Patience MacTavish. I dinnae marry you because I needed an heir. I married you because I could nae live without you."

The fierce declaration made tears form in her eyes as she stared up at him. His harsh expression softened as he shook his head, then kissed her gently.

"You belong tae me, Patience." A possessive note rang through his whisper as his gaze roved its way across her bare body before returning to her face. "Dinnae ever forget that."

Patience nodded and cupped his cheek with her hand. Julian turned his face into her palm and pressed his mouth hard against her skin.

"Show me I'm yours," she whispered. Desire darkened Julian's face as the back of his hand brushed its way across the base of her neck.

"With pleasure, *mo leannan*. With pleasure," he uttered hoarsely before his mouth captured hers in a passionate kiss.

Chapter 2

The rattle of china pierced Patience's sleep, and she sat up to see Julian seated at the breakfast table next to their bedroom window.

"Do you intend to spend the rest of the day in bed, Mrs. MacTavish?" he said without looking at her.

The amusement in his voice made Patience toss a pillow at his head. For the past three days, he'd been the one insistent on spending most of the day in bed. Julian easily batted the stuffed headrest aside and turned his head to grin at her. She arched her eyebrows at him.

"I think I will, Mr. MacTavish. I feel quite spent," she said with a feigned sigh of exhaustion. "Won't you join me?"

Patience deliberately allowed the sheets to fall to her waist as she smiled sweetly at him. The newspaper in his hand fell carelessly onto the table as desire swept across his face. A wicked smile curved his sensual lips while his hot gaze caressed her until her entire body ached for him to touch her. His smile widened, obviously aware of her arousal, before regret swept across his face. With a sigh, he shook his head.

"I can think of nothing that would give me greater pleasure, *mo ghràdh*. But if I come back tae bed, I'll nae leave it for the rest of the day." Julian's eyes darkened. "And as much as I would love pleasuring you until you truly *are* spent from my touch, I must meet with Lord Mayberry this morning."

"I thought you said your meeting with him was tomorrow afternoon," she said with a surprised frown. For a brief instant, she could have sworn Julian looked guilty before he smiled and shook his head.

"Did I? I obviously confused my dates," he said with a sinful twist of his lips. "But how can I be faulted for forgetting the order of my appointments when my wife bewitches me so?"

"If I'm so bewitching, how are you able to resist me now?" she teased as she crawled out of bed and moved toward him. She smiled at the desire in her husband's eyes as his gaze roamed over her naked body.

"God help me, Patience. You'll be the death of me," he muttered as she sat down in his lap.

One arm wrapped around his neck, she ran her hand across his shirt and bent her head to kiss his cheek. His hand warmed her skin as he lifted her bare breast to suckle her. A soft mewl escaped her lips, and she arched backward, enjoying the delightful sensation of his mouth tugging on her nipple. With one last nip at the tip of her, he pulled her head down and kissed her hard. Then, in an authoritative move, he set her back on her feet, turned her around, and swatted her bottom.

"Either get dressed or get back in bed. You're are tae much of a distraction *mo leannan*, and it's nae just Lord Mayberry I have tae meet," he growled with frustrated affection. "I have several matters of business to attend tae for my father as well."

"All right," she said with disappointment. "I have correspondence I've neglected for the past three days. When I'm finished, I'm sure I can find something to occupy my time while you complete whatever business you need to do for your father."

Patience circled the bed to pick her night robe up off the floor. The mere mention or thought of her father-in-law always put a damper on her mood. No matter how often Julian reassured her that his father wouldn't come between them, it didn't make her father-in-law's contempt for her any easier to bear. She slipped her arms through the sleeves of her robe, biting her lower lip.

The last time she'd seen Fergus MacTavish, Laird of Crianlarich, had been a few weeks after she and Julian were married. The Crianlarich had made her stay so unpleasant she'd vowed not to go back. Although Julian had shielded her whenever he could, it had not stopped his father's vicious taunts and insults when they were out of Julian's hearing.

Not even the occasional presence of Julian's younger sister, Muireall, had provided any real buffer from the Crianlarich's acerbic tongue. Patience's fingers fumbled with the sash of her robe at the painful memory. A strong hand gripped her shoulder as Julian forced her to turn around.

"I've told you before, Patience. My father will *never* come between us." Reassurance reverberated in his voice as he cupped her face with his hands and kissed her gently. "I married you because I love you."

"He might not come between us, but I'll never come close to having his approval if I don't give him a grandson. Your heir," she whispered as she wrapped her arms around his waist and pressed her cheek against the soft, lightweight wool of his jacket.

"I told you the other night that it takes time, *mo leannan.*"

"How much time?" She pulled away from him as tears welled in her eyes. "How long before you believe what I already know? I've fulfilled your father's prediction. I'm an Englishwoman who will never give you a son."

"That's enough, Patience." Anger darkened Julian's face as he eyed her sternly. "A son—or daughter for that matter—was *never* a condition of my marrying you."

"But you can't say you're not disappointed."

"Can you?" he asked gently. "I know you want tae give me a son, *mo ghràdh*, but if it doesn't happen, I'll nae stop loving you."

Patience leaned into him again, and Julian engulfed her in his embrace. Even though she might be barren, he still loved her. The realization eased some of her heartache, but not completely. She longed to have Julian's child.

"I must go, *mo leannan*," Julian said with a tender kiss. "I cannae miss my meeting with Lord Mayberry about the land values tax, and if I stay here with you, I'll most definitely nae be meeting with the man."

"Go, I'm sure you'll be as persuasive with his lordship as you always are with me."

Patience smoothed the lapels of his jacket, her fingers brushing across the Clan MacTavish brooch his mother had given him as a child. Her husband was far from a vain man, but the jewelry was one of his most cherished belongings, and he wore it always.

With one last kiss, Julian strode from the room. Listlessly, she moved to the breakfast table to scrape butter on a piece of toast. Patience took a bite, and hoping for one last look at Julian, she parted the window curtains slightly and looked down at the street. A hackney pulled up to the sidewalk just as Julian reached the bottom of the front steps.

About to let the sheer material fall back into place, Patience froze as she saw a woman lean forward to extend her hand to Julian. Fiery auburn hair and a creamy complexion highlighted the woman's beautiful face. Una Bensmore. She'd met the woman during her first and only stay at Crianlarich Castle.

The Scotswoman was a childhood friend who the Crianlarich had made clear was the bride he'd hand-picked for Julian. The woman's flirtations with Julian had been just as upsetting as her father-in-law continuing to point out Patience's inadequacies whenever possible. Why was Una in London, and why here at their house? Her attention swiftly jerked back to Julian, who nodded at something the woman said.

The instant she saw Julian start to look upward, Patience dropped the curtain and drew away from the window. When she believed it safe, she peeked through the slit in the curtains again. She regretted doing so as she watched Julian climb into the two-seat cab with Una. Worse, she saw the woman looking up at her with a smile that reminded Patience of a cat who'd stolen cream from the pantry.

Patience immediately dropped the window curtain as jealousy reared its head. Why hadn't Julian mentioned he would be seeing Una this morning? It was a rhetorical question. He'd most likely chosen to remain silent so as not to upset her. No doubt he'd remembered the fight they'd had about the woman during Patience's one and only stay at Crianlarich Castle. They'd been married only two weeks before Julian had taken her home to meet his family. Except for the raw passion that existed between them, they'd known little about each other. Their short courtship meant misunderstandings had been inevitable. She flinched at the memory of the dinner party her father-in-law had arranged.

When Robert Bensmore and his daughters had arrived at the castle, Fergus MacTavish had spent the night subtly pointing out Una's exceptional qualities whenever Julian was out of earshot. It didn't help matters that Una had the face of an angel. The woman had captivated Julian the entire evening. It had been the most painful thing Patience had ever experienced, and she was grateful when she was able to say goodnight. She'd hadn't been in her room more than a couple minutes when Julian entered with a frown on his face.

"Are you nae feeling well?"

"I'm fine," she said coolly.

"You barely spoke to anyone during the meal," he said with a frown. "Even Una mentioned it when saying good night."

"I find it difficult to believe the woman even realized I was in the room," Patience said without any trace of the bitterness that was eating away at her insides.

She was grateful for her ability to respond in a calm, even tone of voice when what she wanted to do was scream at him. Not bothering to look in Julian's direction, she sat down at the dressing table and undid her hair to brush it. Julian came to stand behind her and touched the side of her neck.

"There's nae need to be jealous, *mo leannan.*"

His soft laugh infuriated her. The man had no idea what it had been like to watch Una fawn over him, all the while sending her the occasional gloating look. Patience looked up at him, and his amused expression made her spring to her feet as anger flowed hot and fast through her veins. Patience's movement was so fast it sent the dressing table bench toppling to the floor and caused Julian to stare at her in stunned surprise. She glared at him.

"Do *not* laugh at me," she bit out fiercely. Julian's gaze narrowed.

"I am nae laughing at you, Patience." His body was stiff with resentment as his brogue thickened with irritation.

"You *are*," she said in a tight voice. "Do you think I don't know why your father asked the Bensmores to come this evening?"

"The Bensmores are family friends." Julian shook his head with exasperation. "Caitriona, Una, and I played together as children. My father has them for dinner quite often."

"She isn't *just* a family friend. She's the woman your father chose to be your bride."

"It dinnae matter what my father wished. You're the one I married," Julian said angrily. "Una has never been anything more than a close family friend."

"Close friend?" she sneered and glared at him for being so obtuse where the other woman was concerned. "From Miss Bensmore's manner tonight, I would have supposed your relationship much more intimate."

"You go tae far, Patience." Fury made his voice hard and flat.

"Do I? The woman made it quite obvious you had only to ask, and she would slip into your bed," she bit out as fear and suspicion became an insidious vine snaking its way through her.

"You dinnae have much faith in your husband's love, Lady Patience." The formal address stung. He'd never spoken to her like this before. His expression was grim, and she saw the flicker of painful disappointment in his dark eyes.

"No more than you have in me when I point out the obvious," she snapped as she fought to keep the tears out of her voice. She turned away from Julian and moved toward the bed, but he followed her, the heat of him warming her back. His fingers trailed a light path across her shoulder.

"I love you, Patience. I have since the moment I first laid eyes on you."

"That is the crux of the problem," she bit out as she whirled around to face him. "We barely know each other."

Patience shook her head. How could she make Julian understand how painful the evening had been for her—how inadequate she felt, even now when she was with him? Throughout the meal and afterward, his father had continued to point out Una's qualities to Patience. Virtues, the man had made clear, she lacked.

Julian and Una shared a common past, and the woman didn't have an ounce of English blood. The woman had flirted with Julian the entire evening and ignored Patience. Something the Crianlarich had encouraged by having Una share tales of when she and Julian were children. Patience had been the only one excluded from the stories Una had regaled everyone with this evening.

Even Julian's younger sister Muireall had heard of Julian's and Una's escapades before tonight. This evening's dinner party had illustrated just how out of place and unwelcome Patience was at Crianlarich Castle. Worst of all, it made her believe the old adage of marrying in haste only to repent at leisure was true in their case. They knew very little about each other.

"We have the rest of our lives tae learn about each other, *mo ghràdh*," he said with quiet reassurance.

"But *she* already knows all about you. She knows your past. I don't. Una Bensmore knows what makes you happy. I saw that tonight when you laughed at almost everything she said," Patience said as her voice quavered. "I understand now what your father meant when he said I'm unworthy to bear the MacTavish name."

"Unworthy—I dinnae give a damn what my father says," Julian snarled as his hands grasped her by the shoulders, and he tugged her close. "You are *more* than worthy of bearing my name, Patience. You have Stewart blood in you, and dinnae forget that. But the only thing that really matters is that you make me happy because you chose me."

Patience was abruptly jerked back into the present by the quiet knock on the bedroom door. Maggie, her maid, entered the room when Patience called out for the servant to enter. Patience forced a smile to her lips and gestured toward the tray.

"I'm done with breakfast, Maggie."

"Yes, my lady." The maid picked up the tray then turned toward her. "Shall I come back to help you dress, Lady Patience?"

"No, I can manage. Thank you," Patience said in a distracted voice.

She didn't even hear the maid leave the room. All she could see in her mind's eye was Una staring up at her with a triumphant expression on her face. Until this moment, Patience had not realized how insecure her father-in-law's vicious insinuations had made her feel about her marriage. Inwardly, she'd told herself to dismiss the man's cruel words. She'd worked hard to forget the innuendos the laird had levied in her direction.

Patience found it hard to believe the man she loved had married her just to spite Fergus MacTavish and defy the laird's demand that Julian make Una Bensmore the next lady of Crianlarich Castle. But it was now clear how much damage the man's words had done. The Crianlarich had cultivated doubt in her as to Julian's love for her.

"You're worried about nothing, Patience MacTavish," she said to an empty room. "Julian told you the woman was nothing more than a friend."

An insidious voice in her head reminded her that Julian had made no mention of a meeting with Una.

"Of course he wouldn't," Patience asserted with false confidence to the empty room. "He knows how much it would upset you. And the last thing the man wants is another argument like the one you had at Crianlarich Castle."

"Yes, but what about his appointment with Lord Mayberry? You must admit that the man appeared somewhat guilty when you questioned him about his appointment." replied a surreptitious voice in the back of her head.

"*Now* you're being ridiculous," she snapped as she sat down at the dressing table and glared at her reflection. "When Julian comes home, you'll simply ask him why Una had met him at their front door and why he'd gone with her in the cab."

A short while later, she was seated at her secretaire, working on her correspondence. As she worked her way through the stack of letters and invitations, she saw one from Louisa. Eagerly, she opened her sister's letter and read the short note. It was an invitation for them to join the family at Westbrook Farms at the end of the week for a family celebration of Constance and Lucien's engagement.

Julian and she always enjoyed the Rockwood family gatherings, and in a brief note, she accepted her youngest sister's invitation. Finished with her correspondence, she decided the spring weather was lovely enough to spend the afternoon reading in the park.

Book in hand, she made her way to Hyde Park. A number of acquaintances were enjoying the spring day like her, and their short conversations were pleasant interruptions to her reading. It was late in the afternoon when she decided to return home.

She closed her book and looked up to see Lord Mayberry heading her way. With a smile, she rose from her bench and walked along the park's graveled path toward the elderly gentleman. As they reached each other, he bowed in her direction.

"Good afternoon, Lady Patience," he said with a jovial smile. "I see I'm not the only one enjoying the late afternoon warmth of this delightful spring day."

"It is lovely out, isn't it," she said with a laugh. "I'm certain you're happy to be outdoors after a long day of parliamentary matters."

"Indeed. It has been a most contentious day." Mayberry winced as if remembering something unpleasant.

"Well, I do hope Julian wasn't one of the more argumentative moments of your day. My husband can be quite passionate about things that are important to him."

"MacTavish? Was I supposed to meet with your husband today, Lady Patience? I know we met this past Thursday to discuss the land value tax, but I don't believe we had an appointment for today." Mayberry's startled response made her heart slam into her chest with fear.

Julian had met with Lord Mayberry last week. Two days before he'd returned home to her. Julian had lied to her. He'd lied about meeting with Lord Mayberry today, and he'd said nothing about returning to town this past Thursday. Of course, he'd never said he'd arrived on Saturday either. She'd simply assumed he'd returned from Crianlarich that afternoon and met her at Marlborough House for the royal couple's annual ball. But he'd not bothered to mention it to her either.

Why would he lie? The memory of Julian climbing into Una's hackney cab earlier in the day had never been far out of her thoughts. Now Lord Mayberry's words had renewed the fears she'd managed to dismiss this morning. Her gaze met the elderly gentleman's puzzled look, and she realized she'd been silent far too long.

"I must have misunderstood Julian. I thought he'd said something about meeting with you today," she said as her throat threatened to swell shut.

"I don't recall our discussing the need for another meeting when we met last Thursday or was it Friday?" the man mused more to himself than Patience. The frown wrinkling his brow suddenly vanished to reflect confidence. "No, it was Thursday as it was the afternoon I met with Her Majesty's cabinet."

"Perhaps he simply meant to come by your office to make another appointment," she said quietly. Lord Mayberry's conviction that he'd met with Julian on Thursday confused and alarmed her. It also heightened her fears about Julian climbing into Una's hackney cab.

"Are you on your way home?" Lord Mayberry asked.

"Yes, Julian and I are to have dinner with the Dumbartons this evening."

"Twilight will be upon us shortly. Perhaps I should walk you home," Lord Mayberry said with a note of concern in his voice. "I would hate for something untoward to happen to you."

"Oh no, that's quite all right. Our house is only a few minutes away," Patience said with a quick shake of her head. The prospect of having a polite conversation with anyone at the moment made her head ache. She forced a smile. "But thank you all the same."

"All right then. If you're certain," the man said with obvious reluctance. Patience patted his arm in a reassuring manner.

"I promise you, I shall be fine."

Her response made the concern on his face ease somewhat, and with a smile, he squeezed her hand. The man was about the age her own father would have been if he were alive, and Lord Mayberry's fatherly manner was endearing.

"Very well," he said. "Tell MacTavish that I look forward to seeing him soon."

"I shall do that," she said with a nod as she turned away and headed for home.

With each step she took, Patience tried hard to dismiss the possibility that Julian might have lied to her about his meeting with Lord Mayberry. But the man's certainty that he and Julian had met on Thursday and not today increased her fears. Then there was the fact she'd not seen Julian until Saturday evening. Where had he been all that time? An image of Julian stepping into a small hackney cab with Una filled her head. Patience bit down on her lower lip as she slammed the door close on the ominous direction of her thoughts.

There *had* to be a reasonable explanation for everything. She simply needed to trust Julian. The idea was good in principle, but her emotions still made it difficult to keep her mind from running amok with the worst of all possibilities. Patience arrived home eager to have Julian set her mind at ease. Their butler, Hobbs, met her at the door as if he'd been expecting her.

"Has Mr. MacTavish returned?" She removed her hat and glanced at the man.

"No, my lady," the butler said with a shake of his head. "But a letter arrived for you a short time ago, and it appears to be Mr. MacTavish's handwriting. I placed it on your secretaire."

"Thank you, Hobbs."

Heart pounding wildly in her chest, Patience hurried into the small salon and retrieved the letter. The parchment crackled softly as she pulled the note out of the envelope.

Patience,

> *Forgive me, mo leannan, but my father's business has run longer than I expected. I shall not be home in time to accompany you to the Dumbartons party. Go without me, and I will see you when you return. I miss you mo ghràdh. I will be home as soon as possible.*

Your loving husband,
Julian

The paper crackled as her fingers crumpled the note. The sudden image of Una Bensmore sent a wave of fear crashing over her. The invisible force of emotion dragged her downward until she was certain she was drowning. Was she losing Julian? She swiftly crushed the thought.

Julian loved her. He'd said so numerous times over the past few days. Patience smoothed out Julian's note to read it again. None of the words had changed. There had to be an explanation, and only Julian could answer her questions. Suddenly, the idea of going out for the evening was far from palatable.

She wrote a quick note to the Dumbartons that she was unwell and that Julian had refused to leave her side. The irony in her excuse was not lost on her. Her husband was at the moment far more devoted to his father's business affairs. Affairs that seemed to include Una Bensmore. The fact that she was questioning even his note made her chest tighten. The Crianlarich would be pleased to know how much doubt his words had instilled in her.

Mrs. Smathers prepared a roast chicken for her dinner, but she was too heartsick to eat. On the fireplace mantel, the clock chimed one hour after another until she was growing frantic with worry. At ten o'clock, another note from Julian arrived. This one stated the meeting he was in was at a critical stage and would run into the early morning hours. When he finished, he would sleep at the club as he didn't wish to disturb her by coming in so late. Although she was relieved he wasn't the victim of thieves, lying in a gutter somewhere, she found herself questioning every word in the note. Was he lying to her?

Eyes closed to hold back her tears, she didn't want to believe all the horrible thoughts racing to confront her. All she could think about was the memory of Una's smug expression as she'd looked up at Patience from the cab this morning.

Lethargically, Patience slipped into the cold, lonely bed. The tears she'd been holding back all day began to flow, and she sobbed herself to sleep. It was a fitful sleep, and she woke up several times during the night until she finally rose at the first light of dawn. When Maggie arrived with her breakfast, the maid stared at Patience in surprise.

"You're up bright and early, my lady."

"I didn't sleep well," she said quietly as she picked up the newspaper off the breakfast tray.

"He'll be home soon, my lady. I'm sure of it."

"Thank you, Maggie." She dismissed the maid with a small smile.

Patience poured herself a cup of tea then pushed aside the plate of eggs and bacon Maggie had brought up to her. She had no appetite at all. The society pages rustled in her hands as she skimmed the gossip columns. Reading the columns was a vice, but it usually afforded her a laugh at the ridiculous antics of people. As she read the column, a small paragraph caught her eye, and she stiffened.

> *A certain Scotsman was seen in the company of an auburn-haired beauty not his wife or sister on maple street looking at houses. has the man decided to take A mistress? we wonder what lady P would say?*

For a moment, Patience remained frozen in her seat as the newsprint fell from her fingers. He was looking for a house with Una. And she was certain it was Una. It had to be. Bile rose in her throat. Men did not look at houses unless they were with a wife—or mistress.

"Don't be ridiculous, Patience MacTavish. You know quite well how gossip can change the most innocent of events into something far more ugly," she muttered as she rose to her feet and proceeded to dress for the day.

Patience spent most of the day lethargically going about her daily routine. It kept her occupied until later in the afternoon when she was in the salon. She was hopelessly attempting to repair the needlepoint on a chair cover when she heard voices at the front door. Setting aside her botched embroidery, she rose to her feet as Hobbs announced Una Bensmore. Patience had no time to recover from her amazement as the woman sailed into the room. Hands clasped in front of her, Patience met the woman's calculating gaze with what she hoped was an expression of detached serenity.

"Good afternoon, Miss Bensmore," Patience greeted the woman politely.

"I'm here to see Julian," the woman said in a musical brogue that was as beautiful as her face.

"I'm sorry, but he's not here at the moment," Patience said with a forced smile. "Would you care to leave a message?"

"No, it can wait," Una said as she stared at Patience with a crafty expression on her face. "You were surprised to see me yesterday morning."

The direct confrontation made Patience flinch, but she managed to maintain her composure. With a shrug, she frowned as if confused by the woman's statement.

"You're a friend of Julian's. Why would I be surprised?" she lied.

"This is true, but I would have thought this morning's society page would have explained why I was with Julian yesterday."

Panic careened through Patience. Was the woman actually confirming the gossip? Had Julian really taken Una house hunting yesterday? If that was true, there was only one conclusion she could draw from the knowledge. She immediately rejected the idea. Julian wouldn't take a mistress. Desperately she fought back the growing fear inside her and struggled not to let the other woman see it.

"My husband is a thoughtful man and always willing to help his friends. I hope you manage to find something to your liking."

"Aye, I did, but then Julian is, as you say, a thoughtful mon, but I think you already know Julian and I are much more than friends." The woman's sly expression made Patience swallow hard as fear snaked through her. An artful smile curved Una's lovely mouth. "Do you nae wonder why he came back to town early without telling you or why he didn't come home to you last night?"

"I'm afraid I don't understand," she lied. "Julian sent me a note saying he'd been detained on business."

"As you know, we were childhood sweethearts. The Crianlarich and I were certain Julian would marry me, but he dinnae," Una said as loathing twisted her lovely features in an ugly mask. "He married an Englishwoman. Nae a Scotswoman."

"I might have English blood, but I have Stewart blood too. *Royal* blood," Patience bit out with fierce pride. "And I didn't steal Julian away from anyone."

Patience shook her head as she remembered Julian's whirlwind courtship. She had come to accept the fact that every man who'd ever courted her had eventually left without making an offer. The last thing she'd expected when she'd been perfectly happy sitting on the shelf had been a romance with a Scotsman whose voice was sin itself. A man whose kisses made her melt. But it also pointed out once again how little she knew of her husband.

"Does nae matter. I've stolen him away from you. Tis my bed he sleeps in now," Una said with a smile that reminded Patience of a beautiful rose full of thorns dipped in poison.

"Why should I believe you?" Patience said with what she hoped was a look of annoyed disbelief. The woman had to be lying. Julian would never betray her.

"Because I can prove Julian was in my bed." The confidence in the woman's voice sent a shiver of fear through Patience.

"And how do you propose to do that?" she scoffed.

"Because I know about his birthmark." Una's words sent ice sluicing through Patience's veins.

"Birthmark?" she whispered as the image of the birthmark on Julian's left hip flitted through her head.

"Aye," Una said with a malicious smile. "'Tis a reddish mark that looks like a bird in flight."

It was as if the woman had ripped Patience's heart out of her chest. Only a woman who'd shared Julian's bed would know about his birthmark. In shock, Patience jumped slightly as the other woman extended her hand.

"I also have the brooch his mother gave him. I thought you might need further proof that I have convinced Julian we belong together."

"His brooch?" Patience said hoarsely as her disorientation forced her to grasp the back of the chair at her side.

"Aye, he left it behind last night, when…"

"When he spent the night with you," Patience choked out despite the knot threatening to close her throat shut.

"Aye."

The woman's mouth curved in a smug, satisfied smile as she pulled something from her purse. She extended her hand and offered the large, round pin to Patience. Her hand shook as she reached for the silver piece of jewelry bearing the familiar crest of the MacTavish clan. Julian's mother had given him the brooch just before she'd died. He'd only been seven at the time, and he cherished the large pin, always wearing it on his shoulder whether he was wearing his fly plaid or not. It was not something he would lose.

As her fingers brushed against the other woman's, Patience sucked in a sharp breath at the image that flashed in front of her eyes. Una holding a baby. A split second later, the vision changed to the familiar images of spinning carriage wheels and the out-of-control blaze that surrounded her.

The chaotic imagery lasted only a few seconds, but it made Patience even more unsteady on her feet. She swayed, and her fingers dug into the chair's cushion. Her gaze met the woman's startled expression.

"You have the *an dara sealladh*," the woman breathed, her voice filled with awe before the woman paled and an uneasy look swept across her face.

"Leave, and never come back here again," Patience said in a cold, flat voice. "If you do, I'll have the magistrate order your arrest for threatening me."

"You would nae dare," Una said with a swaggering look of contempt. "Julian will nae let you."

"Is that a challenge?" Patience said as a sudden rage swept through her. Steadied by a wave of anger unlike any she'd ever known, she stepped toward the other woman keeping her voice low and intimidating. "If there's one thing a Rockwood never refuses, it's a challenge. Now leave."

Fear crossed Una's face as Patience pointed toward the salon door. With an abrupt nod, the other woman headed toward the exit. As she reached the doorway, Una looked over her shoulder with a sneer curling her lips.

"And you should remember this, my lady. If there's one thing, I can give Julian that you cannae, tis an heir."

Patience drew in a sharp breath as the image of Una and her child filled her head again. The moment the woman was gone, Patience staggered to the couch to collapse into it with a soft sob. The pain ripping through her was almost unbearable. How could Julian have said he loved her then betray her in such a deplorable manner?

No, how could she believe Una? Julian had told her that he loved her. Just yesterday morning, he'd made love to her with the same passion she felt for him. It was difficult to believe he could share another woman's bed when he was so tender and loving every time he touched her. Patience trembled as she remembered their passionate lovemaking over the past several days since his return from Scotland. The man had barely allowed her to leave his sight. Had those moments been nothing but a dream—a drama played out by him and for what purpose? None of it made sense, and yet all the pieces connected to form a picture of betrayal.

Confused, hurt, and desperate not to believe Una's cruel words, Patience stared down at Julian's brooch as tears slid down her cheeks. The disappearance of his brooch might have been easy to dismiss. It could have fallen off in the cab. Una could have found it, and Julian would be none the wiser. But the most damning evidence of all was Una's knowledge about Julian's birthmark. How else could she have known about it unless she'd seen Julian undressed?

The knowledge taunted Patience with a horrifying intensity that threatened to bring her to her knees. She shook her head. No, she wouldn't allow that to happen. She was a Rockwood. Slowly, she wiped the tears off her face and stood up.

Patience listlessly walked around the room, trying to reject the evidence Una had shared. She drew in a sharp breath at the memory of her vision. The woman had said she could give Julian a child. The fact that she and Julian were childless was a terrible source of pain to them both. Had he betrayed her because he wanted a son?

Although he'd consistently brushed aside his need for an heir, she found it hard to believe he wasn't disappointed she'd failed to have a child. Nausea gripped her insides. His lie about his appointment with Mayberry and his failure to tell her that he'd returned to town early, yet hadn't come home, was damning enough. She sent up a fervent prayer that somehow Julian would have a rational explanation for everything.

She had no idea how long she'd been standing at the window attempting to sort things out when she jumped at the sound of Julian's voice in the hallway. Patience froze at the window as a sense of impending doom made her mouth go dry. She loved him so much, and yet she knew she would never be able to live with him if he really had betrayed her.

But she refused to find him guilty without hearing what he had to say. She could only hope his explanation would destroy the doubt stirred to life by his father's cruel insinuations, Una's claims of Julian's infidelity, and the lies her husband had told.

Chapter 3

J ulian's step was filled with weariness as walked along the sidewalk leading home. The sun would be setting soon, and he couldn't remember the last time he'd been so tired. He'd missed falling asleep with Patience in his arms last night, but tonight would be different.

With a grimace, he remembered where he'd spent the last thirty-six hours. If it hadn't been for Una yesterday morning, he would never have found Caitriona on his own, nor would he have uncovered the truth of her situation.

Of all the people she could have asked for help, Caitriona had written to her sister. But at least Bensmore's eldest had sent for someone rather than refusing to ask for help at all. The two women had never been close, but Una had surprised him in her efforts to care for her older sister. She'd been good to Caitriona. Five months ago, Caitriona left Bensmore Farms saying she intended to stay with friends in Edinburgh.

When Bensmore didn't hear from her after a week, he'd gone to Edinburgh in search of his daughter. He'd returned home a broken man. After more than a month of searching, Bensmore had not found any leads as to Caitriona's whereabouts. It was at that point that the Crianlarich had decided Julian was to lead a new search for his old friend. For almost the past two months, Julian had been searching Edinburgh and the Highlands for Caitriona.

His efforts had led him to London late last week, where he followed up on two separate leads. Unwilling to worry Patience or explain his late-night visits to the seedier parts of town, he'd quietly taken up residence in a small hotel. Ever since his father had tasked him with finding Bensmore's eldest child, Julian had found it odd that his father was so adamant about sparing no expense in the search for Bensmore's daughter.

Now he understood why, and the reason behind his father's insistence that Julian find Caitriona disgusted him. A noise of outrage bellowed softly out of him. His father had a great deal to answer for when it came to Caitriona's downfall. The memory of walking into the slums where she'd been living had horrified him. Worse, she'd been in the beginning stages of labor when he'd arrived.

It had taken all of yesterday morning to find a competent doctor of discretion as well as a new home for her and her child. They'd moved Caitriona into the house Julian had rented shortly after her labor had begun to intensify. Julian was certain the move had made Caitriona's labor more difficult despite the doctor's reassurances that moving her would do no harm.

She'd died little more than two hours ago, leaving her son in his care. The memory of her wan features and final confession struck deep at the very core of him. In hindsight, he realized he should never have sworn an oath not to reveal Caitriona's secret. It was bad enough his father had extracted an oath of silence from him about his search for Caitriona. He didn't like keeping secrets from Patience, especially when Caitriona's confession would impact them both in the future.

He grimaced. Una had disappeared shortly after Caitriona's death. He'd assumed she wanted to grieve in solitude and left him to make funeral arrangements. He understood why Caitriona had entrusted the boy's care to him. Una was far too irresponsible to be the child's guardian.

Not that it mattered because Una had already declared she had no intention of taking the child home with her. At least the wet nurse had agreed to care for Caitriona's son until he could make other arrangements.

Wearily, he climbed the steps of the house and walked through the front door. Hobbs appeared from the back of the hall as Julian dropped his hat on the half-moon table pressed against the wall of the small foyer.

"Hello, Hobbs," he said quietly. "Is Mrs. MacTavish in?"

"Yes, sir," the butler gestured toward the salon. "I believe she's in the salon, reading."

"Thank you."

Julian frowned at the other man's observation. There were at least another two hours of sunshine left, and it was still beautiful outside. He knew Patience loved to read in the park when the weather was like today. For her to be inside meant something was wrong. He opened the door to the salon to see Patience standing at the window.

Every time he looked at her, he remembered the first time he'd seen her. The sound of her laughter had lured him to her. But it had been the golden warmth in her beautiful brown eyes and the touch of her hand in his that had sealed his fate.

His father was wrong. Patience was the best thing that had ever happened to him. It didn't matter that they had no children. All that mattered was that she was his to love. If he ever lost her, it would destroy him. As she turned to face him, Julian's body hardened with tension. She looked as if there had been another death in the family.

The loss of her sister-in-law in childbirth last year had been difficult for the entire Rockwood clan, but Patience had been extremely fond of Georgina. It had been almost as devastating for her as it had been for her brother, Caleb.

Now, as he stared at her pale, stoic expression, he feared the worst.

"What is it, *mo ghràdh*? What's happened?"

"Where have you been?" she asked hoarsely. The question caught Julian off guard, and he stared at her in surprise as his insides twisted with guilt.

"I sent a note explaining where I was. Did you nae receive it?" The fact that he was skirting her question with misdirection made him uncomfortable, but there was little he could do about it without breaking his oath of silence to Caitriona.

"I received it," she said in a flat voice.

"Will you forgive me, *mo leannan*?" Wearily, he rubbed the back of his neck.

"Did your business with Lord Mayberry go well?" The quiet question set off a warning bell in his head. He frowned as he met her cold gaze. Never in the entire time they'd known each other had she ever looked at him like that. It was almost a look of contempt. She turned away from him to stare out the window once more.

"Aye," he said as another twinge of guilt lashed at him for lying to her. "You were right about my appointment with Mayberry. It was this afternoon."

He pinched the bridge of his nose and rubbed his eyelids. He should have risked telling Patience the truth and making her worry instead of lying to her over the past two days. If he'd told her business had brought him to London last week and he'd met with Mayberry when he'd returned to town, things would be less complicated. Instead, he was lying about Mayberry now. Damn his father for putting him in such a difficult position. No, he'd done that all by himself when he'd failed to trust his wife.

"So you saw him today," her voice was strained, and he frowned at the pain he saw flickering in her beautiful brown eyes.

"No, my father's business was nae complete until just a short time ago." He drew in a deep breath of sadness as he remembered Caitriona's hopeless struggle to live.

"And was Una Bensmore part of that business?" she asked in a tight voice. The unexpected question made him stiffen in surprise as he stared at her in amazement.

"Why would you ask such a thing?" He shook his head slightly as a sense of foreboding streaked through him at the frosty glare Patience cast in his direction.

"Because of this," she said fiercely as she thrust her hand outward and opened her fist. Fear snaked through him the moment he saw the blood pooling in her palm.

"*Christ Almighty, Patience*," he bit out. "What the hell have you done tae your hand?"

Obviously surprised by his harsh response, she shifted her gaze downward. A puzzled look crossed her pale features as she stared at her bloodied hand. Julian strode forward.

"It's your brooch," she murmured in a strained voice.

"I can see that," he growled as he took the jewelry from her hand to drop it on the table. Julian snatched a napkin off her lunch tray. It made a loud crack as he snapped it open and dabbed at the blood on her palm. "What the devil possessed you tae hold it like that?"

The blood that had made her injury look so severe was the result of several deep pricks to her palm. The amount of blood had made it look far worse than it really was. It would give her slight discomfort for a few days, but she would heal easily. As Julian cleaned the blood from her hand, he looked at her in a silent demand for an explanation.

"I wasn't thinking," she said woodenly. The dispassionate response made Julian shake his head as he tried to comprehend how his brooch had come to be in her possession, to begin with.

"Where did you find this? I thought I'd lost it."

Relief that she was unharmed mixed with gratitude that he'd recovered the brooch. He would have mourned its loss. His mother had given it to him on his seventh birthday a few months before she'd become sick and died. The last time he'd seen it had been yesterday morning on his coat. It must have fallen off on his way out the door. A second later, he looked into Patience's eyes, and an icy blast of fear chilled him to the bone. Her face was pale, and her expression devoid of emotion. Normally his wife was an open book to him, but she'd closed herself off to him. Julian frowned at the flicker of emotion darkening her soft, brown eyes. What the hell had happened while he'd been gone.

"Una Bensmore delivered your brooch in person," Patience's voice held the sharp brittleness of glass shattering. With a quick, vicious tug of her hand, she jerked free of his grasp. Bone tired, it took Julian several seconds to comprehend her words.

"Una? She was here?" He frowned in bewilderment.

"Is she your mistress?" The question blindsided him.

"My mis—*God in heaven, Patience.* I dinnae have a mistress."

Bloody hell, what would make her even contemplate the idea he was involved with Una? His gut twisted like a hung man hanging in the wind. Una had always been one to make mischief, but God help the woman if she'd been malevolent enough to suggest she was his mistress.

He'd have Una's head for making Patience question his fidelity. Caitriona's sister had been nothing but trouble since the day she turned seventeen, and Fergus MacTavish had planted the idea in her head that she'd one day be the lady of Crianlarich Castle. She'd been trying to seduce Julian ever since. Despite denying his involvement with Una, he saw the look of disbelief on Patience's face. Sweet mother of God, exactly what had Una told Patience?

"Then why did you ride off in a hansom cab with her yesterday morning, and why were you seen house hunting with her?"

"How in the hell do you know about that?" he exclaimed.

The instant the words spilled out into the air, he realized how damaging they sounded. Whatever Una had told Patience had only exacerbated his wife's fears. The memory of their argument at Crianlarich shortly after they were wed made his gut twist viciously as another wave of guilt rolled over him. Patience had seen through Una all along, and he'd dismissed her fears. No doubt, his beautiful, sweet wife had spent most of the night imagining the worst of him. He wanted to bang his head against the wall out of frustration for being such a thick-headed dolt.

"Anyone who reads the society page knows about it by now. But it still doesn't explain why you were looking for a house with the woman you say isn't your mistress."

Each word she spoke crackled with anger and humiliation. Christ Jesus, everyone they knew, including her family, would think the worst. But the only thing he cared about was what Patience believed. His sluggish brain tried to frame an answer without betraying his oath to Caitriona or the word he'd given his father as to his search for the young woman.

"Tis difficult to explain, *mo ghràdh*," he muttered. Julian saw Patience flinch, and he took a step forward only to see her recoil from him. Her retreat cut through him like a knife.

"It's not difficult at all, Julian. Either you did or didn't go house hunting with the woman." The brittle note in her voice echoed between them like the sound icicles made when they snapped free of a tree limb.

"I did," he growled. "But tis nae what it looks like, Patience."

47

"What is it *supposed* to look like?" The question was delivered with a cold, detached bluntness that made him feel as though she'd kicked him. "You took the woman house hunting, and you were with her last night."

How in God's name was he supposed to explain he'd been with Una looking at houses for her sister? The mere fact that Una was in the same room as Caitriona's labor progressed made it impossible to deny being with the woman. Worse, it meant betraying Caitriona's confidence if he explained why Una had been with him last night as they waited for her sister to give birth.

"I give you my word, Patience. She is nae my mistress. I dinnae sleep in Una Bensmore's bed last night. I never have," he said quietly and firmly.

It was the truth as far as sharing the woman's bed, but omitting the fact that she was with him as Caitriona had given birth didn't sit well with him. For a fleeting second, he could have sworn an expression of hope softened her features before her expression hardened with distrust.

"Then tell me where you were." Patience demanded sharply. Julian shoved a hand through his dark hair.

"'Tis difficult to explain," he muttered. His words made Patience wince, and he took a step forward only to see her retreat from him once more. A vise wrapped around his chest the moment she drew back.

"Then explain about your meeting with Lord Mayberry," she said softly. Something in her voice said he was treading treacherous waters.

"I told you, I dinnae meet with Mayberry—"

"Liar." The sharp accusation made him freeze as he stared at the cold rage in his wife's eyes. He tilted his head slightly to study her warily.

"I am nae a liar, Patience," he said quietly, knowing full well he was exactly what she'd called him. "I dinnae meet with Lord Mayberry yesterday or today."

"But you did meet with him, didn't you?"

"I've already answered the question," he snapped.

"I saw Lord Mayberry yesterday, and he said you met with him last Thursday."

Patience's words crackled like ice breaking beneath his feet. She knew he'd come back to London without coming home. It only made him look all the more guilty. Julian was a man drowning as he stared at her. It was obvious she'd already formed an opinion, and it wasn't good. His tired brain didn't respond quick enough with an explanation, and her mouth thinned into a tight line of anger.

"You were in London for two days before you came home, Julian. Where *were* you?"

"*Bloody hell*, tis nae what it looks like, Patience." He shoved both hands through his hair. His head was starting to hurt as if he'd just awoken from a night of drinking.

"What *is* it supposed to look like, Julian?" She glared at him with a cold disdain that ignited an angry frustration inside him. Julian intended to wring Una's neck for upsetting Patience and making his wife doubt his love for her.

"You don't deny you were with her," she sneered. "So, I'll ask you again. Is she your mistress?"

"*Damn it*, Una is nae my lover," he bit out. It was as if he were a large fish caught in a fisherman's net, and the more he tried to escape, the tighter the net encircled him.

"The woman knew about your birthmark, Julian," she said quietly. There was a note of deep pain in her voice that belied the contempt on her face. "How could Miss Bensmore know about the mark unless you've shared her bed?"

Stunned, Julian stared at her as if he were dull-witted while his brain whirred with a dozen questions all at the same time. He fought through them to the one that seemed the most important. How had Una known about his birthmark when he'd never slept with her? Patience was right. The only way someone could know about his mark was if they saw him naked, and he knew he'd never been naked in Una's presence. Worse, if he couldn't make Patience listen to reason—believe him—he was damned for certain. Julian shook his head.

"Patience, I dinnae have an explanation for how Una knows about my birthmark, but I have *never* been with the woman."

"Liar," she spat out with a quiet, cold fury. "The only explanation is that you were in her bed last night, and God knows how many other nights. You were at Crianlarich for two months. Perhaps the dinner parties your father likes to throw for his *close* friends, the Bensmores, encouraged you to take advantage of my absence."

"Bloody hell, do you nae know me at all? Are you willing tae let the words of a spiteful witch come between us?"

"A woman who says the two of you are lovers."

"*She is nae my lover.*" His words thundered in the salon so loudly he would not have been surprised to see the walls shake. "How many times do I have tae tell you that?"

"Then explain where you were last night if you weren't with her. Explain what you were doing so late that you couldn't come home to me? Tell me why you lied about Lord Mayberry. Tell me why you came back to London but didn't come home to me." The soft plea snagged at his heart as a tear slid down her pale cheek, and the pain in her gaze sliced through his chest.

"I cannae explain, *mo ghràdh*," he said with a shake of his head. "'Tis nae my secret tae tell."

"Do you have any idea how that sounds, Julian?" She closed her eyes for a moment, and he saw her throat flex as if she were trying not to cry. Patience looked at him again. "How can you expect me to believe you weren't with her when I know you've lied to me once already? What am I supposed to think?"

"I expect you tae have a little faith in me—tae trust me and believe that I would nae lie tae you," he ground out fiercely as he took a step toward her. Patience raised her hand to stop him.

"Don't come near me. I don't want you to touch me."

The words knotted his muscles tight with something he'd not experienced since he was a child—fear. Julian swallowed the anger rising in his throat. He turned away from Patience and walked to the window to stare out at the street. Hands clasped behind his back, his brain churned madly as he blindly grasped for an explanation that would ease Patience's fears and honor Caitriona's request.

The burden of Caitriona's secret on his shoulders was causing a deep chasm between him and the woman he loved more than life itself. Even more crippling was that he didn't know what he could say to close the growing gap between them. Bloody hell, why hadn't he simply written to her that an old friend from Crianlarich was desperately in need of his help?

Patience was the most compassionate soul he knew. She would have understood. Instead, he'd lied to her, and agreeing to Caitriona's final request had only made things that much more difficult for him when it came to making Patience believe he was innocent of any betrayal. Slowly, he turned to face her.

"Things are nae what they seem, *mo ghràdh*. I should have come home last week, but I had to conduct my business in the more sordid parts of town." Julian met her gaze steadily as he pleaded his case. "I dinnae wish to worry you when I came home late with no explanation why. My father asked me to help Una in a matter that is of a personal nature. It is the only reason I was with her yesterday."

Disbelief and confusion swept across Patience's face as she pressed her hand to her throat. He stretched out his hand to her.

"Trust me, *mo leannan*," he said fervently, praying she would see he was speaking from the heart. "I swore an oath to an old friend nae tae reveal what I know. Dinnae believe Una's lies."

"You're asking a great deal of me, Julian."

"Aye," he jerked his head sharply. "I am."

"You're asking me to forget everything. You lied to me, Julian, and now you want me to believe you, simply because your answer is that you were helping—"

"*Bloody hell, Patience*. I cannae tell a secret that is nae mine tae tell," he roared as he smashed his fist on the table next to the window. He saw her jump with fear and immediately regretted his fierce reaction.

"What would you believe if you were in my shoes, Julian? What if I'd lied, and I were the one saying I was protecting someone's secret?" she whispered as if in great pain. "I doubt you would be so willing to believe me any more than I am to believe you."

Patience was right. It would be almost impossible to believe in her innocence if the same type of evidence was presented to him. Angry with himself for his lies and stupidity in agreeing to Caitriona's request, he shook his head.

"I know the evidence makes me look guilty, Patience, but I am nae," he rasped. "But I must honor my oath."

"Please stop," Patience said in a strained whisper. "I can't think straight, Julian."

One hand pressed against her temple, Patience closed her eyes and shook her head. A second tear slid down her cheek. Unable to help himself, he closed the distance between them in three quick strides. This time she didn't retreat, but he could see the raw pain in her eyes. With a gentle touch, he wiped the tear off her cheek. If someone had beaten him until he lay dying in a ditch, it would have hurt less than to see the anguish in her gaze. He caught her hand in his and carried it to his lips.

"I love you, Patience. I made a mistake. If I'd come straight home last week, I would nae have had a reason to lie about Mayberry. I was wrong, *mo ghràdh*. Dinnae let Una's lies come between us."

"I need time to think," she whispered. "I'm going to Louisa's for the next few days. I can't stay here right now."

The lifeless look in her brown eyes tightened the vise wrapped around his chest until it was painful to breathe. He wanted to plead with her to stay, but Patience, like the rest of the Rockwood clan, could be stubborn. As much as Julian didn't want to let her go, he knew it would only make matters worse if he insisted she stay. With a sharp nod, he released her hand and stepped back from her.

"If that's what you wish. But know this, Patience, you're my wife. I'll go tae hell and back tae keep you. I love you. Nothing will change that. Nothing." Something flashed in her eyes, and it gave him hope he would be able to win her trust again.

"I'll leave in the morning for Westbrook Farms." A pained look crossed her face. "Please sleep in the spare bedroom tonight. I do not want you near me."

Her words made his head snap back as if she'd hit him. What had he expected? Patience walked past him and headed toward the door. He turned to watch her leave him, hoping against hope she'd look back at him. If she did, he would know he had a chance to win her back. Just as she walked through the door, she glanced over her shoulder. Hope flared in him. She did love him. He was certain of it. There was no doubt he would have a fight on his hands regaining her trust, but that one brief look meant he stood a chance.

Chapter 4

Patience took a sip of the Madeira Louisa's husband, Devin, had poured for her and sat opposite her sister in the drawing-room of Westbrook Farms. Dinner hard been a festive affair. Yet despite the jovial manner of the family gathering, all Patience could do was think about Julian. She missed him terribly, and the more she thought about him, the worse her heart ached.

"Really, Patience. It's been two days now. If you continue to look so down in the mouth, the rest of the family will start meddling in your affairs. Particularly Constance, who is grateful for your interference in her and Lucien's happiness and would gladly like to repay the favor." Louisa nodded toward their sister and her future husband, who were watching Sebastian and Devin's intense chess game. The youngest of the Rockwood clan's astute observation made her flinch.

"As I recall, I was quite cheerful at the dinner table. That's hardly the sign of an ill-tempered demeanor," Patience said quietly.

"At a dinner party anywhere else, I'd say you would have easily fooled all the guests. But you forget your family has far too many special talents for your unhappiness to go unnoticed," Louisa said with a sympathetic look. "Even Sebastian, who doesn't have the sight, noticed you're despondent, and he asked where Julian was."

"Julian had business to attend to," she lied. Louisa's penetrating gaze made Patience feel as though she'd been placed under a microscope.

"You know there isn't a single member of the family who believes that ridiculous story in the paper, dearest."

As her youngest sister's statement of reassurance, Patience drew in a swift breath of horror. Her family had said nothing about the article since she'd arrived at Westbrook Farms, which had led her to hope none of them had read the article or made the connection. Now, as she met Louise's gaze, a wave of humiliation swept over her.

"No one said…"

"Of course we wouldn't, darling," her sister scolded gently. "At least not until now when you look so miserable. It's obvious you're taking this gossip to heart, and you shouldn't. If there's one thing everyone in the family agrees on, it's that Julian loves you. He would never betray you. There has to be a logical explanation for it. You just need to ask him."

"I did ask him." Patience closed her eyes for a brief moment at the memory of their argument and his deception.

"I see," Louisa said in a cautious tone of voice. "I take it this whole matter has to do with a red-haired woman I keep seeing?"

The remark made Patience flinch. With as much nonchalance as she could, she leaned forward and set her wine glass on the round coffee table in front of the settee.

"I don't have to ask how you came by that knowledge," she murmured with resignation. Her sister offered her a small, knowing smile.

"When it comes to those we love, the Rockwood gift is something to be cherished."

"As someone who has a wee bit of the *an dara sealladh*, I must agree with Louisa. It is troubling tae see ye so verra unhappy, dearest."

The soft lilting sound of Aunt Matilda's brogue floated over Patience's head as her maternal aunt circled the settee to sit next to her. The Scotswoman patted Patience's knee. With a wince, she glanced at first her aunt and then her sister.

"Who else—or would it be better to ask who *hasn't* seen something?"

"Other than me and Aunt Matilda, no one else has mentioned anything. At least for the moment, they haven't," Louisa said with added emphasis on the last part of her statement.

Patience released a quiet gasp at the idea of her heartbreak becoming a family matter. If left unchecked, it would take no time at all to get out of hand and everyone would be offering advice as to how to fix her marriage. It was the last thing she wanted. Determined to stop her aunt and sister from saying anything further, Patience turned her head toward Caleb, who seemed attached to the liquor cart.

He'd drank heavily at dinner and had imbibed at least two full snifters of cognac since the family had retired to the salon. Her brother's unrelenting sorrow had been evident to her all evening. She shook her head with concern.

"I think the one we should all worry about is Caleb. It's been a year since Georgina's death. Every time I see him, he's drinking." The most handsome of her brothers, Caleb's excessive drinking was beginning to take its toll on his health and appearance.

"We've tried to convince him to stop, but it only enrages him when we mention it," Louisa said with an unhappy frown. "And he wants nothing to do with the children.

"Aye, the poor bairns dinnae lose just a mother. They lost their father too." Aunt Matilda's expression was one of sorrow as she shook her head in dismay.

"Does he even visit the nursery?" Patience asked as her gaze shifted to Caleb, who was pouring himself another drink. Her brother had been devastated by the loss of his wife in childbirth, and she hated to know that his children were suffering for it.

"Seldom," Louisa said. "I know they miss him terribly. Although I'm not Caleb, I make every effort to give Alma and Braxton as much attention as I do Charlie and William. Greer is too young to understand, but it is Caleb who is missing out. They're all growing so fast."

"Well, perhaps I can at least coax him away from the liquor cart for the rest of the evening," Patience said as she rose to her feet.

"Tread lightly, Patience," her aunt warned as she touched Patience's arm. "Ye brother is nae always pleasant when he's been in the drink."

"I'll avoid any mention of our concern for him." With a squeeze of her aunt's hand, Patience crossed the room to her brother's side.

"Would you indulge me in a game of cards, Caleb?" she asked. With as cheerful a smile as possible, she tucked her arm in his. "You used to trounce me easily, but my skill has greatly increased since we were children."

"You know good and well I had to earn every one of those games," her brother said with a small smile. From across the room, Sebastian's wife, Helen, laughed.

"Patience, if you're able to convince Caleb to play cards, I insist on playing as well. It's been too long since I've enjoyed a good round of Euchre."

"I'm in as well," exclaimed Percy, the second oldest of the Rockwood clan. He pressed his fingers to his temple and closed his eyes as if thinking hard. Eyes opening, he grinned. "And I predict I shall win."

For the first time since leaving London, Patience laughed. Beside her, Caleb chuckled as well. He looked down at her, and the sorrow in his hazel eyes made her heart break.

She had a small inkling of what he was feeling. Patience forced a smile to her lips.

"Well, are you going to play, or are you afraid I shall beat you," she asked as she arched her eyebrows. Caleb's eyes narrowed as he met her gaze, then nodded.

"You know bloody well I wouldn't be a Rockwood if I let that challenge go unanswered," he said with a quiet resolve and slight smile.

At his agreement to participate, Helen clapped her hands, and Louisa went in search of cards while Caleb pulled away from Patience to pour himself another drink. She knew better than to protest his doing so. The fact that she'd convinced him to play cards was an achievement itself. To push for another change so quickly could easily undo the little she'd already accomplished.

With cards in hand, Helen joined Caleb, Percy, and Patience at the card table. Sebastian and Devin were deeply involved in their game of chess and waved them away. Despite her protests, Louisa convinced Aunt Matilda to join her, Constance, and Lucien at another table. For the next hour, laughter filled the air as everyone merrily taunted one another when a hand or game was won.

Despite his brooding demeanor, Caleb seemed to be enjoying the game. But to Patience's dismay, he continued to drink more and more wine as the evening wore on. Patience had just taken a trick when Louisa's butler appeared at her side.

"There is a messenger for you, my lady," Hughes bent over to discreetly whisper in her ear. "They say it's urgent. I've shown them into his lordship's study."

"Thank you," she said with a nod as she took another trick. Had someone come to tell her Julian had been hurt? Her heart slammed into her chest before she tried to dismiss her fear. She wished she could feel nothing, but she did.

"Are you all right, Patience?" Caleb laid his hand over hers as an odd frown darkened his handsome features.

"I'm fine." She smiled with a cheerfulness she didn't feel. "It's just a message for me."

"Isn't it rather late for someone to be delivering messages?" Helen murmured. The worried expression on her sister-in-law's face made Patience's heart lurch, but she shook her head. "I'm sure it's nothing. I'll be back in a moment. Sebastian, Devin, will one of you take my place until I return?"

Her eldest brother looked up from his chess game with a scowl as Devin announced checkmate with a jubilant cry of victory. With a grimace of self-disgust at his loss, Sebastian grunted his agreement to Patience. As he stood up, he warned Devin a rematch would be expected at a later date as he moved toward Patience's seat at the table. Her brother bent to kiss his wife's cheek then straightened to smile at her.

"Are you and Helen winning?"

"Yes," she said with satisfaction as she arched her eyebrows at Caleb. Percy simply groaned with amused disgust that he and his brother were losing the match. Caleb shook his head.

"Your winning streak is about to end, Patience. We both know Sebastian is not a very good player," Caleb taunted, his slurred speech indicating he was well on his way to being completely drunk. Sebastian frowned at his youngest brother's condition but didn't say a word, despite his obvious desire to chastise Caleb.

"Then I'll return as quickly as I can to prevent any real damage." Patience went up on her toes to kiss Sebastian's cheek. "Please do your best not to muck up what I've achieved, Sebastian."

"I shall rely on Helen to keep me in line," he said with an arched look at Patience.

"Something I do every day, my love," Sebastian's wife said with a teasing laugh.

Satisfied her winning streak was fairly safe, Patience left the drawing-room and hurried to the study. God help her if something had happened to Julian. His betrayal was devastating, but she still loved him no matter what he'd done to cause her pain. The study was softly lit by the blaze in the fireplace while a small gas lamp spread its light over one of the reading tables.

Patience looked around the empty room with a frown of puzzlement. She was certain Hughes had said the messenger was waiting for her in the study. Behind her, the soft thud of the door closing made her whirl around in surprise. One hand pressed to her stomach, she froze at the sight of Julian. For a moment, she thought he was a hallucination. Patience blinked as if that would erase the image in front of her. When he didn't disappear, she drew in a breath of relief. He was all right. Nothing had happened to him.

"Why are you here?" The tremor in her voice angered her. She didn't want him to know she'd been worried about his safety or how he could still make her heart flutter when they were in the same room together. She drank in the sight of him. He looked tired. Tired and dusty. Dressed in breeches and his riding jacket, it was apparent he'd ridden to Westbrook Farms rather than taking the train. The realization made her think he'd been eager to reach her—unwilling to wait on the train.

"Your sister sent word for me tae come."

"Louisa should not have done that," she said hoarsely.

"I would have come with or without her invitation." The resolute note in his words made her heart skip a beat. God, how she wanted to run to him, but the fear of being hurt again held her back. He'd lied to her, and she couldn't forget that.

"I said I needed time to think, Julian," she said warily.

"Aye, that you did." His lips were thinned in a grim line as he nodded. "I've had time tae think as well, and the same question keeps nagging at me like a fishwife. I want tae know why you're willing to believe the worst of me."

"Isn't that obvious," she snapped.

"I dinnae dispute the fact that I deceived you, Patience, but it was with good intentions. I also know the evidence against me is damning. But none of it is true, and I can prove it."

Startled by his observation, Patience stared at him for a moment before she shook her head.

"I don't know how you think you could possibly do that." At her brittle reply, Julian eyed her carefully.

"Let us consider the gossip column first," he said quietly as he clasped his hands behind his back. "Gossip requires a source, and I've learned that a woman with red hair supplied the newspaper with the lies they printed in the column."

"How do you know that?" she scoffed with a disbelieving frown.

"Because I threatened tae thrash the man who wrote the article until he told me where the story came from." The fierce expression on his face made Patience certain Julian had terrified the newspaper reporter into believing he would make good on his threat.

"Even if what you say is true, there's still the brooch and Una's visit," she said scornfully.

"Aye, the brooch," he said softly. "The estate agent who showed us several houses said he found the brooch, and Una claimed it as hers."

The terse note in Julian's voice emphasized his restrained fury, and his handsome, rugged features were dark with a dangerous emotion that caused her heart to skip a beat. If she didn't know him better, it wouldn't be unreasonable to suspect him contemplating doing injury to the woman.

"Naturally, she dinnae return it tae me, but delivered it tae you instead."

Patience stared at him in silence as she contemplated everything he'd told her so far. When she said nothing, Julian frowned.

"Do ye nae have something tae say?"

"What would you have me say?" she asked with an aching heart. "You've explained two things, but you've failed to explain why you were house hunting with her or how Una knew about your birthmark, which is the most damming of all the evidence."

"Christ Jesus, Patience," he snarled. "I cannae explain how Una knows about my birthmark, but I have nae been with her or any woman since we met. Whatever lies Una told you are nothing more than that—they're lies."

"The *an dara sealladh* showed me a baby. The woman was holding a child, Julian," she choked out in a hoarse voice. At the accusation, Julian stiffened, but his gaze did not leave hers as he shook his head.

"'Tis nae my child, *mo ghràdh*," he said firmly, but it was the endearment he used that made her flinch.

"*Don't call me that*," she exclaimed fiercely. "I am *not* your love. You don't know the meaning of the word."

"And you dinnae know the meaning of trust," he snarled viciously.

Her heart skipped a beat. She'd never heard Julian speak so harshly to her before. Savage anger hardened Julian's face, and she was certain dark angels could not have looked more fierce. As she met his furious gaze, bitterness welled up inside her.

"You're not asking for trust, Julian," she said through clenched teeth. "You're asking me to believe *she's* the liar, not you."

"She *is* lying," he ground out with restrained fury

"But she's not lying about the birthmark," she said softly, and her words made Julian jerk.

"Nae," he said in a flat voice.

"I asked you once before, but you didn't answer me," she rasped. "Put yourself in my place and answer me honestly. Would you believe me if our positions were reversed?"

"I hope I would choose tae believe you," he said in a voice devoid of emotion.

"But you're not certain that you would."

"*Nae,*" he bit out in a harsh voice and with great reluctance.

"I need more time, Julian," she whispered. "Whether your lies were well-intentioned or not, you still deceived me. You're asking for blind faith, and under the circumstances, that doesn't come easily to me, any more than it would for you."

With a shake of her head, she started toward the door. The moment she tried to pass him, his hand snaked outward to wrap around her arm. With a swift tug, he pulled her into his arms. Instantly, her body was on fire, and the air left her lungs as a longing deep inside her wished this nightmare wasn't happening. The scent of the outdoors flooded her senses as he pulled her tight. He always smelled good. Tonight he smelled of horse, leather, and the crisp night air. She trembled at the way his scent assaulted her senses.

"How many times have I showed you how much I love you?"

His warm silky brogue wrapped its tendrils around her in a way that had always been her undoing. Julian bent his head to brush his lips across her cheek until his teeth grazed her earlobe. The shudder rippling through her had to have told him the effect he was having on her. And it was a potent effect. Her mouth was dry, and she was on the verge of losing herself in him.

"What reason would I have tae bed another woman when the only woman I want is the one I'm holding in my arms?" The softness of his voice mesmerized her. The sincerity in his words made her want to believe him.

"Let me go, Julian," she whispered. It frightened her how easily he was seducing her into forgiving him. Or was it exactly what she wanted?

The dark growl rumbling in Julian's chest should have warned her that he had no intention of releasing her, but her senses were taking control, overriding her ability to think clearly. As much as she hated to admit it, her body was betraying her as easily as he'd lied to her. A tremor swept through her as his lips grazed across the edge of her jaw downward until his mouth lightly touched hers.

"Answer me, *mo leannan*. Why would I bed another woman when you're the only woman I want? The only woman I'll ever want."

"Please don't do this, Julian."

"Dinnae do what, *mo ghràdh*? Love you? That would be like asking me tae stop breathing," he whispered as his mouth brushed over hers again. His words hypnotized her. Deep inside, she didn't question his sincerity, only her own inability to believe him.

Sweetly, tenderly, he kissed her. The light touch of his mouth on hers was that of a lover unwilling to do anything that might frighten her. In the back of her mind, a voice warned her not to give way, but she did. Just as she always had whenever he touched her, Patience melted into him. He murmured something just before his mouth hardened on hers. The moment his tongue slipped into her mouth, she knew she was lost.

As her tongue mated with his, her body hummed a familiar rhythm. Her hands spiked in his silky, dark hair as she pressed her body into his. The warmth of him seeped its way into her until she was aware of nothing else but him. He was all male, and for this particular moment in time, he was hers. The pain in her heart eased at the tender kisses he planted on her face.

He whispered words of love. Words that sank their way into her subconscious and told her to forgive his transgressions. His hands slid across her shoulder in a loving caress as his mouth blazed a path across her cheek then down her neck.

"I love you, *mo leannan*. Forgive me. Come home tae me."

Sanity returned to her the moment he asked for her forgiveness. With a hard shove against his chest, Patience broke free of his embrace.

"No, Julian. You cannot seduce me into forgiving you or believing what you say. I need something more than sweet words whispered in my ear," she said quietly.

"Something more than my *sweet words*?" Julian's voice was tight with anger. "What is it you really want, Patience? Do you expect me tae grovel? That I will nae do. Nae even for you, *mo leannan*."

"No, I don't want that," she said with a shake of her head. The thought of his pride being stripped from him appalled her.

"Then what do you want?" he bit out as he stared at her with eyes that could have been dark mahogany ingots.

"What I want is to trust you again, and I don't know how to do that." Sorrow swept through her. It was as if a part of her was dying, and she didn't know how to revive it.

"Nor do I, Patience," he ground out with a viciousness that made her flinch. The heel of her palm pressed to her forehead, she closed her eyes for a moment. When she looked at Julian again, his features were chiseled stone.

"I'll have Hughes find you a room for the night." With those final words, Patience walked to the door. Her hand had just touched the doorknob when Julian's voice filled the air.

"Understand this, Patience. I'll nae give you up," he said in an inflexible, resolute voice. "Dinnae think tae ask for a divorce. I will nae give it tae you."

Patience looked over her shoulder at him, but he wasn't looking at her. His profile could have been etched in marble for how severe his expression was. Her heart skipped a beat. If he didn't love her, would he be so set in his determination not to let her go? His fiery refusal to divorce her made her question whether it was possible for him to betray her? The fact that she didn't have an answer is what terrified her the most. It meant she didn't trust him, and without trust, how could their marriage survive? Without replying to his words, Patience fled the room.

Chapter 5

Patience woke up coughing. Half-awake, she reached for the glass of water at her bedside and swallowed the liquid. The mantel clock chimed four, and she pushed aside a strand of hair that had escaped her braid. She coughed again realizing the air was heavy with smoke. The scent made her whisper a short prayer the damper in her fireplace had fallen closed rather than something far worse.

She slipped out of bed, and the moment her feet touched the floor, dread spiraled through her. The floor was warm, almost hot beneath her feet. Embers in the fireplace sparked then flared into a flame that illuminated small tendrils of smoke swirling gently in the air. In the distance, she thought she heard cries. Patience ran to the door and touched the brass nod in a quick movement. It was still cool to the touch, and she cautiously open her bedroom door. Smoke billowed into her room from the hallway and set off another bout of coughing.

Dread tightened her chest as she stepped out into the corridor and looked toward the main staircase. Patience's eyes widened in horror as she saw a wall of flames at the stairs. Terrified, she let out a wild scream of fear. On the opposite side of the burning staircase, she saw Sebastian fling his arm around Helen to prevent her from racing through the flames toward Patience. Devin and Lucien were doing the same with her sisters as all three women struggled with their husbands and screamed mad wails of terror.

"Oh dear God," she whispered as she remembered the nursery was behind her. "The children."

The door across from hers opened, and Aunt Matilda emerged from her room coughing. As the Scotswoman looked toward the stairwell, she blanched with fear before a calm expression settled on her face. She touched Patience's arm.

"I'll see to the children," her aunt said in a quiet but urgent voice. "Rouse Caleb."

With a nod, Patience hurried through the smoke to Caleb's room, which was closest to the fire. Through the flames, she saw Percy shove Julian against the corridor wall to keep him from plunging through the fire engulfing the floor at the top of the staircase. Terror spiraled through her with the speed of a serpent striking out. Her gaze met Julian's for a brief moment before she turned away and threw Caleb's door open. It crashed against the wall to reveal her brother, still dressed, sprawled across the bedcovers. The smoke was stronger in Caleb's room, and her coughing worsened. Racing toward the bed, Patience shook her brother hard.

"*Caleb, get up,*" she shouted. "The house is on fire."

His response was to push her hand away with a grunt and continue sleeping. In the hallway, she heard more shouts and cries of fear.

"Caleb, please," she pleaded as she shook him again. "Wake up."

He grunted but still didn't move. Frantic to wake him, Patience glanced desperately around the room for something that might awaken her brother. A vase of flowers on a nearby table made her leap forward. The blooms scattered beneath her feet as she yanked them out of the vase and raced to the bed, where she dumped the water on Caleb's head. Her brother came to with a loud snarl and jerked upright in bed to glare at her.

"What the devil is wrong with you, Patience?" he shouted in a slightly slurred voice.

"The house is on fire," she screamed at him. For a long moment, Caleb stared at her as if she were mad. Then in the next instant, he was wide awake and off his bed in a flash of movement.

"The children," he ground out with visible fear on his face as he headed toward the door.

The two of them ran into the hallway, and Patience saw the fire had crept even closer toward Caleb's room. Aunt Matilda had reached the nursery and, with Nanny Smythe's help, was hustling the children out into the hallway. Both Patience and Caleb reached their aunt at the same time. The Scotswoman held her namesake in her arms while the nurse held Caleb's baby girl, Greer. The older children had taken charge of the younger children, and her brother knelt next to Alma and Braxton to give them a quick hug.

"It's all right, my darlings. Papa is here. Everything's going to be all right."

The little boy and girl clung to Caleb as he tried to stand. When they wouldn't let go, he rose up with them still in his arms. Coughing, he looked at Patience and then their aunt.

"We'll go down the servants' staircase," Caleb said with a calm she would have expected from Sebastian, never from him. Before he could move forward, Aunt Matilda shook her head, her mouth thinned in a tight line of worry.

"The fire has reached there as well. It's blocked."

"The window," Caleb bit out as he strode toward the end of the corridor with Alma and Braxton still in his arms.

From where she stood, she saw his back grow rigid. He whirled around and returned to where the group of them was huddled in a small tight group. The children were beginning to cough at closer intervals now, and Patience met her brother's worried gaze.

"The flames are shooting out from the dining-room window below. We'll not be able to get out that way." Her brother's voice was grim as he looked at first Patience and then Aunt Matilda. "The whole downstairs on this side of the house must be burning out of control. None of the windows below us will be free of the flames."

Patience's heart sank down into her stomach before it pushed upward into her throat and threatened to choke her. A young hand slipped into hers, and she looked down to see Devin's and Louisa's oldest child at her side.

"My feet are hot, Aunt Patience," Charlie said amid a coughing spurt.

"Mine are too, darling. But we'll find a way out of here, all right." Patience bent over the boy and kissed his forehead. In her head, she whispered a fervent prayer the night would not make a liar out of her.

"Then we'll have to brave the lion's mouth," Aunt Matilda said with a tightening of her mouth. Caleb and Patience looked at her then followed her gaze. In disbelief, Patience looked back at her aunt as she shook her head violently.

"There has to be another way," Patience exclaimed with horror.

"There's no way out on this end, child," her aunt said softly. "The servants' stairs at the other end of the house are still usable. They've already formed a fire brigade to try to reach us."

Patience looked over her shoulder and saw Sebastian empty a bucket of water on the fire before Julian passed him another one. Lucien, Devin, and Percy were passing buckets they were receiving from someone in the servants' stairwell. She looked back at her aunt and Caleb, who was contemplating the grim prospect.

"How will we keep the children—or us— from being burned?"

"We will cover the wee bairns with wool blankets from the nursery. Wool does nae burn fast, and we can wet them down with water from our rooms." Confidence filled the Scotswoman's voice, and Caleb nodded in agreement.

"We'll do it. Aunt Matilda, let Sebastian know what we're going to do. Patience and I will fetch—" A loud crack interrupted Caleb, and they all turned toward the end of the hall where the nursery was. Flames flew upward as a small portion of the floor broke away and gave the fire room to breathe.

"Saints preserve us," Aunt Matilda whispered, and for the first time, Patience saw fear on the Scotswoman's face.

"Move the children toward the main stairs, Aunt Matilda," Caleb commanded with a sharp precision their eldest brother would be proud of. "Patience, come with me. We'll need water to wet the blankets."

Following his orders, Patience left her aunt and the nurse to usher the crying children toward the middle of the house. Caleb pointed to her bedroom and her aunt's in a silent command for her to get what they needed while he moved toward the nursery. Fear created a knot in her throat, and she coughed hard as she entered her aunt's smoke-filled room. One arm covering her nose and mouth, Patience hurried toward a vase of flowers to merge the water with what was in the pitcher sitting beside the washbasin.

Pitcher in hand, she grabbed the wool blanket off the bed and returned to the hallway. She hurried to where her aunt and the nurse had gathered the children and set the water and blankets on the floor. The heat of the fire had forced them to stop several feet away from where the main staircase was on fire.

For the first time, Patience was able to see the gap between them and the rest of her family. She drew in a breath of horror and froze as she saw how narrow their path to safety was. There was less than a third of the hallway floor remaining for them to walk across. Patience's heart pounded with fear as she watched Sebastian throw one bucket of water after another onto the hallway floor in a desperate race to keep the fire from devouring their escape. Her oldest brother's grim expression as he looked up to meet her gaze from across the flames made her throat close in terror. She had never seen Sebastian afraid before, and the fear in his dark eyes emphasized how dire the situation was. He jerked his head in a silent command for her to continue gathering water and blankets from the bedrooms. Without a word, Patience turned and raced back down the hall to continue retrieving water and blankets.

The smoke in her room made her eyes sting, and it was almost impossible to breathe. Seconds later she'd returned to the hall where she met Caleb on his way back to the frightened group of children. His grim expression was no different from that of the men on the opposite side of the stairwell.

"We'll send the oldest children across first," Caleb shouted at his oldest brother over the roar of the fire.

Sebastian nodded and turned his head as Devin broke away from the hall brigade. Her brother-in-law said something to Sebastian and pointed toward the section of wood that still laid between the two sections of the upper hallway. Her brother nodded, and Devin stepped toward the edge of the wood as Caleb returned to their small huddle.

"Jamie. Theo. Imogene. The three of you are to go first," Caleb said as he used a knife he'd retrieved from his room to begin splitting the blankets they had in two. The three children looked at their uncle with terror in their eyes, and her brother bent his head toward them. "I know you're scared, but you don't have to be. Do you remember when we used the stepping stones to cross the stream at Melton Park?

This is almost the same thing. Uncle Sebastian and the others will be there to help you those last few steps. You can do this."

"Come on, Gene," Jamie said as he straightened and reached out for Imogene's hand. In the far reaches of her mind, Patience remembered how Constance despaired of Jamie's nickname for Imogene. The girl, who'd been trembling only seconds before, slipped her hand into Jamie's as she nodded at Caleb's calm reassurance.

"We'll be okay, Uncle Caleb," Theo, Sebastian's oldest child, said with just a touch of fear in his voice.

"I know you will," her brother said as he squeezed the young boy's shoulder.

"Who will take Greer across," Imogene exclaimed. The girl had become attached to the baby, and Patience understood her fear for the infant.

"We'll see that she gets across as well," Caleb said in a reassuring tone. A tenacious look settled on Imogene's face as she rejected the response with a firm shake of her head. If Patience hadn't known better, she would have thought the child a Rockwood by birth.

"I will carry her." Without waiting for anyone to object, Imogene went to the nurse and took the baby from her hands. "Come along, Greer. You'll be safe with me."

Caleb stared helplessly at the young girl holding his baby girl in her arms. Patience could tell he didn't know what to do, and she touched his arm in a gesture of encouragement. With a grimace, he hurried Imogene back to the oldest boys. Caleb dampened blankets for the three children ordered them to keep the protective covering over their heads as they crossed the narrow strip of wood. With instructions to keep their heads down and stay close to the wall, he sent Imogene with the baby first, followed by Theo and Jamie just a few steps behind.

Lucien greeted Jamie and Imogene with thankful enthusiasm on the other side as Devin handed the children off to him. The instant Devin handed Theo to her eldest brother, Sebastian hugged his son tight, and Patience saw him shudder in relief. With a kiss on the boy's forehead, Sebastian set his son down and pointed toward the stairs at the end of the hall. Her nephew nodded and set off at a run.

Satisfied the children and the baby had reached safety, Caleb ordered Aunt Matilda to carry Tilly across. In a voice that dared anyone to argue with her, the Scotswoman insisted Nanny cross the small stretch of wood with Charlie in her arms first. An odd expression crossed her brother's face as he gave her a grim nod. For the first time, Patience realized her aunt and Caleb didn't think all of them would reach the other side. They were sending the heirs to safety first.

She dragged in a sharp breath of fear and coughed hard as smoke filled her lungs. Caleb urged Nanny forward, who pulled a blanket over her head and Charlie's, who was sobbing with fear. Sebastian paused in his efforts to keep their path to safety wet as he watched the nursemaid crossed the narrow section with in slow, careful steps.

Seconds later, the nurse delivered her small charge into his father's arms. Devin kissed the boy, hugged him, then handed his son back to the nurse and directed her to the end of the hallway. When Nanny had reached safety, Sebastian resumed throwing water on the floor keep it wet. His pace increased as he jerked a bucket out of a footman's hand and splashed water onto the boards. The moment the water hit the boards it sputtered and sizzled as the fire continued to eat away at the flooring.

"Aunt Matilda—" Caleb didn't get to finish before the Scotswoman shook her head.

"Patience is tae go with Braxton, I'll—"

"*No,*" she shouted over the noise of the fire. "Take Tilly. Caleb will need help to ensure the rest of the children are safely across. *Go. Now.*"

With a look of resignation on her face, her aunt closed the space between them and enveloped her in a tight hug. The Scotswoman pressed a tender kiss to Patience's cheek, then stepped back and wrapped a wet blanket tight around her and Tilly.

The four remaining children clung to Patience's nightgown as she watched Aunt Matilda slowly carry her precious cargo to safety. As her aunt reached the other side, Patience noted the wood flooring had narrowed even more despite Sebastian's frantic efforts to keep the fire at bay. If possible, Caleb's expression had become even grimmer as he turned toward Patience, and she offered him his son.

"Take Braxton."

Caleb jerked his head in a sharp nod. Throwing a blanket over his head, he scooped Braxton up into his arms and moved through the flames toward safety. When he was within arm's reach of Devin, he handed Braxton to the other man and returned to where Patience and the remaining children waited.

Without a word, she picked up Angus and handed him to her brother. Caleb winced as he glanced down at Alma. Patience met his gaze then looked down at the little girl clinging to her nightgown. She knew her brother understood the male spare was considered more valuable than his own daughter.

Patience saw the horror in his eyes as she saw him struggle with whether or not to override her decision. It was a heartbreaking choice. A choice she'd made for him because she knew it would be too much to ask of him at the moment. Fighting back tears, she shook her head.

"*Go,*" she ordered in a sharp voice. "*We're running out of time.*"

Caleb nodded then turned and moved as quickly as he could across the narrow strip of wood by the second. His foot slipped, and for a moment, she was certain he and Angus would fall into the roaring fire. Devin said something to him with a vicious gesture of both hands. Her brother hesitated, then in one swift movement, he tossed the child to Devin more than three feet away.

Horrified, Patience pressed her hand against her mouth to cover her scream. Devin caught the child without difficulty and handed Angus to Sebastian. Her heart pounded painfully in her chest as she saw the fire biting at Caleb's trousers. Sliding his way back across what was left of the plank of wood, her brother jumped past the flames beginning to threaten the last of the flooring. He landed a short two feet away from her and she glanced down at the two blankets left. Patience's heart sank as she realized what would be required of her in another moment. Before Caleb could speak, she pointed to her nephew.

"You have to take Willie then come back for Alma. I'm not as strong as you if it becomes necessary. . ." Her voice trailed off at the thought of having to throw Willie or Alma to safety.

Caleb didn't argue and picked up another blanket, lifted Willie into his arms, and started back across the narrow strip of wood. The flames seemed to lick even harder at her brother's feet as he moved toward the other side of the gap, and Patience watched with horror as he struggled to keep his footing. When her brother tossed Willie into his father's arms, Patience watched as Devin hugged the boy while Caleb made his way back to her. Picking up the last blanket, she met her brother as he passed through the fire that had expanded and was eating away at the flooring only a few feet away. Without a word, she handed Alma and the last wet blanket to him. His gaze swept the floor, and his jaw hardened with tension.

"I'll be back for you."

"No, I'll come after you."

"For the love of God, Patience. You need some form of protection."

"Look at the flooring. It's already broken between here and where Sebastian and the others are. Go now," she said in a calm voice as she resigned herself to whatever fate had in store for her. "I'll follow you. I can jump, but I won't risk Alma's safety if I'm forced to do that. I'm not strong enough."

"Then I'll meet you halfway," he snarled.

"*No,*" she shouted over the roar of the fire. "The floor might not hold us both. I'll be right behind you."

Horror, pain, and fear glazed her brother's beautiful dark eyes as he stared at her for a moment. Like her aunt, he pulled her into a tight hug, then with a kiss to her brow, he released her and headed back toward the fire. Patience's gaze flitted away from Caleb's tall figure to look across the barrier of flames to see Julian staring at her with an agonized look on his face.

Her heart sank into the pit of her stomach, and she looked away. Patience couldn't bear to think that she might never be in Julian's arms again. Quickly ripping the material of her nightgown at the knees, she stepped out of the lengthy piece of material and tore it again, then doubled it into a shawl. With the shawl covering her head and face, Patience stepped forward to follow Caleb through the fire. Her heart in her mouth, she saw Alma fly through the air to land in Devin's arms.

A small measure of relief swept through her. The children were safe. She closed her eyes for a brief second before she heard Caleb roar with anger. In horror, she saw another piece of the floor begin to buckle beneath him. He flung his arms out in an involuntary effort to save himself. In the next precious instant, Devin caught her brother by the hand and pulled Caleb toward him.

Relief surged through her once more before the sound of snapping wood echoed over the crackling of the fire. Horror held her rigid as she saw the flooring beneath Devin's feet give way. As he fell, Devin twisted his body and caught the edge of the flooring with one hand as Caleb weighed him down with his other hand. Sebastian, Julian, and Lucien rushed forward to reach for Devin, but the flooring beneath his hand gave way, and a split second later, Devin plummeted with Caleb into the fire below.

Wild screams pierced the air relentlessly, and Patience thought they would never fade until she realized they were coming from her. Sobbing, she sank to her knees as she tried to forget the image of her brother and Devin plunging into the flames. Arms wrapped around her waist, she rocked back and forth as a web of fear wrapped itself around her leaving her paralyzed.

Once again, the sound of wood breaking beneath the onslaught of the flames rent the air. Patience's head jerked up, her eyes widening with horror as she saw the last piece of the ledge to safety fall into the inferno. Suddenly icy cold, she realized she was all alone. From across the flames and the gap where the main stairs had once been, she saw the panic in Sebastian's face. Her brother never panicked. It was an odd thought to have when she was facing certain death.

"*Patience*," Julian shouted over the crackling fire. "You have to jump, *mo ghràdh*. You must jump *now*."

Horrified at the death that waited for her below, she shook her head vehemently. He was asking her to do the impossible. Sebastian called out to her from across the hole in the floor.

"*Patience, look at me*," her brother shouted in a voice filled with an authoritative anger she'd only heard once or twice in her life. Sebastian never lost control of his temper.

"Julian will catch you. Lucien and I will hold on to him, so the two of you don't fall."

He didn't have to say the words, but she knew he meant they wouldn't let her fall into the flames as Caleb and Devin had. She shook her head again, looking around her for another escape route. Behind her, she saw the floor outside the nursery groan and fall inward as the fire ate its way toward her.

"*For the love of god, Patience.*" Anguish filled Percy's voice as their gazes met. "You have to jump, sweetheart."

Percy had been her idol growing up. She'd followed him like a puppy everywhere he'd gone. Patience closed her eyes for a brief moment before she opened them and looked at Julian. His expression was one of pleading and encouragement, and she took a step forward. Suddenly, flames exploded from the wall on her left. In the next instance, the material on her face burst into flames.

Pain twisted through her as she screamed and frantically fought to pull the flaming material off her head. Terrified, she jumped away as part of the wall collapsed near her feet, and the fire lashed out at her again. She raised her arm to cover her face, and the flames viciously flayed her skin while licking her cheek in a silent taunt. She was going to burn alive.

Patience staggered away from the flames that took the place of where the wall had once been. Dazed with fear and pain, she stared across the fiery divide at the men watching her with looks of horror and helpless fury. Sebastian turned away from her and slammed his fist into the wall. Scorn suddenly crossed Julian's features as he folded his arms across his chest and glared at her.

"I thought a Rockwood never refused a challenge, Patience MacTavish." Julian's shout was loud, strong, and arrogant as he met her startled gaze. "Are ye about tae let this little fire beat ye?"

The cynical look on Julian's face sent a streak of anger through her. The bastard wasn't happy he'd caused her pain by lying to her. Now he had to ridicule her as well. Anger swept through her at the disdainful sneer on his lips. The fury it aroused in her battled its way past the excruciating pain threatening to render her unconscious. Julian was right. A Rockwood *never* backed away from a challenge. Her gaze met his, and she saw a flash of emotion sweep across his face. She didn't try to identify it because she knew it would be her undoing.

Slowly, she turned and walked as far back along the hallway as she could. Just as she'd reached the furthest spot in the hallway, a roar split the air over her head. Fire erupted out of the ceiling, and a piece of flaming lumber crashed down on top of her left side. She screamed with pain as the wood drove her down to the floor, and the flames ate away at her skin. With a loud cry, this one of panic and fear, she gathered her strength to push the burning lumber off her.

Free of the wood's weight, she fell backward on the floor and remained still. In the distance, she heard people calling her name. It would be so much easier to ignore them and simply remain here until the fire took her. It was then that she heard Julian's voice piercing the roar of the flames as he called her name several times in the brogue that had seduced her when they first met.

"*Well, Patience?*" Julian's shout of derision punched its way through her pain and despair. "Are ye going tae just lie down and die, or are ye going to show us what a *true* Rockwood will do tae survive?"

She slowly sat up and looked over her shoulder at him. She saw Sebastian say something to Julian, but her husband waved her brother away without his gaze straying from hers. With a casual, deliberate motion, he folded his arms across his chest. The arrogance of his stance enraged her. For the first time since she'd laid eyes on Julian, she hated him.

Hated him for mocking her when she was in pain. Hated him for lying to her. And hated him for being here to watch her die. But worst of all, she hated herself for not telling him one last time how much she loved him.

"*Dinnae make me come for ye, Patience MacTavish.*" His angry shout was filled with a fury that made her stagger to her feet.

His words instilled a fear in her greater than anything she'd felt tonight. If Julian were to come after her, he'd die just like her. That was something she refused to let happen. She would not let him die because of her. Patience turned around to meet Julian's gaze across the distance. If she were to die tonight, it would be running toward the man she loved. A sudden bolt of energy zipped through her, and with a primal scream, she leaped forward into a fast run. Patience's gaze didn't leave Julian's face as she raced forward. Her feet pounded against the hot floor as she sped toward the wall of fire and the gaping hole where the staircase had once been. The moment she reached the edge of the flames and the opening between her and safety, she closed her eyes and flung herself into the air toward Julian.

Hands outstretched, she prayed he would catch her. What seemed like an eternity, but was only a brief second, strong hands latched onto her wrists and pulled her to safety. The pressure on her burned wrist pulled a screech of agony out of her throat, and she fell into a deep hole free of the pain.

A cacophony of sound assaulted her ears as she emerged from the darkness. Her entire left side felt as if she were still in the burning house. Through the pain, she realized someone had carried her outside. The noise here was as loud as the roar of the fire had been only moments before. Bells clanging, shouts, the sound of Louisa screaming wildly with grief, and the men of the family trying to bring order to the chaos echoed madly in her ears.

The fresh scent of grass mixed with the stench of wet wood and smoke. It made her gag as it filled her nose. The cool night air brushed over her burns like icy cold water, and she shivered. A blanket was thrown over her, and she shrieked as the wool scraped across her blistering skin. It was immediately jerked off her as, through a blur of tears, she saw Percy and Julian kneel down, one on either side of her.

"*Christ Jesus, look at her face,*" her brother exclaimed in a low voice of horror. "She has burns down her entire left side."

Somewhere in the back of her mind, Patience remembered the *an dara sealladh*. The visions of her burns. The scars. Why hadn't she known what they meant? She could have saved Caleb. Devin. The salt in the tears running down her cheek intensified her pain, and she choked on her sobs.

"You're safe, *mo ghràdh*. I'm here." Julian said softly as he stroked her unmarred cheek. "It will be all right."

She moaned her protest. It would never be all right. Her gift had failed her. No, she'd failed Caleb and Devin. Nothing would ever be the same again. Despite the pain, it caused her to move, she reached out to grasp Percy's shirt in a tight fist and pulled herself upward. "Percy, please…home…Melton House."

"Yes, Patience, we'll take you home to Melton House."

At her brother's reassurance, she fell backward onto the grass again. Her eyes fluttered shut for a moment, then opened again as Julian brushed his mouth against her unmarred hand. He didn't say a word, but the anguished hopelessness in his gaze made her sob again before the pain dragged her down into a dark place where she felt nothing.

Patience woke with a cry of pain on her lips. A stranger was wrapping her arm with a wet bandage, and the pressure made her want to push the man's hand away. Tears rolled down her cheek, but the salty droplets didn't burn. Groggily, she reached up with her free hand to touch her face. A strong hand caught hers in a firm, but gentle grip, to prevent her from touching the bandage covering the side of her cheek.

"Nae, Patience. You need tae lie still, *mo leannan.*" Julian's voice wrapped its way around her in a light caress. He was here. Her fingers moved against his as she licked her lips.

"How…long?" she asked hoarsely. Her eyelids felt heavy, and she struggled to keep her eyes open.

"Two weeks, me darlin' girl. Doctor Branson thought it best that we keep ye sedated for a while."

As if from across the moors of Callendar, she heard her aunt's voice. Her gaze shifted toward the sound, and the soft rustle of silk filled the air as Aunt Matilda bent over her. A smile curved the Scotswoman's lips, but she could see the concern in her aunt's gaze.

"We thought we had lost ye, Patience," her aunt said as she gently squeezed her shoulder.

"You're healing nicely, Lady Patience," the young doctor said in a quiet voice as he continued to dress her burns. "But you still have a long road to recovery. We'll need to begin stretching exercises as soon as you are more fully awake. It will be painful, but it's necessary to avoid contraction of the limbs."

Patience's eyelids brushed her cheeks as she realized the bandage the doctor had applied must have contained something to ease her pain as her arm no longer felt as if it were consumed in flames. It simply throbbed in a way that made her stomach roil. Images of the blaze at Westbrook Farms filled her head, and she drew in a sharp breath of fear.

The air made her chest hurt until she coughed violently as she remembered watching Caleb and Devin plunging to their fiery deaths. Patience released a sob.

"Vision… didn't…understand."

"*Christ Jesus*, Patience." Julian's voice was thick with an emotion she couldn't decipher. "'Tis nae your fault, *mo leannan*."

"You cannae blame yourself, dearie." Aunt Matilda's fingers stroked her unmarred cheek. "The *an dara sealladh* is nae always clear. There was nothing ye could have done."

"Caleb," she breathed her brother's name. "Devin."

"They are in a better place now, my darlin' lass." Her aunt's mouth brushed across her brow.

Patience's eyes fluttered shut. Her visions hadn't been able to help her save Caleb or Devin, but the scars she'd seen were a reality. She would never be the person she'd once been. Her scars would be her penitence. They would make her a monster to the children.

Worst of all, she'd be pitied. It was no less than she deserved. She'd survived, and two fathers had not. She had no children to leave without a parent to love them. Nausea rolled over her. How could she expect Julian or her family to look at her again without flinching? God, how she wished they'd left her to die in the fire.

"Dinnae *ever* let me hear ye say something like that again," Julian growled fiercely.

Her eyes opened at his low rumble of anger, and she realized she'd spoken out loud. Patience met Julian's gaze, which was dark with emotion. Pity? The thought was unbearable. She tried to pull her hand free of his, but he held fast to her fingers. The strength of his grasp made her heart ache while giving her the courage to do what was necessary.

"Leave," she whispered hoarsely. "I don't want you here."

"I'm nae going anywhere, Patience," he said as he tightened his grip on her hand. "Everything will be all right, *mo leannan.*"

"Liar."

The word was a soft condemnation, and Julian paled beneath her gaze. He was wrong. Nothing would ever be the same for her—or for him. Not only was she barren, but she was also now an object to be pitied. He was better off without her. Patience tugged at her hand, but Julian refused to let it go as a stubborn expression crossed his face. Angry that he refused to listen, she came up off her pillow to tugged viciously against his grip.

"I *don't* want you here," she cried out. The movement of her mouth tugged at the burns on her cheek, and a scream of pain escaped her.

Tears blurred her vision as the room erupted in a rush of sound. Her heart shattered as Julian did as she'd ordered and released her hand. Exhausted, Patience closed her eyes, barely hearing Julian's harsh whisper as he argued with her aunt and Doctor Branson. Another voice joined the others, and she recognized Sebastian's calm presence. Her brother would take care of everything. Sebastian always brought order to chaos. He would convince Julian to leave. The thought made Patience's heart constrict painfully in her chest. She wanted to take back her words but knew she couldn't. It was the last thing she remembered as she slipped back into the depths from which she'd come.

Chapter 6

S he's my wife. She belongs with me," Julian exclaimed with angry frustration.

"And she's *my sister*," Sebastian said with an implacable coldness and stubbornness reminiscent of Patience's temperament. "I'm abiding by her wishes. Patience has made it clear she wants to remain here at Melton House."

"For how long? It's been six months since the fire. She's refused tae see me since the day she—since the day she first woke up."

"I'm sorry, Julian," Sebastian said with a disgusted shake of his head. "Our coaxing her to change her mind only seems to make her all the more adamant in her refusal to see reason."

"Aye, tis nae a surprise," he bit out. "Patience's always been stubborn, but nae more than I. If I thought it would help matters, I'd simply drag her out of the house and take her tae Crianlarich."

"I am glad to hear ye have nae intention of doing something as foolish as that."

Matilda Stewart eyed him with disapproval from her seat on the couch. Julian met the Scotswoman's gaze, and her condemnation dissolved into sympathy. He didn't want anyone's commiseration. He wanted Patience to come home.

"Staying locked up in her room isn't healthy," Julian ground out.

"Don't you think we know that?" His brother-in-law eyed him with irritation. "Aunt Matilda is the only one allowed in her room on a regular basis. She's convinced herself she's a monster people will run from."

"Bloody hell," Julian muttered with frustration. "I had nae doubt her burns would leave her scarred, but nae so bad as tae have her believe others will think her a monstrosity."

"Her burns *are* disfiguring, but nae to the extent she believes. Give the lass time, Julian. She's been through far more than any of us could imagine. She still blames herself for Caleb and Devin's deaths." Matilda Stewart met his gaze with an expression of sympathy. He shook his head.

"She cannae continue to hide from the world *or me*. I don't care what she looks like. I love her. I simply want her tae come home so I can take care of her." Julian heard the same amount of stubbornness in his voice that matched Patience's, and Sebastian uttered a sound of frustration and sympathy.

"Your feelings for my sister are without question, but I have reason to believe Patience's refusal to see you isn't simply about her scars." His brother-in-law pinched his nose and closed his eyes for a brief moment before meeting Julian's gaze. "I don't know—nor do I wish to know—what happened between the two of you before the fire, but she's asked me to begin proceedings for a divorce."

"I won't give her up." Julian's hard-edged response made his brother-in-law nod in understanding.

"I didn't think you would, which is why I've not done anything about it," Sebastian said with a wry twist of his lips. Before he could say another word, the salon doors opened, and Percy strode into the room, his expression dour.

"Helen and I have managed to convince Patience to come out of her room."

"Thank God," Aunt Matilda said with a relieved sigh while Sebastian and Julian stared at Patience's brother in amazement.

"How the devil did you and my wife manage that miracle?" Sebastian asked with an open display of heartfelt relief. Julian didn't bother to look at the patriarch of the Rockwood family as he studied Percy's troubled expression.

"How did you convince her? Is she coming down now?" Julian asked as an overwhelming relief swept through him, followed by an uneasy sensation.

He didn't expect Patience to speak to him, but just seeing her again would be enough for the time being. Impatiently, he waited for his brother-in-law's answer. The other man avoided looking at him, and Julian's gut twisted with dread. One hand rubbing the back of his neck, Percy finally raised his head to look at Julian with a wary expression.

"She has a condition." At Percy's words, an uncomfortable silence filled the room.

"She'll come out provided I'm nae here." Julian clamped down on his teeth until his jaw felt as though it would crack under the pressure. Percy grimaced as his gaze met Julian's.

"Actually, she said you're never to come here again."

"*Saints preserve us,*" Patience's aunt exclaimed in horror.

"Bloody hell," Sebastian muttered as he looked in Julian's direction.

The moment his brother-in-law shared Patience's stipulation, Julian went rigid. Despite Patience's rejection of him shortly after the fire, hope had kept him going over the last several months. But the condition she'd just tied to her agreement to leave her room had pulled the rug right out from beneath him.

"I'm sorry, Julian," Percy said with obvious frustration. "We've been arguing with her for more than a week now. But God help me, she's as obstinate as a mule."

"I see you've told them," the Countess of Melton said as she entered the salon. She looked directly at Julian with compassion and shook her head. "I'm so sorry, Julian. I know we've been saying this for months, but I really do believe she simply needs time. The doctor says her reaction is not unusual. We simply need to be patient."

Julian's gaze flitted from one Rockwood to the next before he stalked across the salon to one of the windows overlooking the street. Outside, the avenue was busy with the day's traffic, but all he could see were images of that terrible night. The images still had the power to make his muscles tighten and grow hard as a tree trunk.

The memory of the anguish and fear on Patience's face as they'd all watched Devin and Caleb plummet to their deaths. Then her screams of grief and fear afterwards. The sound of her cries still echoed in his head whenever he thought about that night.

What had been all the more gut-wrenching had been the expression of surrender he'd seen on her face only seconds after her brother fell to his death. She'd been terrified but resigned to dying like her brother. The memory of it made him fold his arms across his chest and dig his fingers into his biceps.

It had been his bullying that made her jump through the flames, but he wasn't sure she'd forgive that or anything else he was guilty of. The thought filled him with a despair he'd not felt since the day his mother had died. If he lost Patience, life would hold little meaning for him. He turned to face the people he'd come to cherish as a part of his own family.

"If it means Patience will come out of her seclusion, then I'll abide by her wishes," he said through clenched teeth.

"It will pass, Julian," Aunt Matilda said with what he believed was an overabundance of confidence. "Patience is a strong woman, she will come around, and all will be well."

"Nae," he said with a vicious shake of his head. "Percy said it well, she is as stubborn as a mule, and I cannae make her forgive me. I'll leave and will nae return unless she asks for me."

With a nod, he walked toward the salon door. He had little doubt that his current state of unhappiness could have been avoided if he'd simply been honest with her. But he'd been so exhausted the day they'd argued that he'd not been thinking clearly enough to realize Caitriona had only made him swear not to tell *her father*. She'd not sworn him to keep the truth from anyone else.

He could have told Patience everything that day without really breaking his word to Caitriona. It would have stretched the boundaries of what was honorable, but at the moment, he'd gladly give up everything he owned, including his honor, just to take his words back. His failure to stretch the confines of his vow had cost him everything he held dear. Every inch of him ached as if he'd been in a boxing match. But he had lost. The only woman in the world he would ever love had condemned him to a prison he would never escape from unless she produced the key.

"Julian." The manner in which Aunt Matilda called his name made him stop, but he didn't turn around. Silk rustled quietly as the Scotswoman moved to his side to touch his arm. "The lass loves you. I'm certain of it."

"Does she? She's made her decision, and I will abide by it," he said as the words ripped at his insides. Julian drew a harsh breath into his lungs and looked over his shoulder at Sebastian. "I have a condition of my own. I will never give her a divorce. I'll fight it with everything I own."

"I'll make that quite clear to her, Julian." Something akin to satisfaction crossed his brother-in-law's face.

Nodding, Julian didn't say another word and left the room. In the hallway, he accepted his hat from Madison, the Rockwood butler. A brief whisper of sound made him jerk his head up as he saw Patience's unusually slight figure in the dark shadows of the second-floor landing. *Christ Jesus*, she'd lost weight. It was impossible to see her face in the shadows, and he longed to see her.

Without thinking, he crossed the floor to the staircase. As his hand settled on the bannister, and he put one foot on the steps, her horrified gasp fluttered down to him. In a flash of movement, she disappeared. Frozen in place, he heard a door slamming. He didn't have to hear the grinding of a metal key to be certain she'd locked her door. Locked him out of her life for what he feared would be a lifetime. The thought was enough to bring him to his knees. His body rigid with pain, he walked out of Melton House, leaving his heart behind him.

The train rolled to a stop at the Crianlarich station. Julian pulled his bags down from the overhead rack with suppressed anger, then threw open the compartment door and stepped down onto the station's narrow, roughly hewn platform. In front of him, craggy hills towered over the forest that made up the rest of the landscape. The gray sky cast a pallor over the hills giving the land a stark appearance that was as ominous and threatening as it was hauntingly beautiful.

Whenever he came home to Scotland, he was always in awe of his country's harsh yet resplendent majesty. The few people who had gotten off the train with him had already begun their walk into the village. His gaze fell on the carriage that had been sent to bring him home. It carried him one step further away from Patience and one step closer to the man who'd help destroy his life.

The vehicle's door swung open, and he saw the Laird of Crianlarich step out onto the road. Fergus MacTavish's plain brown work kilt was offset by the MacTavish tartan fly plaid he wore on his shoulder. His father was a tall man, falling just shy of Julian's own height. Fergus MacTavish was a handsome but dour-looking man with his neatly trimmed, peppered beard, and Glengarry dipped low over his forehead. His stern, weathered features eased slightly as he directed a small smile at Julian.

"'Tis good tae have ye home, lad," Fergus said as he shook Julian's hand then gestured toward the carriage.

Julian quietly thanked Drummond, their driver, as he handed his bags off to the man. The longtime servant touched his cap deferentially as he accepted the baggage. The vehicle's interior was cramped, and seated across from his father, the combination of their long legs made it all the more confining.

The carriage rolled forward with a jerk, and Julian stared out the window. Why had he come back to Crianlarich Castle? Because the house he'd shared with Patience had become a tomb without her.

"I take it your wife will nae be coming any time soon?"

"No," he said crisply, unwilling to listen to the Crianlarich belittle Patience.

His father's indiscretion was one of the reasons he was no longer with his wife. God, how he missed her. The memory of how Patience had fled from him yesterday when he'd glimpsed her on the second-floor landing of Melton House still haunted him. He'd always loved his wife's full curves and lush thighs. The silhouette he'd seen standing in the dim light of the upstairs corridor was a mere shadow of the woman he'd married.

His jaw clenched as he remembered the lies he'd told Patience to protect Caitriona's shame. At the time, it had seemed the right thing to do. Now it made everything all the more painful knowing the lies he'd told might mean Patience would never return to Crianlarich or the house they had shared in London.

If he'd simply told her the truth, he would have had a much better chance of convincing Patience of his innocence and that Una was a liar. He had no idea how the woman knew about his birthmark. Not even when he'd unleashed his wrath over Una's head more than a month after the fire had the woman offered up any explanation as to how she knew about the mark.

"Where's your head, lad? I asked you a question."

"My apologies, sir." At his stilted reply, Fergus shook his head slightly.

"I asked how well Patience was mending?"

"What?" Julian stared at his father in amazement before he narrowed his gaze at The Crianlarich. "Since when did you give a damn about Patience?"

"I am nae always a hard-hearted man, Julian," Fergus said in a strained voice. "I might nae have liked ye taking her as a bride, but I hae never wished her harm."

"I find that surprising since you did your best tae convince her that she wasn't good enough for me," he bit out as he glared at his father. The Crianlarich flinched before an implacable mask of stone hardened his features. Silence drifted between them for several moments as Julian returned his gaze to the landscape outside the carriage.

"I received a note from Lady Westbrook thanking me for the flowers I sent tae her husband's funeral. The fire was a terrible thing." His father's attempts at conversation puzzled him as he bobbed his head without looking at Fergus.

"And Patience's scars? Are they—"

"Why this sudden interest in my wife, Crianlarich," he snarled as he used one of his father's less formal titles. He glared at the man who'd played a part in his unhappiness.

"Because ye are my son, and I know ye love the woman. I also know tis nae been easy on ye or any of the Rockwoods. Two deaths and Patience's injuries are nae something tae heal from quickly."

"It's hellish," he said sharply. "The family has found it extremely difficult tae deal with Caleb's and Devin's deaths as well as their concern about Patience."

"I dinnae envy Lady Westbrook left alone tae raise her children," his father said with a note of sorrow in his voice. "When I lost your mother, I dinnae know what tae do."

"I doubt your cock remained soft for too long." Julian's crude comment made his father jerk his head back in astonishment before his face reddened in anger.

"I loved your mother, lad, and dinnae ye ever forget that," the Crianlarich snarled. "Dinnae confuse love with a mon's baser needs."

A small nugget of regret lodged in Julian's throat at the insult he'd thrown at his father before he remembered Caitriona. He gritted his teeth and jerked his gaze back to the passing scenery. Caitriona had loved her father deeply, and Bensmore had always doted on both his daughters.

In her confession to him, Caitriona had made it clear that Julian was never to tell her father about the child. She'd told Julian that she'd left home because Caitriona knew it would have killed her father to know what she'd done. Her worst fear had been what her father would say when he discovered the child's father was Fergus MacTavish.

"How is the boy faring," he asked quietly without looking at Fergus.

"He's going tae be a strapping lad just like his older brother." There was a note of pride in his father's voice that filled Julian with anger.

"You should have married her the moment you bedded her," Julian said with outrage and disgust as he turned his head back to meet his father's startled gaze. A split second later, the Crianlarich narrowed his eyes at Julian.

"I dinnae pursue the lass," Fergus said. "She entered my bed without invitation. I had nae wish tae marry again, and I told her that."

"As I said, your cock has nae remained soft."

"Caitriona dinnae tell me she was carrying my son. If she had, I would have done the honorable thing by her." His father's voice echoed belligerently in the air as he refused to accept any blame for what had happened to Caitriona.

"And have you told Bensmore the truth?" At the question, Fergus moved uncomfortably in his seat.

"'Tis been hard enough on the mon, losing Caitriona. I dinnae need to add tae his pain."

"In other words, you have nae had the courage tae tell him you were the one who sullied her, left her with child, then abandoned her."

"I dinnae abandon Caitriona. I dinnae know the lass was with child until ye sent the bairn to Crianlarich with the letter that I was the father," Fergus said indignantly. "I have done my duty by the child."

"But nae tae Bensmore. The man deserves tae know his grandson," Julian said between clenched teeth.

"Ye can tell him the truth," Fergus said with a crafty look. Julian glared at him.

"You know damn well I gave my word tae Caitriona nae tae tell her father."

"And yet ye dinnae have a problem breaking ye word when it came tae telling me the boy was mine," his father sneered.

"Caitriona dinnae ask me tae hide the truth from you—only her father, and I'll nae break my word tae her. But you're a coward for nae telling the man the truth." Julian's scorn made his father's face grow dark with rage.

"Dinnae judge me, boy. Tis better Robert believes Caitriona's child died with its mother in childbirth. The mon has been humiliated enough."

"And what about Aiden? Has Bensmore nae even questioned Aiden's sudden arrival at Crianlarich Castle?"

"I told him the child is yours and Patience's. He thinks ye sent the boy here because of the fire and Patience injuries."

"*You did what?*" he snarled.

Julian stared at his father with raw fury. The bastard had no shame. Worse, he'd made Patience a pawn in his charade. He wanted to wrap his hands around his father's throat and squeeze until the man was on the brink of death.

"I thought it a perfect solution," Fergus shrugged. "Ye and your wife have yet tae have a child, but Bensmore and everyone else dinnae know that."

"And what do I tell Patience? Do you really think for one moment she'll accept the child as her own?" Julian ground out with the same fury he'd wielded over Una's head for her part in destroying his marriage.

"Aye, for all her lack of Scottish blood, she loves you," the Crianlarich said with confidence. "She'll take the babe as her own."

Disgusted by his father's actions and lies, Julian stared out the window once again. How in the hell was he supposed to explain his father's lie to Patience? What would it do to her when she learned everyone believed her to be the mother of Caitriona's and her father-in-law's baby? A child she might think was his. He closed his eyes for a moment.

When Caitriona had begged him not to tell Bensmore who her lover had been, Julian had instinctively known she was pleading with him to tell no one about the baby. But she'd only mentioned her father, not anyone else. The morning he'd returned home, he'd been awake for almost two days. Lack of sleep was the only explanation for why he'd chosen to keep Caitriona's secret from Patience. He'd been a fool.

If he had foreseen the ramifications of not telling Patience the truth, he would have chosen differently. His inability to see what had been in front of his eyes all along said how little regard he'd had for his wife's fears about Una and the malicious mischief the Scotswoman might cause. Perhaps worst of all, he'd failed Patience in not confronting his father about the seeds of doubt the Crianlarich had planted in his wife from the moment he'd brought her home to meet his father. But it was too late to undo the damage, and it emphasized what a fool he was. It was a steep price to pay for the knowledge.

Julian grimaced. He'd accused Patience of not being able to trust him, and yet he'd repaid the debt in kind by lying to her. Even worse was the havoc Una had added to the wretched mess. His jaw hardened at the thought. Not even when he'd confronted the woman had she been remorseful. Instead, she'd scornfully dismissed Patience and suggested that he divorce her and take a true Scottish wife. That Una had actually thought he would do such a thing reinforced his anger and disgust for his father. The Crianlarich had filled Una's head with hopes of one day being Mistress of Crianlarich. Una's successful attempt to destroy his marriage revealed the woman would go to great lengths to achieve her goal.

The carriage wheel hit a deep rut in the road, and it jogged Julian out of his thoughts. He glanced out the window opposite his seat. They were on the narrowest stretch of road leading to the castle. On his father's side of the carriage, the byway bordered a drop-off of almost a hundred feet. Across from him, Fergus uttered a low growl as he leaned forward to stick his head out the window.

The Crianlarich shouted at Drummond, but before Fergus could retreat into the cabin, one of the wheels at the back of the carriage cracked loudly. The wheel wobbled violently in a manner that made the vehicle teeter precariously toward the edge of the small cliff. Outside, the horses were whinnying loudly while Drummond called out to them in a voice filled with fear.

"Father, move tae this side of the carriage," Julian snapped as the vehicle tilted further toward the cliff.

The Crianlarich moved quickly to do as Julian ordered, but his shift in position destabilized the vehicle more. With a loud screech of wood and metal, the carriage tumbled off the short craggy incline. He heard his father cry out while the horses screamed in terror. Instinct made Julian brace himself against the wall of the vehicle as it rolled downward.

Tossed to the opposite side of the carriage, his head slammed against the side of the wall that had been pierced by a large rock. The moment his head hit the granite, he could have sworn someone had taken an ax to his skull. Patience's face filtered through his pain to hover in front of him like a shimmering light. In that brief moment, he thanked God she wasn't with him. It was the last thing he remembered before he passed out.

Shouts echoed in the distance, and Julian slowly regained consciousness. He had no idea how long he'd been senseless. Opening his eyes, he realized it was nighttime. The moon had to be behind the clouds as there wasn't a single drop of light in the carriage, making it impossible to see his father. Julian touched his throbbing forehead and suppressed a groan. The knot on his head was the size of a large egg, and there was blood from a cut close to his temple. Christ Jesus, his head hurt. A sharp pain radiated from below his knee, which was trapped beneath his other leg. The moment he straightened the leg, pain streaked up it with the force of a hammer blow.

"*Fuck*," he snarled as he slammed his fist into his upper thigh and waited for the knifelike sensation in his calf to ease.

Julian hovered on the edge of consciousness for a moment before the pain dissipated to a persistent stabbing sensation. The tension in his body slowly abated, and a slow breath of relief rolled past his lips. He didn't need a doctor to know his leg was broken. Julian uttered another oath as he stretched out his hand to search for his father in the darkness.

"Father, are you all right?"

After groping for several seconds, his hand found the Crianlarich's arm. Gently, he squeezed his father's shoulder. He tried to shift his position, but this time it was his head that protested with a vicious stab of pain. The voices were almost at the shattered vehicle, and Julian realized he'd fainted again. Furious that his body wasn't cooperating with his desire to move, Julian steeled himself for more pain as he reached out to touch his father. His fingers brushed the side of his father's face, and he tapped him lightly on the cheek.

"Father, *answer me*," he snapped. He smacked harder at the Crianlarich's face. The instant he did so, his father's head lolled to one side, and Julian drew in a sharp breath of shock. Despite their differences, Julian loved his father. It seemed inconceivable that he might truly be gone.

"Crianlarich, Mr. MacTavish, are ye all right?"

"Who's there?" His leg protested viciously the instant he shifted his position. Pain pulled a loud grunt from him as he struggled to remain conscious. In the back of his mind, he tried to understand why the man didn't have a light.

"Do ye nae recognize me, Mr. MacTavish? It's Croft. Ainsley is with me too."

"How badly is my father injured?" he asked, hoping his initial assessment was wrong.

"I'm sorry, sir." Croft hesitated before his tone shifted to one of sympathy and regret. "The Crianlarich has met his maker."

Julian closed his eyes at the words as grief dug into his senses. It penetrated his physical pain to lash at his heart. Frozen in place, it was as if someone had suspended him in the bleakest of nights with the realization he was the new Crianlarich. The thought only reinforced the fact that his father was dead, and grief tugged at him again. He pushed his sorrow aside as he remembered the driver of the carriage.

"Drummond. Is he all right? The horses?"

"Aye, Crianlarich, Drummond will be fine. He has a broken arm and a gash on his leg, which needs stitching. The horses are the only ones who escaped any injury, although I dinnae ken how tae explain that miracle."

In the back of his mind, Julian noted Croft had addressed him by the honorary title that was now his as the new Laird of Crianlarich. With a nod, Julian suppressed a sound of pain as he tried to find a more comfortable position to recline in.

"Crianlarich, we need tae get you out of the carriage," Croft said.

"My leg is broken," he said hoarsely as his every word sent pain jabbing through his forehead to the back of his head. "You'll need a board. I cannae walk or ride."

"Right. Ainsley off with ye now tae the castle and fetch help."

"And bring lights," Julian snarled through his pain. "How the devil were you able to see anything out on the moors at this time of night?"

"Night, Crianlarich?" Puzzlement mixed with worry in Croft's words.

"Yes, night. I cannae see a damn thing in this infernal darkness." Julian frowned with anger. Was the man daft for being on the moors without a lantern when it was so dark?

"But, Crianlarich..." as Croft's voice died away, a whisper of something insidious slithered its way through Julian.

"What time is it?" he demanded.

"'Tis a little after four, Crianlarich."

"In the morning?" he snapped, unwilling to believe what the voice in the back of his head was suggesting.

"Nae, Crianlarich," Croft said in a worried voice. "'Tis the afternoon. Ainsley and I were out on the moor when we saw the carriage roll off the road."

"Four in the afternoon..." Julian growled like a wounded animal.

With a growing sense of doom, he roughly rubbed his eyes, hoping to erase the black abyss that had replaced his vision. When he opened his eyes again, all he saw was darkness. Anger and fear weighed against his chest with the heaviness of a tree trunk. Desperately, he struggled to suppress the shout of fury rumbling in his chest.

The result was a low groan of pain breaking free from his lips. It barely eased the tightness in his chest, but it hid the dread rising inside him. Eyes closed again, he willed himself to obliterate the darkness. When Julian opened his eyes to nothing but blackness greeted him, and another cry of rage rose in his chest. He was blind.

Shock wrapped its arms tightly around him, causing him to go rigid as he fought to contain the rising stem of dread. Panic struck deep at the core of him. He pushed back against the terror as he rationalized the reason for his blindness. The only blood was from the gash on his temple. It was obvious his eyes themselves were uninjured. That left his head injury as the only logical reason for his blindness. Temporary blindness, he told himself, despite a growing fear that it might not be temporary at all.

Croft seemed to understand he had no desire to talk as they waited in silence for Ainsley to return with help. Images of Patience filled Julian's head, and once more, he experienced gratitude that she hadn't been with him. The thought of her suffering more injuries or perhaps even death made him choke back bile. Would she be worried about him if she learned of the accident?

Suddenly he remembered Patience's vision of a spinning carriage wheel and fire. Twice the *an dara sealladh* had shown her disaster, and yet both accidents had been unpreventable. Again he uttered a silent prayer of thanks to the Lord that she wasn't with him. She blamed herself for Caleb's and Devin's death. Knowing Patience as he did, she might easily blame herself for this accident as well. Muireall would want to send word to Patience, but he wouldn't let her. Patience had endured enough pain and suffering in the past six months. He refused to add to her misery. Julian wasn't sure how long they waited, and at the sound of approaching voices, he experienced a small measure of relief.

"*Julian,*" his half-sister's voice filtered through his pain, and he frowned. "Julian, are ye all right? Is father all right?"

"Damn it, Muireall, what are you doing here," he snarled, not wanting her to see their father's body like this. "Croft, get her out of here. *Now.*"

Muireall protested vehemently, and suddenly he caught the scent of heather and lavender breezing into the broken carriage. Her dissension quickly became a wail of sorrow. Furious that he'd been unable to shield her from the truth a little longer, he shot upright in an attempt to grab her hand. When he found nothing but air, the pain wracking his body slammed through him like a fast-moving train. A fraction of a second later, he lost consciousness.

Chapter 7

J ulian."

Patience screamed his name as she awoke and jerked upright in her chair. The book in her lap fell to the floor as the fire crackled in the fireplace. Running feet pounded against the foyer's marble floor, their sound announcing Percy even before he charged into the morning room.

Her gaze met her brother's, who moved quickly to her side. As he knelt in front of her, she turned her scarred cheek away. Gently, he turned her head toward him and brushed tears off both sides of her face. Startled by the touch, she realized she'd been crying.

"Another dream?" Percy asked gently.

The worried frown on his face made Patience wince. The doctor had said her nightmares about the fire would eventually fade with time. He'd even said the one or two instances when she'd walked in her sleep would run its course. But this dream had not been about the fire.

This time they'd been filled with nothing but images of Julian lying in a dark space with his leg awkwardly bent beneath him. Was it a dream or a vision? It was impossible to tell the difference anymore. She swallowed the knot of pain that had quickly formed in her throat and shook her head.

"I'm fine. Dr. Branson said it would take time for the nightmares to disappear."

The soft whisper of feminine footsteps moving quickly across the main entryway made Patience turn her head to see Louisa enter the room. Dressed in mourning black, her sister's life with Devin had been a good one, and she had been desolate since that terrible night. Now, as she met her sister's gaze, Patience experienced guilt at causing Louisa to worry. The youngest of the Rockwood siblings hurried to the settee and sat down next to her. She clasped Patience's hand in hers and squeezed it in a gesture of comfort.

"Another one?"

The concern in her sister's voice made Patience nod. The fire in the hearth suddenly crackled and popped loudly. Patience jumped violently at the sound, and Percy quickly moved to the fireplace to spread out the coals in an effort to deaden the sound the flames created. She was certain it was his attempt to alleviate any reminder of the fire for all three of them.

"I'm fine," Patience said softly as she gently pulled her scarred hand free of Louisa's grasp.

She covered the marred flesh with her other hand while dipping her head slightly to minimize the scars her sister could see on her face. Patience wanted to spare her sister as much pain as possible. Her burnt flesh was simply a reminder to Louisa that Devin was dead and Patience wasn't.

"*Don't*," Louisa said sharply as she uncovered Patience's scarred hand. "Don't you ever be ashamed of those scars, Patience Rockwood MacTavish. If it weren't for you and Caleb, the family would have lost our future that night. Devin would say the same thing to you if he were here. Our children were more important to him than life itself."

Patience's eyes widened with surprise as she met her youngest sister's fierce gaze. A stark pain filled Louisa's hazel eyes. But the strength displayed on her lovely features was an expression she knew well. It was the same look Patience had witnessed on the faces of her entire family as each of them had dealt with their grief over the past nine months.

Yet despite Louisa's reprimand, Patience found it unbearable to look in the mirror. Last week in an effort to stop Sebastian's badgering, she'd ventured out with her brother for a morning ride. They'd rode out just after dawn, but their effort to avoid people had been to no avail, and it had proven painfully obvious why she should never go out in public.

Several family acquaintances had been out as well, and despite the netting attached to her riding hat, she'd endured looks of horror and revulsion. But it was the looks of pity that had made her withstand Sebastian's growing insistence that she ride with him again. From the fireplace, Percy cleared his throat as he clasped his hands behind his back.

"Several of us were wondering—"

"Patience, I'm planning to go with Aunt Matilda when she returns to Callendar Abby in a few weeks," Louisa interrupted her brother with a nasty glare before she turned back to Patience. "I hope you'll reconsider going with us. We're taking Greer, Alma, and Braxton with us."

"We've discussed this before. I'm content where I am," Patience said as she cast a glance in Percy's direction for a brief moment.

It was obvious the family thought she should go to Scotland, but there were two reasons why she refused to do so. The first was that the journey meant being out in public where she'd be the subject of scrutiny no matter how much she tried to cover her scars. Secondly, Crianlarich was little more than an hour north of the abbey. She had no intention of enduring the possibility of Julian coming to visit her aunt.

"It will be good for you, Patience," her brother said in a coaxing voice.

"I'm quite happy here."

"Louisa could use the help, and you know the children adore you. They don't care about your scars any more than the rest of us do. We all love you."

Her brother's blunt words made her flinch. She averted her gaze as she struggled with the idea that her family members might really not care about her disfigurements. Patience swallowed hard at Percy's words. Perhaps it was time to accept herself as she was. Her throat tightened. No, her family might see past her scars, but society would not, and the thought of going out of the house was almost paralyzing.

"I've given you my decision. I no longer wish to discuss the matter," Patience said in a quiet but firm voice. Percy could plead all he wanted, but she had no intention of going to Callendar Abby.

"Are you afraid?"

Percy's confrontational question told her that he knew precisely why she refused to go to her aunt's Scotland estate. Tension tugged painfully at the scarred skin on her cheek while her hand ached as the stiff scars protested as her hand tightened into a fist. Patience tried to relax to ease her discomfort as she narrowed her gaze at her brother.

"No, but Julian might take it in his mind to call on Aunt Matilda, and I have no wish to see him."

"For the love of God, Patience," her brother exclaimed angrily. "When are you going to forgive the man for whatever wrong he's done you?"

"Whatever happened between Julian and me is our affair and no one else's, Percy," she said coldly as she rose to her feet. "But I have my reasons. Good reasons."

Regret swept across her brother's features, but she ignored his obvious remorse and walked out of the morning room. With each passing day, one family member or another gently pressed her to reconcile with Julian. She resisted vehemently, not because she couldn't forgive him.

Patience had forgiven Julian his small lie and accepted how important his honor was to him. It made her heart ache for not believing him. She'd allowed the Crianlarich and Una to make her question Julian's faithfulness. But what kept her from going to him was the thought of being the recipient of his pity. Even if he still loved her, it would be impossible for him not to feel pity for her. Worse, he might view her and their marriage as one of duty.

She'd already earned more than her fair share of pitying looks. The burns from the fire had left horrific scars on her arm, leg and face from the edge of her cheekbone back to her ear. She was grateful that she'd not suffered the loss of hair. But the last thing she wanted was for Julian to see her like this. It would be unbearable, particularly when there was the possibility of seeing Una.

Compared to the woman's beauty, she would look like a beast if she were ever in Una's company again. Her stomach lurched at the thought. She had no wish to suddenly face the Crianlarich or Una and become the target for their ridicule or pity. Patience winced as she crossed the floor to the main staircase. She paused at the foot of the stairs, acknowledging the fear that held her paralyzed for a brief moment.

It had taken time for her to go up and down the stairs without the vivid memory of fire engulfing the staircase of Westbrook Farms. The memory of being trapped had proven crippling on more than one occasion. She started up the stairs and winced as the tight scars on her leg were forced to stretch with her movements. She'd been lax in her exercises and was paying the price.

Behind her, she heard the door knocker hitting the metal plate on the front door. A streak of panic spread through her. She never accepted callers and always hid when someone arrived at Melton House. Ignoring the pain in her leg, Patience moved quickly up the stairs as Madison opened the front door. She was halfway to the second floor when she heard a voice pleading with the family retainer.

"Please, I need tae see Mrs. MacTavish."

"I'm sorry, miss, but Mrs. MacTavish is not receiving callers."

"Oh, please. Tis verra important. I cannae leave without seeing her."

The soft lilting brogue filled Patience's ears, and her heart stopped. Slowly, she turned to see Muireall attempting to push past the stalwart servant. Her sister-in-law was almost seventeen, and Patience drew in an appalled breath that Muireall stood on the doorstep without a chaperone.

Her heart skipped a beat. Was Julian waiting outside and had sent his sister inside to act as an emissary? Conflicted as to what to do, Patience stared down at the small altercation at the door. The moment Percy and Louisa emerged from the morning room, Patience made up her mind before her siblings did so for her.

"It's all right, Madison. This is my sister-in-law. You may let her in."

No sooner had she given the order than Muireall pushed her way past the butler with the rough strength only available to the young. The girl charged forward as Patience slowly descended the stairs. Muireall's eyes widened in horror the moment she saw the scars on Patience's face. Unable to help herself, she flinched in the face of the girl's dismay. Tears formed in the girl's eyes, and as Patience reached the foot of the stairs, Muireall raced forward to fling herself into Patience's arms. The girl didn't say a word. She simply clung to Patience in a silent message of sympathy for what Patience had suffered. Gently, Patience pushed her sister-in-law away from her and wiped the tears from the girl's cheeks.

"Enough tears, sweetheart. Where is...who's with you?" If she'd said Julian's name, everyone would hear the tears in her voice.

"No one," Muireall said with a contrite expression before she frowned. "Julian would nae have let me come."

Louisa's gasp of dismay matched her own consternation as well. Percy uttered something unintelligible beneath his breath. Despite her appalled reaction, she experienced great relief that Muireall had arrived at Melton House unharmed.

"Come, we'll go into the morning room." Patience looked at the butler, whose face was one of fatherly disapproval and concern for the girl. "Madison, would you see to it that someone brings a tray into the morning room? Also, please arrange for a telegram to be sent immediately to Crianlarich Castle. Let Mr. MacTavish know his sister has arrived here safely, and we will send her home tomorrow with a chaperone."

"Of course, Lady Patience," Madison said

As Patience guided the girl past her siblings, Percy touched her arm in a silent question, and she shook her head. Whatever had possessed the girl to come here alone, it had to be important, and she knew Muireall's actions were connected to Julian in some way. Her heart constricted at the thought. Was Julian miserable without her? The thought warmed and pained her at the same time.

"When did you last eat?" Patience wrapped her arm around the girl's waist as they walked toward the morning room.

"Cook gave me porridge this morning before Julian was up. I told her I was going to Callendar for the day as I have a friend there," Muireall said with satisfaction at her ingenuity before she grimaced. "Although I dinnae expect the train tae take so long tae reach here. Julian will worry when I dinnae return home."

"The telegram Madison sends will reassure everyone at Crianlarich that you're safe," Patience said in a soothing voice.

"He will nae be happy with me," the girl said with a troubled frown furrowing her brow.

"I should think not," Patience said as she chastised her young sister-in-law. "What if something terrible had happened to you on the way here? Julian would be inconsolable to lose you as would I."

"You would?" The disbelief in Muireall's voice made Patience frown in puzzlement.

"Why would you think I wouldn't?"

"Because you never came back tae Crianlarich," Muireall said in an injured tone.

"I'm sorry, sweetheart, but it was difficult for me." She didn't know what else to say without speaking ill of Muireall's father. "But you did come to spend a month with us last spring."

Us. Just saying that word made Patience think of happier times. Muireall reached out to touch Patience's hand.

"I know my father was nae kind to you, Patience, but everyone in the castle loves you. Julian, most of all." The moment Muireall mentioned Julian's feelings for her, Patience pulled her hand back. God how she wished she'd had the courage to go home to Julian. Life was miserable without him. Patience shook her head and abruptly changed the topic.

"When you arrived, you made it sound urgent that you see me."

"Aye," Muireall nodded as a look of deep sorrow darkened her sweet features. "I know Julian would be furious, but I cannae bear to see him suffering."

"Muireall, if you—"

"No, you dinnae understand," her sister-in-law said fiercely. "There was an accident. My father…he was killed…"

"Oh, I'm so sorry, dearest," Patience exclaimed softly as she caught Muireall's hand in hers and leaned forward to press a kiss against the girl's forehead.

"I know he was a hard man, but he loved us, and I miss him," Patience's sister-in-law said quietly before she shook her head. "But it is Julian. He was in the carriage, too."

"Carriage?" she barely breathed the words, and she could feel the blood draining from her cheeks.

Her heart slammed to a stop in her chest before it began to race inside her breast. The *an dara sealladh*. The image of a carriage wheel spinning madly in the air filled her head. She'd seen both the fire and Julian's accident but had been helpless to stop either one. Patience suddenly felt light-headed, but the dizziness passed after a few seconds. She focused her gaze on her sister-in-law.

"When did it happen?"

"A little less than three months ago. It happened the day he returned to Crianlarich."

"Why didn't he..." she whispered as a chill spread across Patience's skin. He believed she didn't care what happened to him.

"I *knew* Julian was wrong. You *do* still care for him." Satisfaction brightened Muireall's face as she squeezed Patience's hand. "You must come home tae Crianlarich."

"I...it's not quite that simple, Muireall," she stumbled over her words as her sister-in-law's expression mirrored one she'd seen many times on Julian's face. Despite having two different mothers, the brother and sister possessed the same stubborn nature.

"Julian needs you, Patience. He was hurt."

"*How?*" she whispered hoarsely.

"He's blind."

Muireall's quiet reply made Patience grateful she was seated as a tremor rocked her body. It was the worst thing that could happen to a man like Julian. He would be unable to function without someone's aid, and if there was one thing her husband didn't like, it was feeling helpless. She recalled the instance shortly after they'd married when he had slipped on the stairs and sprained his ankle.

During that short time of healing, a lion would have been easier to manage than Julian's frustration at not being able to do things for himself. No one had been spared his sharp tongue, not even her. She grimaced at the thought. The soft clink of china announced one of the maids arriving with Muireall's luncheon tray. Patience gestured for the servant to set it on the coffee table and thanked the woman. Her gaze returned to Muireall's hopeful expression.

"Eat your lunch."

"Will you come home with me?" Once again, Muireall's persistence illustrated how much she was like her brother. Patience could only assume their headstrong nature was a trait they'd received from their father.

"I shall consider it. In the meantime, I want you to eat," Patience said firmly. "I need to ensure that telegram to your brother has been sent."

"He's dismissed several nurses, and the last one only lasted a week, Patience. He needs you more than you know."

"I said I shall consider it. Now eat." At her instruction, Muireall nodded and leaned forward to pick up a plate. She stopped and turned her head toward Patience. "I am sorry for your loss, Patience, and I'm sorry you suffered so terribly."

"Thank you, Muireall. Now stop dawdling and eat. I'll return in moment."

Patience choked out her words as her throat closed up with tears. She stood up and hurried toward the morning room door. As her hand touched the doorknob Muireall called out to her.

"Julian says you're the bravest woman he's ever known." Muireall's words wrapped themselves around her heart and squeezed it until she thought it would stop beating. Patience looked over her shoulder at the younger woman. Her sister-in-law stared at her with something close to hero worship. "He's right, Patience. Your scars prove how brave you are."

Patience responded with a sharp nod then pulled the morning room door closed behind her. With her back pressed into the wood door, she closed her eyes for a moment. What was she going to do? Did she have the courage to go to him? Would he even want her? Julian thought she'd sent him away because she believed him unfaithful. How could she explain the real reason and her own lie? He would be justified in throwing her out the door of Crianlarich Castle.

"Well?" Percy's voice echoed quietly in the foyer, and her eyes flew open to see her brother studying her from the salon doorway. "What did she have to say?"

"Julian's been hurt." Patience started forward, her body feeling wobbly and weak.

"Good God," her brother exclaimed in a low voice. "Is he all right?"

"He's blind." Just saying the words made Patience's stomach churn. Percy was across the foyer in seconds as he wrapped his arm around her waist.

"Come sit down before you faint."

"I'll be fine," Patience said with a shake of her head. But she didn't object as her brother guided her into the main salon. As they entered the room, Louisa, her aunt and sister-in-law, Helen, all stood up with expressions of curiosity.

"What's happened?" her sister asked quietly.

"Julian and his father were in an accident the day Julian returned to Crianlarich. Muireall's father is dead, and Julian is now blind."

"Sweet heavens," Aunt Matilda exclaimed as Helen and Louisa echoed her dismay.

"But why did Muireall wait until now to tell you?" Helen exclaimed in dismay. "And for that reason, why did she come to Melton House to tell you when a telegram would have been easier?"

"She wants me to go home with her to Crianlarich," Patience said as closed her eyes in pain and fear for Julian. What would Julian do if she returned to Crianlarich? "She says Julian needs me."

"What was your reply?" Louisa's gaze was probing as she studied Patience's face.

"I said I would consider it." At her response, the entire room was filled with a silence that she recognized as one of shocked surprise. Patience's gaze scanned the faces of her family and grimaced. "I know I have been adamant about my refusal to see Julian, but this is different."

"What you really mean is that when he wanted to remain at your side, you sent him away. You pushed him away because you thought he only wanted to stay and care for you out of pity and his sense of duty," Louisa scolded. "And what if he thinks you've returned to him for the same reasons? How do you think he'll react to that?"

"But I thought they had a fight before the—"

"For heaven's sake, Percy, do be quiet," Louisa snapped with irritation without bothering to look at their brother. Her sister narrowed her gaze at Patience. "Well, Patience?"

"He will be like a lion in a cage, ready to eat me alive. But I have no choice but to win his heart again."

The moment her words drifted through the air, Patience knew she had decided to return to Crianlarich the moment Muireall had pleaded with her to return. She would go to Crianlarich Castle. While her task would be difficult, if Julian still cared for her, as Muireall said he did, she would find a way to make him believe she loved him. The silence in the room lasted only a minute before her brother exhaled a loud breath.

"About bloody damn well time," Percy muttered. Louisa eyed him with annoyance before she moved forward to take Patience's hand in hers.

"I think I can speak for the rest of the family when I say we're relieved."

"Aye, that we are," Aunt Matilda said as she moved forward to kiss Patience's cheek.

As she studied the expressions on her family's faces, she shouldn't have been surprised at their relieved expressions, but she was. They clearly believed she'd made the right choice, but she was far from certain of that. Julian could be even more stubborn than she was. Her heart rose in her throat. He would fight her every step of the way when it came to her convincing him pity had nothing to do with her return. The thought made her wince, and Aunt Matilda squeezed her arm.

"Ye are a Rockwood, lassie," the Scotswoman whispered in a reassuring tone. "Challenges are something we thrive on. The mon will never know what hit him."

Patience turned her head to see a twinkle in the older woman's eyes. For the first time since she'd decided to return to Crianlarich, a small measure of confidence sought to suppress her uncertainty. Perhaps Aunt Matilda was right, but only time would tell.

Chapter 8

"*loody hell*," Julian snarled as he hobbled to an abrupt stop and bent to rub his throbbing shin. Behind him, the sound of running feet made him quickly straighten upright. He turned toward the sound.

"Are ye all right, Julian?" Worry made his sister discard proper English as she came to a halt in front of him. He dismissed her question with a sharp wave of his hand, mindful to keep the gesture as far above Muireall's head as he could visualize. The last time he'd swung his arm outward, he'd hit her.

"I'm fine, lass," he snapped, unwilling to admit what had just happened. His blundering only reinforced Muireall's argument that he needed a nursemaid. It was a proposal he'd been fighting tooth and nail since the last nurse he'd discharged.

"Ye didn't sound fine a moment ago." The relief and irony in his sister's response made his mouth twitch with a small smile despite his irritation at her escapade more than a week ago.

"No, I suppose not," he said reluctantly as he fought to see Muireall's face. Unable to do so, a furious frustration snaked its way through him until he wanted to hit something.

"What were you trying to do? Marry your leg to the chair behind you?"

"And why would you make that assumption?" he asked through clenched teeth.

"Because the chair has been knocked a kilter," his sister said with a sigh as she brushed past him to push the chair back into its normal position.

He tried to follow her movements, but all he saw was a slender black shape against the light gray landscape that was all that remained of his vision. Silently, he shouted with rage at his inability to see his sister's face or the displaced chair that had betrayed his clumsy attempt at independence.

"You've been avoiding me," he growled.

Muireall's adroit methods of staying out of earshot over the past week illustrated her awareness of his anger. But it also displayed a shrewd understanding on her part that time would ease his outrage. His sister had known he was furious, and she'd stayed out of his way until now.

"I knew you were angry with me," she said in a matter-of-fact voice. "I thought it best to wait for your anger to become irritation before I threw myself at your feet begging forgiveness."

"You have a touch of the devil's tongue, Muireall MacTavish," he said with amusement before he frowned with disapproval. "You shouldn't have gone to London without an escort."

"What you mean is that I shouldn't have gone to see Patience."

Her impertinent tone made him look heavenward as if he could actually *see* heaven. But that realm had disappeared the day Patience had sent him away from Melton House. With the cane he'd been using to find his way around the castle, he searched for the chair his sister had adjusted. When the wood stick connected with the side of the chair, Julian sank down into the seat. With a sigh of frustration at his sister's meddling, Julian rested both of his hands on the eagle-shaped metal cane top.

"You should nae have gone. It is dangerous for a young woman tae go tae London without an escort," he bit out with a trace of the fury he'd experienced when they'd received the telegram from Melton House. "Anything could have happened to you, Muireall. If you'd been hurt…you were reckless, and it's nae tae happen again."

"Don't you want to know how Patience is?" The sly note in his sister's voice made him twist his lips in a bitter smile.

"*Nae*, I dinnae want tae know how Patience is." It was a lie, but his pride wasn't about to admit he wanted more than anything to hear everything his sister had to say about his wife.

"I asked her to come home."

"*You did what?*" Without thinking, Julian was on his feet and reached out for his sister. His fingers bit down into soft shoulders, and he bent his head until he felt the warmth of her breath on his face. "How *dare* you interfere in something you know nothing about? If Patience wanted to come home, she would have done so long ago."

"Nae, Julian. You haven't seen her face. *Nae* woman would want her husband to see her with such scars. It has to be the reason she sent you away. She loves you. I saw it in her eyes. She loves you just as much as you love her."

"*Enough*," he snarled despite the way his gut wrenched at the thought of Patience not trusting him enough to love her no matter what she looked like. "Dinnae *ever* interfere in my affairs again."

"Yes, Julian." There was a note of trepidation in his sister's voice, and he stretched out his hand until his fingers touched a wet cheek.

"I'm sorry, lass," he said with a sigh of regret. "But you cannae fix people like you can a piece of broken furniture."

"Well, she did say she would consider coming," Muireall whispered with a small trace of defiance.

"And what makes you think I want her here?" Julian asked sharply. "I have nae need of her pity."

"But if she came, it wouldn't be because she pitied you, Julian. She loves you."

"I'm done with this conversation, Muireall. Dinnae interfere in this matter again. Is that understood?"

"Aye." It was a clipped answer that indicated she was unhappy with his decision, but he knew she'd abide by his order. "But I dinnae regret asking her to come home."

Julian snorted with mild disgust at his sister's defiant reply. The sound of muffled voices in the foyer outside the library made him stiffen. Since the accident, he'd refused to accept callers. He had no use for anyone's pity. Before he could speak, Muireall's hand squeezed his arm before he could object to the visitors.

"Dinnae argue with me about this, Julian," his sister said with a hint of steel in her voice.

In that split second, he knew his sister had arranged for another nursemaid candidate to come meet with his approval. He'd already rejected four previously, and the one nurse he'd agreed to hire had left after just one week. Julian knew it was his temper that had driven the older woman to leave, but he had little use for someone who treated him like a child.

"You've arranged for another nursemaid to come interview for a job.

"Aye," Muireall said softly. "You *will* be nice to this lady, won't you, Julian? Lorne has said you have been exceedingly rude to the other candidates."

Although he appreciated the efforts of Muireall and his childhood friend, who now served as his estate manager, he knew it was an exercise in futility. There was only one woman he would even consider for the post, and the thought of her coming here out of pity filled him with anger. He had no need of her pity or her help. The thought that she would come at all almost made him snort with incredulity. Muireall squeezed his arm again in a silent plea.

"Aye," he bit out with a sharp bob of his head. "I'll be cordial."

"Thank you," his sister said. There was an odd note in her voice that any other time he might have thought was excitement, but he dismissed it as her relief he'd agreed to be polite. With a grimace, he patted the small hand on his sleeve.

"Go see to our guest," he said in a quiet voice.

"You *promise* to be nice?"

"I promise," he said with a slight smile.

Interviewing another candidate was the last thing he wanted to do, but he knew Muireall was deeply worried about him. Worse, he knew she was right, but he'd hoped his vision would have returned by now. In the first few weeks after the accident, his vision had gone from nothing but the stark darkness of a moonless night to the beginnings of shapes against a fuzzy white background.

The doctor had expressed optimism at the change, but at his last visit, the man had indicated it was possible Julian's vision would never return. It was one of the reasons he was unwilling to reject this latest candidate outright. As much as he resented the idea of relying on someone, it was time he thought of Muireall.

Losing their father had devastated her. Adding to her grief was the burden she'd taken on caring for him. She never complained, but it was too much to ask of her. She was a young girl who should be enjoying the attentions of suitors at a dance or visiting Edinburgh or London for a spring wardrobe. He was not a rich man, but he was more than capable of ensuring Muireall had a proper wardrobe.

As he heard his sister leave the room, Julian reached behind him to touch the chair that had gotten in his way. He wanted to throw it across the room. Instead, Julian leaned his cane against the back of the chair before he slowly skirted it and headed toward the wide expanse of windows that to him resembled nothing more than cloudy patches of white. He paused for a moment as he stumbled slightly next to the settee. His fingers skimmed the soft velvet upholstery until he found what he was looking for.

The pillow in his grasp, he visualized where best to place it. Moving into the open space between the settee and the large expanse of windows, he dropped the stuffed roll of fabric onto the floor. His foot noted where the pillow was, then he counted off the steps to the window. Satisfied with the test he'd engineered, he faced the wide expanse of white that was his only view of the scenery beyond. In his mind, he saw the rolling moors stretched out in front of him.

There was a chill in the air today. It penetrated the glass to brush over Julian's legs and hands despite the warmth of the room. No doubt the sun was hidden by clouds. It reflected his sullen mood. He heard someone enter the salon, but he didn't move. Judgment day was at hand.

"Crianlarich—"

"Leave us, Lorne." He didn't allow his friend to finish his introduction. When he sensed his estate manager was about to object, Julian stiffened his back with displeasure. "*Now.*"

"As you wish," Lorne said in a soft voice.

The sound of his friend retreating from the main salon left silence in his wake. It hung thick and heavy in the air. With his back to the woman his sister had brought in for an interview, he heard the soft rustle of silk as if she'd shifted her weight where she was standing. It made him think she might be nervous or intimidated by him. The thought gave him satisfaction. At least he still possessed the ability to unsettle people despite his affliction.

"Sit." The harshness of his command cracked through the air.

"I prefer to stand."

Patience. He froze, suddenly unable to move. Why had she come? Muireall. His sister's pleas had made his wife feel obliged to return to him. Julian clamped down on his jaw until it ached as he slowly turned to face his wife.

"What do you want, Patience?"

He heard a small sound escape her, and he frowned. Was his work kilt or jacket askew? With great restraint, he prevented himself from tugging at his jacket. He stared at the dark, softly curved shape against the light gray background in front of him. When he considered the wraith in the shadows of Melton House, it pleased him to know her curves had returned. He immediately scoffed at himself for caring. Julian saw what must have been her arm move as if she had pressed her hand to her throat.

"I…I thought…"

"That I might need your pity?" he lashed out with a bitterness he'd kept locked up inside him over the last three months.

"*No,*" she exclaimed softly. "I came to tell you I was wrong, Julian."

"Wrong?" he sneered. "What pray tell were you wrong about, madam?"

"I should have believed *you* and not…Una." Simple and clear, her words rang out across the space between them. For almost a year, he'd long to hear her say those words, and yet now, they seemed hollow.

"I have nae need for your apologies, Patience," he said in clipped tones.

"But you *do* have need of my help." The quiet determination in her voice sent a surge of anger coursing through his veins.

"You're mistaken. I can see well enough to move around quite easily," he lied in a cold voice as he strode forward, intent on sending Patience on her way.

"*Stop*," she exclaimed. Startled, Julian stopped in his tracks while keeping his features hard and inflexible as he glared in her direction.

"What?" he snarled.

"There's a pillow directly in your path," she said quietly. "If you continue forward, you'll trip and wind up sprawled on the floor like a newborn foal."

Julian scowled as he realized he'd forgotten about his test for the candidate he'd *been* expecting. Patience was the first one who'd passed it. None of the other candidates had ever thought to give him oral commands. They'd all rushed to his aid as if he was a child incapable of doing anything on his own. But then Patience was his wife.

She knew him well enough to know he would never tolerate being treated like a child. Julian strode straight to where he'd left the pillow, kicked it to one side, and then closed the distance between them. The soft lilac scent she wore was a familiar one, and he breathed in the sweetness of her. God help him. She smelled wonderful. It took every ounce of self-restraint he possessed not to pull her into his arms. Patience wasn't to be trusted. She was here simply because she felt pity for him. She'd said she believed in his innocence, yet it was all too easy for her to say what she thought he might want to hear.

Desperately, he tried to see her face, but it was nothing more than a round shadow in front of him. Despite his determination not to touch her, the urge to stroke her cheek was strong. He stretched out his hand to her. Even though it had only been three months since the accident, his other senses were already compensating for his lack of sight, and he heard the sharp intake of her breath. He could almost feel the tremor that shook her body before she recoiled from him.

Raw fury barreled through him. She'd said she'd been wrong not to believe him, and yet she still found him repulsive. The last time he'd been near her, she'd called him a liar, but she was the liar. She was here out of duty and pity, nothing more. It was the one thing he didn't need from her. He wanted nothing from her at all. A mocking laugh echoed in the back of his head. He straightened.

"Leave, Patience. There's nothing for you here."

"I'm not leaving, Julian. You're my husband. I belong here—with you."

"Go or stay, it matters nae tae me," he said in an icy voice.

"Then I choose to stay."

"As you wish." Julian shrugged, then stepped around her, intent on picking up his cane from where he'd left it at the chair. She didn't move as he found the stick and headed toward the door.

"Julian."

The melodious sound of her voice caressed his ear just as her lips had done in the past. He wanted to strangle her for the way she could make his body respond to her so easily. Ignoring her, he continued making his way toward the door of the library.

"*Damn you, Julian MacTavish*, don't you dare walk away from me. Do you have any idea how difficult it was for me to come here?" Her words made him come to an abrupt halt, and he whirled around to face her.

"If you came seeking redemption, you'll nae find it here, Patience."

"I came to Crianlarich Castle because I *wanted* to, not because I had to."

"Then your trip was a waste of time," he said with open hostility.

"You forget how stubborn I am, Julian." The determination in her voice made him lock his jaw in anger.

"I've forgotten neither your stubbornness nor your request for a divorce," he sneered. "I suggest you return to

London and have your attorney draw up the papers. I'll sign them as soon as they're delivered."

Patience's gasp held what might have been a note of pain, but he ignored it. The idea that he might have hurt her with his agreement to give her what she wanted wasn't worth a second thought. Without another word, he walked out of the library and lurched his way to the staircase. He was almost at the top of the stairs when Muireall called out to him from below.

"Julian, where are you going?"

"To my room," he snarled. "Thanks to your damned interference, 'tis the only place I can go where I will nae be nagged by a wife who's suddenly developed a conscience where I'm concerned."

Julian didn't wait for his sister's response. He simply turned and made his way down the hallway to his room. What the hell had his sister been thinking to ask Patience to come here? His cane beat a harsh rhythm as he walked along the corridor. When the tip of his cane connected with his bedroom door, he fumbled slightly as his hand sought to find a firm grip on the doorknob.

With a violent push, he thrust the door open, and it crashed backward into the wall with a loud crack. The swish of air it made as it bounced back in his direction made Julian raise his hand to stop the door from hitting him. He stepped deeper into the room and took immense pleasure in slamming the door shut behind him.

"*Damn her,*" he said with a bitterness that had been slowly eating away at him for months until he no longer cared whether he lived or died.

He'd been dying in bits and pieces since the day his marriage had fallen apart. The fire a few days later had only made matters far worse. For two weeks, he'd not left Patience's side. She'd drifted in and out of consciousness, but he'd refused to leave her. At times she'd seemed to hear his voice, and her hand always tightened around his just before she sank back into her drug-induced sleep.

But it had been those moments when Dr. Branson had changed her bandages that her hand had gripped his so tightly. It had made him believe she needed him. He'd been wrong. It had simply been the response of a woman in pain. When he'd heard her call him a liar through her agony, he'd realized he might never hear her heartbeat against his chest again.

Julian staggered his way toward the chair in front of the fire and sank down into it. Patience's refusal to leave Crianlarich meant he'd find few places where he could avoid hearing her voice or breathing in her delicious scent or, worse, stumbling into her exquisite curves. That would be the worst possible thing of all because he wasn't sure he'd be able to keep his hands off her.

Julian snorted at the thought. He would have no problem keeping his distance from her. All he had to do was remember how she'd recoiled from him earlier. That memory alone would keep him from touching her. Once more, a mocking laugh echoed in the back of his head. He ignored the way the voice reminded him that he was a liar.

With a grunt, he closed his eyes and rubbed his temple. He could feel the beginnings of one of the headaches that occurred regularly since the accident. Even his fully healed leg ached. The doctor had said that was something that would never go away despite the way the bone had knitted together so well. The ache was something he could deal with rather than the pain from a constant limp. He was fortunate where his father had not been.

The memory of his father came with a mixture of regret and resentment. The Scotsman had been a hard man to love. Things had only been made worse by his adamant rejection of Patience as Julian's bride. He'd never understood why his father had opposed his marriage so stridently, but it mattered little now. His marriage had fallen apart just as Fergus MacTavish had always maintained it would. His temple had begun to throb more insistently, and Julian forced himself to relax in an effort to reduce the strength of the headache. His last thoughts before he dozed off were of Patience's laughter and her sparkling eyes.

He wasn't sure how long he'd been asleep when the persistent knock on his door pierced his consciousness.

"Come," he commanded in a sharp tone.

The sound of the door opening was preceded by the clinking of china. Was it dinner time already? No sooner had the question popped into his head than the clock on the mantel began to chime. The chime ended on the eighth ring, and he realized he'd missed dinner.

"Muireall, is that you?"

The only reply was the sound of his dinner tray scraping softly across the table Muireall had arranged to be placed at the window. The smell of succulent roast beef made his mouth water. A moment later, the door to his bedroom closed, and he frowned. Muireall usually remained behind in case there was something he wanted. With a grunt of irritation, he rose from his chair to move to the table. Seated in front of his plate, he picked up his fork to stab at a piece of the beef. Where he'd expected bite-sized morsels was a large hunk of meat.

"*Damnation*," he muttered. Mrs. Drummond had failed to cut up his meat for him. His fork hit the table hard, knowing his meat would be cold by the time he rang for someone to come cut up the meal.

"You're quite capable of cutting it up yourself." The sound of Patience's quiet yet firm voice echoed behind him, and he jerked with surprise before he stiffened. Why the devil hadn't he realized she was in the room? Because his head was still wooly from his headache.

"Is there nae room sacred in my own home that you won't enter, madam?" he snapped.

"If you had come down for dinner, it wouldn't have been necessary for me to intrude on this hiding place of yours." Patience's voice was a mixture of amusement and irritation.

"I want my meat to be cut as it usually is," he said sharply. "Take it downstairs and have Mrs. Drummond cut it up."

"You may cut it up yourself." Her retort was short and crisp.

"What did you say?" he growled deep and low as anger swelled up inside him.

"If you're so desperate to be independent, why haven't you learned to do more things for yourself?" Patience said with exasperation. "Cutting your meat up is one of those things. Otherwise, you're little more than a babe in the woods."

"I am *nae* a babe in the woods," he bit out fiercely despite knowing she was right.

"Then prove it by learning how to cut your meat up. I've ordered Mrs. Drummond to fix your plate a certain way from now on," Patience said in a matter-of-fact tone. "Your meat will always be at five o'clock on your plate. Vegetables will be at eight, ten, and two. Soups and stews will always be at six o'clock when it's served. Desserts will also be at six o'clock when served after the meal. If you have a tray, dessert will be to the left of the plate at the hour of eight, while your bread plate will be just above it at ten. Your wine and water goblets are where they always have been at one and two, and your coffee or tea will be to the right of your plate at three o'clock."

The explanation was so logical he wondered that he'd not thought of it himself. The fact that Patience had done so but not him irritated the hell out of him. The quiet sound of silk brushing against the carpet echoed in his ear, indicating she was headed toward him. Julian heard her sit down opposite him.

"Well?"

Her voice was quiet, but there was enough mockery and challenge in the one word it made him wrap his hand around his fork in a grip almost tight enough to bend the metal. He didn't answer. He simply picked up his knife and attacked the meat. The utensils scraped viciously against the china plate as he stabbed at the roast beef. He'd cut several pieces up before she sighed.

"If you cut up the entire piece of meat, it will make it more difficult for you to know how much is left to cut," she said quietly.

There was nothing in her voice that resembled pity. For a brief second, Julian allowed himself to hope she'd come to Crianlarich for a reason other than duty before crushing the notion. He didn't respond to her comment. He simply stopped cutting the meat. Julian took a bite of the beef then gently probed the areas on the plate where she'd said his vegetables would be. The skirlie Mrs. Lester had prepared was to the left of the roast, and he took a bite of the mashed potatoes mixed with onions and oats.

As always, Mrs. Lester's cooking was exceptional. She'd won numerous pie-baking contests at the local fair, and he knew there were many who'd tried to lure her away from him. But he paid her well to ensure she didn't leave him. He took a bite of the cauliflower, cheese, and whiskey casserole the woman had made.

The three flavors mixed and mingled pleasantly on his tongue. Patience remained silent as he ate, and he remembered the meals they'd often enjoyed at home. There hadn't been silence between them then. The air had been filled with her laughter.

"I'm sorry about your father, Julian." Her voice was soft with sincerity, and he bobbed his head in a sharp acknowledgement of her condolence.

"The fact that you say so is more than he deserves," Julian said with bitterness.

Patience was far more generous with her commiserations than she should be. It was his father who'd set into motion the destruction of her happiness and his. And what would she say when she learned Aiden was here at the castle? His gut knotted at the thought. Patience would think the worst of him for certain.

Anger and resentment erupted inside Julian as he attacked his unseen slab of beef. The old Crianlarich had created a mess, and Julian had been forced to clean it up. In the process, he'd lost Patience. In the back of his head, a small voice whispered that there was the possibility he could be wrong. Muireall had said Patience still loved him. If that was true—he crushed the hope without hesitation.

"Muireall says you don't go outside anymore."

"My sister does nae know when tae hold her tongue," he said harshly before regretting his sharp tone. Muireall only had his best interest at heart.

"She loves you," Patience said softly with the hair's breadth of a pause that made him think she'd been about to say something else. "And you're evading the topic."

"Perhaps you haven't noticed," he said sardonically. "I'm blind."

"And prone to self-pity as well." The dry note of amusement in her voice made Julian clench his teeth.

"I dinnae feel sorry for myself," he growled as he focused his gaze on the dark round shape that was her head.

"No? I'd venture to say you play the martyr quite well," she murmured unsympathetically. "You forget I remember how disagreeable you can be when you're confined in your movements."

Julian ignored the lack of compassion in her voice. It was obvious she was referring to the time he had a sprained ankle. He wasn't about to say it out loud, but she was right. He was a surly bastard when he couldn't move about under his own steam. Silence filled the room as he continued to eat his dinner. Julian reached out to the dessert plate then stopped.

"Do I need a spoon for dessert?" he asked with annoyance.

"I'm sorry," she murmured ruefully. "I should have mentioned that I had Mrs. Lester send up some gooseberry jam shortbread cookies. I didn't know they were your favorites until she mentioned it."

He grunted and bobbed his head at the thoughtful gesture. Unwilling to expand on the expression of gratitude, he cautiously ran his fingers along the rim of the dessert plate to pick up one of the cookies. The sweet taste of the cookie mixed with the tart gooseberry jam in the center for a delicious treat.

It was almost as savory a taste as he remembered Patience's mouth could be. Julian frowned at the direction of his thoughts. The sooner she left Crianlarich Castle, the more quickly he'd forget her. He knew it was an asinine thought even before the jeering voice in the back of his head could chide him for it. Forgetting Patience was impossible. When he'd finished eating, he wiped his mouth with his napkin then dropped it carelessly over the remains of his meal. He leaned back in his chair and tipped his head to one side as if it would help him actually see her face instead of the dark shadow he saw.

"Why are you here, Patience?" he asked in an emotionless voice. He heard her draw in a quick breath of surprise. He immediately remembered times when he'd touched her, and she'd gasped just as sweetly. Julian shoved the memories out of his thoughts to wait stoically for her response.

Chapter 9

Patience sucked in her breath quickly at Julian's question. How was she supposed to answer him? She closed her eyes for a moment before looking at him again. Blindness had not destroyed his commanding presence. If anything, he was even more devastating to her senses. Her heart ached to tell him the truth at this very moment, but she knew he wouldn't believe her. There was even the possibility that Muireall was wrong.

Her lack of trust in him so many months ago could have easily destroyed his love for her. The thought caused a small bout of nausea to roll through her. No, she couldn't believe that. She simply needed to regain his trust, and his entire demeanor today said it would take time to do that.

"I asked you a question," he bit out. "Or are you trying tae determine what lie tae tell me next?"

"I've not lied to you," she said quietly. "I came because you need me. I came because I want to be here."

"I told you earlier—I dinnae need you."

"Don't you," she huffed at his obstinate response. "When was the last time you were outside? When did you last go for a ride, something I know you enjoy immensely?"

"A ride?" Julian laughed loudly, but there was bitterness in the sound. Her heart ached for him, but compassion and pity would not help him. "I think you've gone a bit daft, madam."

"Why? Because I think you can do things that you've convinced yourself that you can't?" she snapped. "I was right about you playing the martyr. You're not even willing to at least try to do things you enjoy."

"Because I can't."

The flat response took her breath away for a second. He truly believed he was incapable of living a full life despite his affliction. The Rockwood family thrived on challenges, and she knew Julian would not be able to turn one down either. She bit down on her lip for a brief second before she stood up.

"You surprise me, Julian," she said with deliberate disdain in her voice. "I never took you for a coward."

Patience started toward the door, and in a flash of movement, Julian was on his feet, one hand braced against the table as his hand reached for her. On the first thrust of his hand outward, his fingers grazed the top of her shoulder. Before she could step out of reach, his hand wrapped around her arm, and he pulled her toward him.

Fury had darkened his features, and if she didn't know him well, she would have thought him capable of beating her. He leaned in close to her, and Patience drew in a sharp breath of surprise before her entire body hummed with a familiar vibration.

The blank, sightless look in his beautiful coffee-colored eyes as he stared at her without seeing her made Patience flinch. It made her wish with every fiber of her being that she had the ability to give his sight back to him. His mouth thin with outrage, she realized she might have pushed him too far.

"Dinnae *ever* call me a coward again, Patience. I'll nae take that from anyone, especially a woman who hid from the world for six months," he snarled. His words cut at her emotions like a finely honed sword. But she would willingly accept the brutality of them if it meant she could give him back his independence. She swallowed the knot threatening to close her throat.

"Then I take it I shall not be riding alone tomorrow morning?" she asked in a careless tone.

"Aye," he growled. "Ye will *nae* be alone."

His grip on her arm relaxed as if he intended to let her go before he tightened his grip again. With a sharp tug, he pulled her into his chest. The sudden proximity of him made her heart do a somersault. Fingers splayed against Julian's chest, she breathed him in. He smelled of warm spice and bergamot. It had been too long since she'd been this close to him, and she trembled with a sudden need that scorched its way through her veins.

His mouth was so close to hers that with just a slight tilt of her head, their lips would touch. Almost as if he'd read her mind, his hand cupped the back of her neck as his other arm wrapped around her waist, and he pulled her tight against him.

"I have nae idea why ye came back, Patience," he said hoarsely. "But ye are treading a dark and dangerous path, lass."

No sooner had he uttered his warning than his mouth captured hers in a demanding kiss. A tremor shot through Patience as her lips parted beneath his. Every bit the arrogant, commanding Highlander, his tongue swept into her mouth to duel tempestuously with hers. She knew it was folly, but she responded eagerly to his hot caress. The tart taste of gooseberry lingered in his mouth and danced across her tongue as his swirled around hers.

Caught up in the raw, sensual maleness of him, the heat radiating off him engulfed her until her body trembled with need. Hard, steely muscles pressed into her body with a powerful, unyielding strength that tempted and aroused her. She ached to feel his skin against hers until she didn't know where she ended or he began.

Hot and erotic, his kiss enticed and claimed her until a hedonistic rush of pleasure spiraled through her veins. It sent a pulse streaking down to the center of her core. The moment it reached the sensitive spot between her legs, a low cry of need rolled out of her throat as her body ached for more than just his kiss. The exquisite need for fulfillment spiraled through her while her heart raced out of control.

She moaned softly as with each stroke of his tongue, she yielded to his silent seduction. The pounding of his heart vibrated against her fingertips as a desire so deep and strong made her blind to everything but his kiss. She forgot all that had brought them to this point and simply gave herself up to the sweet passion of the moment. The low growl rumbling in his chest sent a rush of delight streaking through her. In the next instant, he thrust her from him.

"*Get out*," he said coldly.

Heart beating wildly in her breast, Patience stared up at Julian's stony expression. There wasn't the slightest trace of emotion on his face, and tears welled in her eyes. Was he truly lost to her? Had she come to Crianlarich Castle for nothing? The back of her hand pressed against her mouth, Patience silenced the cry of pain careening through her. She gulped back her tears and raced out of Julian's bedroom.

In the hallway, Patience slowly walked the few steps down the corridor to the bedroom next to her husband's. Although Patience had protested, Muireall had insisted that as the Crianlarich's wife, the bedroom next to Julian's belonged to her. Wiping the tears off her cheeks, Patience quietly entered her room lit by just one candle.

As she'd instructed, there was no fire in the fireplace. Muireall had objected, expressing concern that Patience would be cold. She'd simply shook her head and requested more blankets. In the dim light, she looked around for her trunks. They were tucked away in the corner behind a screen with her things already in the wardrobe and chest of drawers.

Exhausted from her journey and her contentious interaction with Julian, she proceeded to undress. She was certain she would have no problem sleeping through the night. Her nightmares were now fewer and further between, but stressful days like today had a propensity to make her experience unexpected moments of panic.

With a heavy heart, she pulled her nightgown from the wardrobe. She'd just dropped the silk gown over her head when she heard a crash in Julian's room. Without thinking, she raced toward the connecting door between their rooms. Patience's hand touched the cool metal doorknob for a fraction of a second before she jerked it back at the sound of Julian cursing his inability to see what he was doing.

A breath of relief whispered past her lips. He was all right. There was no need to antagonize him any further tonight. And she had no doubt the knowledge that she was sleeping in the room right next to his would definitely anger him. Slowly, she walked back to the bed and sank down onto the mattress.

Patience closed her eyes and pressed her fingers against her lips. She'd been woefully unprepared for Julian's kiss. He'd been as masterful as always, but when he'd pushed her away, his expression said he'd been completely unmoved by their kiss.

Had it been his way of demonstrating exactly how futile her efforts were in coming to Crianlarich Castle? But if he believed she'd come simply out of pity and her duty as a wife, what purpose did kissing her serve? Confusion spread its wings to speed its way through her. Whatever Julian thought, he would not be easily convinced that she'd come to Crianlarich because she still loved him. Patience's lips tightened with determination, and her cheek protested.

Extremely tired, Patience longed for nothing but to slide under the covers. She considered putting off for just one more day the stretching exercises she was supposed to do daily. But her marred flesh had been tight and itchy all day, and it had intensified over the last few hours. She muttered an unladylike curse for not having done her usual regimen of exercise and emollients for more than a week now. Now, when she was fatigued, she couldn't put off her exercises any longer.

Harlan would not be happy with her at all. The thought of Dr. Branson made her mouth twist in a small smile. Immediately, the mottled skin on her cheek sent a signal of pain to her head. It was a vivid reminder that she needed to do her exercises. Harlan had been a regular visitor to Melton House ever since the fire. Although he was still her doctor, he'd become a friend as well. Like her family, there was no horror or pity in his eyes when he looked at her. Knowing he'd be disappointed at her lack of discipline, Patience went in search of her cosmetic case. As she did so, she tilted her head to deliberately pull and stretch the taut flesh of her cheek.

She continued to repeat the exercise as she retrieved the special cream Harlan had prepared for her. It was designed to ease, if not eliminate, the need to scratch at her skin for relief. Jar in hand, she sat down at the dressing table and avoided staring at her reflection. It still pained her immensely to see the creature she'd become. Closing her eyes, she applied the emollient to the tight, dry skin of her cheek.

The soft floral scent of lavender, sandalwood, and something Harlan called aloe wafted beneath her nose as she worked the cream into the scarred tissue. Harlan had said the aloe was a natural ointment to alleviate the pain caused by burns. Relief came quickly, and she sighed as the unpleasant tingling began to subside. Patience continued to do the facial exercises Harlan had taught her as she applied the soothing lotion to her forearm and lower leg. When she'd finished working the cream into her skin, she began to stretch her arm and leg in the exercises that would help keep the skin from retracting.

The movements brought tears to her eyes, and she angrily berated herself for allowing her packing to prevent her from following Dr. Branson's orders. She would not forgo them in the future. After a long time, the tight discomfort of her scars eased, and she stopped her exertions. The jar lid screwed back into place, she set it on the dressing table. As she did so, her gaze settled upon the scarred woman in the mirror.

Although she hated the fact that Julian's blindness had taken his independence, she was grateful he couldn't see the horrid thing she'd become. Patience winced at the thought as she rested her elbows on the vanity and cradled her face in her hands. The journey to Crianlarich today had been long and had started out unpleasantly.

Victoria Station had been a discordant mix of train whistles, shouts, and the loud whoosh of steam engines. Everywhere there was chaos, and her hand had gripped Percy's arm as if it were a life preserver. Her brother knew exactly how difficult being in public was for her.

"You're doing fine, Patience," her brother said in a soothing voice. "Nothing to it. We'll get you on the train, and you'll be in Crianlarich before you know it."

She didn't have a chance to respond as a tall, burly man charged past her, his large shoulder knocking her away from Percy. In her effort to remain standing, her hat became caught in another passerby's jacket, and it was tugged completely off her head, along with the veil that covered her face.

"*Oh, dear God,*" she exclaimed in panic. "Percy...where's my hat?"

"Here you are, miss," the cheerful voice of a boy echoed in her ear.

Not thinking, she lifted her head to meet the boy's gaze. Instantly, the child dropped her hat and recoiled from her with a small cry of horror. At his cry, other people turned their heads, and gasps of dismay and pity assaulted her ears.

Percy growled an oath and leapt forward to scoop up her hat. Deftly, his arm about her waist, he shielded her as she fumbled in her efforts to hide her face again. Terror spiraled through her, and she clung to her brother's tall strength.

"I can't do this, Percy," she whispered hoarsely. "Take me back to Melton House."

"Of course you can do this, sweetheart. You're a Rockwood. Rockwoods never turn away from a challenge."

"No, I just can't," she said with a small sob as she burrowed her face into his chest. Percy held her tight and quietly soothed her as she fought back tears.

"Patience, you're the bravest woman I've ever known, but even better than that, you're my sister," he said against her ear as he held her close. "Do you love Julian?"

"Yes," she rasped.

"Then you have little choice except to get on this train, do you?" At his matter-of-fact manner, Patience pulled away from him. She accepted the handkerchief Percy handed her and slipped her hand beneath the veil to dry her tears.

"This is the hardest part of the journey, Patience," her brother said as he gently guided her along the length of the platform toward the rear of the train. His manner one of solicitous purpose, Percy assisted her onto the train and guided her along the narrow aisle to the private compartment Sebastian had arranged for her.

The conductor was headed toward them as Patience quickly entered the cabin. She heard the low rumble of voices as Percy spoke with the man just outside her accommodations. The compartment was small but comfortable, and she was grateful her oldest brother had arranged for her privacy. A porter had already placed her luggage in the car along with the hamper Mrs. Stoner had instructed Cook to prepare for Patience's journey.

Seconds later, Percy joined her and drew the shade. Slowly, Patience removed her hat, grateful to be free of the veil that made her face itch. Percy sat down on the seat opposite her. His gaze reassuring, he smiled at her.

"You did it, Patience," he said with brotherly pride. "The rest of your trip will be easy."

She nodded but remained silent as fear assaulted her. Aware of her trepidation, Percy caught her hands in his and squeezed them.

"There are only three stops between here and Crianlarich. I've instructed the conductor to see that you are not disturbed. Simply draw the shades as you're pulling into each station. The conductor will arrange for a porter to offload your baggage at Crianlarich. Muireall said she'll send someone to meet you at the train."

"Thank you, Percy," she said softly. "For everything."

"I'm only doing what any brother should do." Percy shrugged. "Just make sure that husband of yours understands you love him. Although I think you might have your work cut out for you. I don't think you'll be received with open arms. He was not happy when he left Melton House the last time, and for a man like Julian, to be struck blind, it will only make things more difficult."

"I'm certain of that, but I'll make him understand I need to be at his side," she said softly. Percy nodded and stood up. Bending over, he kissed Patience on her scarred cheek.

"Try to enjoy your trip, Patience," he said quietly and then he was gone.

Enjoy your trip. Percy had been far more optimistic than her. But she had enjoyed the scenery. Though it was by choice, being limited to the garden at Melton House had made Patience appreciate the countryside she'd seen from the train window. Other than seeing Julian, there was another thing she had been looking forward to about her return to Crianlarich Castle.

Freedom. The freedom to go outside without the fear of meeting friends or strangers. She would even be able to go riding or walking without a hat or veil if she chose. At Crianlarich, the only looks of pity and horror would be from the staff, but that had turned out to be a needless worry.

That much had been true from the moment Drummond had met her at the Crianlarich station. He'd greeted her with the same quiet manner he'd displayed the first time she'd come to the castle. The man had not even flinched at the sight of her. Mrs. Drummond had acted as kind and cheerful as Patience remembered. The housekeeper had made over her like she would a lost lamb. She had no idea if Muireall had informed the staff of her burns, but she was increasingly grateful for their kindness.

Patience lifted her head and turned away from the mirror. She wasn't sure what had prompted her to provoke Julian into riding in the morning. It would not be easy for him. Perhaps she should have gone alone, but she couldn't deny she was pleased he was going. It would allow her the chance to begin healing the breach between them. Being at Crianlarich also gave her a chance to heal herself as well.

Her self-imposed seclusion had created a deep-seated need to feel the wind in her face and the scent of heather beneath her nose. Unlike Hyde Park, Crianlarich was a safe haven. It would be unusual to meet people when she was riding on the moor, and as the family was in mourning, there would be no parties. It meant there would not be any pitying glances or looks of horror.

A yawn parted her lips, and she stood up and crossed the room to her bed. With a gentle puff of air, she blew out the candle beside her bed, pulled back the bedcovers, and slipped beneath the cold sheets. She shivered as she waited for the sheets to warm up around her. With a small tug, Patience turned on her side and pulled the bedding upward until she was snuggled deep under the blankets.

In the process, her fingers brushed across the skin on her left cheek. Despite the cream, the skin was still rough and rigid, and she shivered at the feel of the scarred flesh against her fingertips. How would Julian have reacted if his mouth had touched her marred skin? Patience shuddered again, not wanting to know what his response might be. It was something she would be forced to face when Patience finally convinced him that she'd returned to him because she loved him. With a sigh, her eyes fluttered shut.

The moment she did so, images of the fire filled her head. Patience drew in a sharp breath, and her eyes flew open as she tried to suppress the fear wrapping its tendrils tightly around her. Despite her efforts to steady her breathing, her lungs constricted from a lack of air as panic twisted its way through her at lightning speed.

Fingers curled up into fists, her body became a tight ball as she fought desperately to hold back the paralyzing terror. It was a futile effort as images of the fire swirled in her head until she was there again. As if it had happened minutes ago, she swallowed her screams as she watched Caleb and Devin fall to their deaths. Her heart pounded as she froze where she was.

She could feel the flames licking her skin. Pain seared her cheek and arm, and she gasped at the memory's powerful intensity as the smell of smoke filled her nostrils. The urge to scream barreled upward and out of her lungs, and she buried her face in her pillow as the terror erupted out of her. With each muffled scream, the fear slowly abated until the screaming died a quiet death.

A sharp click filled the air, and the faint moonlight streaming into the room revealed Julian standing in the doorway of the connecting door. He stood there with his head tilted, and Patience tried not to breathe or move as Julian's tall frame filled the doorway. She was certain he'd heard her muffled screams, but his posture said he wasn't sure they'd come from her room.

Frozen in place, she waited for him to say something, but he didn't. Instead, he slowly turned and went back to his room, closing the door behind him. As the door snapped shut, Patience released a soft sigh of relief before tears rolled down her cheeks.

Patience awoke to the sound of a commotion coming from Julian's room. He was as grouchy as a bear, and his voice was sharp to whoever was assisting him dress. Remembering his agreement to ride this morning, she quickly tossed her covers aside and went about the business of performing her daily ministrations.

In roughly a half-hour, she was hurrying down the main staircase dressed in her riding habit. Julian stood impatiently in the front hall, his riding gloves beating a steady rhythm of irritation against his riding breeches. He was the epitome of an arrogant laird annoyed that someone had kept him waiting.

"You're late," he snapped.

"I don't recall our setting a time to ride, but I'm sorry if I kept you waiting," she said quietly.

He grunted his reluctant acceptance of her apology, and with his cane tapping sharply against the foyer's stone floor, he made his way to the door. Patience didn't say a word as he fumbled for the doorknob. When he opened the door, he stood back with his hand holding onto the doorknob with the obvious expectation that she should precede him.

As she passed him, Patience caught the faint scent of his woodsy cologne, and her senses were immediately on alert. She was grateful there were no steps for him to navigate. The thought of him needing her arm made her feel incredibly vulnerable. The last time he'd touched her, he'd unsettled her completely. Lorne, the Crianlarich estate manager, was waiting for them a short distance from the front entrance of the house with Julian's stallion, Romulus, and a horse for her.

Patience smiled as she recognized Remus. The gentle yet fast-paced gelding had been her favorite horse to ride the one, and only time she'd been to Crianlarich. The horse had carried her far away from the vicious taunts of Julian's father. She moved forward to rub the jowls of the animal. The horse nudged her shoulder in a clear request for a treat.

"Later, boy. I've nothing for you at the moment."

"Here." Julian's voice was gruff as he pulled a few cubes of sugar from his jacket pocket and extended his hand toward her. She didn't move.

"I'm approximately three feet away from you and two feet to your right."

She spoke in a matter-of-fact, quiet tone of voice as she waited for him to move closer to her with the cubes in his hand. A frown wrinkled his brow before he slowly advanced on her with the treats. When he was within arm's reach of her, she took the sugar from him and offered Remus the cube. An expression of satisfaction swept across Julian's face as he dropped his hand to his side.

"Where's Romulus?" he demanded.

"He's facing you. Go to your left about five feet, then four steps forward." At her directions, Julian nodded and used his cane to move forward. When he reached the dark red stallion, he ran his hand across the bridge of the animal's nose before he dug into his pocket and fed the horse a sugar cube. A second later, Julian's hands were on the horse's mane as he slipped his cane into the rifle holster attached to the saddle. A moment later, he awkwardly jumped into the saddle.

The stallion pranced a bit, and Patience bit down on her lower lip. Perhaps this had not been the best of ideas. Actually, the challenge had been impulsive and rash. Traits she'd always seemed to excel at almost as much as Caleb. The thought of her brother brought tears to her eyes. Patience blinked them away to focus on the current problem. Romulus.

Her gaze met Lorne's, who arched his eyebrows with skepticism. The fact that the man didn't hesitate to meet her gaze made Patience feel as if she were at home where what she looked like didn't matter. She grimaced as she focused her attention on the matter at hand.

"Lorne, will Remus be able to keep up with Romulus?" Before the estate manager could speak, Julian glared sightlessly in her direction.

"Are you suggesting Romulus will grab the bit, my lady?"

"I simply asked if Remus can keep up with Romulus," she responded quietly.

"Implying I will nae be able to manage my horse."

"I didn't say that," she said with exasperation and a hint of guilt.

"You dinnae have tae," he snapped angrily. "I know Romulus better than anyone. Now, do you intend tae go riding or do I go alone?

At the suggestion he might actually leave her behind, Patience stared at him aghast. With a jerk of his head, Lorne silently indicated she should mount.

"I'm coming," she said with irritation. "Stubborn Highlander."

She muttered the last part under her breath, and Lorne looked at her in surprise before grinning at her broadly.

Patience rolled her eyes at the estate manager and accepted his help in mounting Remus. When she was properly seated, Patience turned her head toward Julian.

"Do you have a preference as to where we ride?" At the question, an indescribable look crossed Julian's face. It was gone in a brief second as his expression became unreadable.

"The falls," Julian said in a dispassionate voice. The air left Patience's lungs as she stared at him in dismay. It was the last thing she expected him to say. *Eas Falloch*—The Hidden Falls. The last time she'd been to the falls had been with Julian. They'd made love in a small glade close enough to the falls that they could hear the water crashing over the rocks. Was his intention to remind her of that time and demonstrate he no longer cared for her?

"As you wish," she said, then looked down at the estate manager. "Lorne, would you ask Mrs. Lester to have lunch ready a little earlier than usual. As I remember, the falls are an hour's ride from here. We should be back by eleven or so."

"Yes, my lady." Behind her, Patience heard running feet. With a skilled pull on her reins, she turned Remus around to see Muireall running out of the castle with a look of apprehension on her face.

"What are you doing, Julian?" her sister-in-law cried in dismay. "Patience, you cannae let him go riding, 'tis too dangerous."

"I'm more than capable of riding," Julian snapped. "I simply need a pair of eyes to show me where tae go and how tae get home."

"Romulus —

"I raised Romulus from the time he was a foal. I trust the horse. I dinnae have any reason tae believe he will fail me as others have."

There was an emotion layered beneath his words that made Patience believe he was referring to her lack of faith in him. Her entire family had told her more than once his reaction to her refusal to see him after the fire had been a crushing blow to him. Percy had been right. Julian was far from willing to receive her with open arms.

Patience could only hope her own betrayal of not believing he was innocent had not destroyed his love for her. She still had no idea how Una had known about Julian's birthmark, but it didn't matter. Patience had forgiven him the night of the fire as she'd run toward him and flung herself through the air into his arms. Patience had known then that if she were to die, she wanted it to be in his arms. And she *had* died that night in a manner of speaking.

The old Patience had vanished, and in her place was a creature people shied away from. The thought of being the beneficiary of Julian's pity had forced her to send him away from her. She'd used the only weapon at her disposal, and it had worked. Perhaps she'd done her job too well.

"It will be all right, Muireall," she said reassuringly as she met the girl's gaze. "I'll see to it he stays out of trouble."

Julian released a low sound of disgust and muttered something beneath his breath. Without any warning, he nudged Romulus forward into a trot. Muireall's eyes widened, and Patience shook her head at the girl as she turned Remus around to follow her husband. Not for the first time, she wondered if she'd made a mistake in suggesting he ride.

Chapter 10

Julian heard his sister's quiet cry of dismay as he rode away, but he ignored it. Although Patience didn't say anything, he heard the clip-clop of Remus' hooves against the front drive's gravel as she followed him. In his mind's eye, Julian could see the landscape in front of him. Even if he wasn't blind, he'd only need to close his eyes to know exactly where he was.

Now, with his eyes open, all he could see were dark shapes mixed with gray ones against the cloudy white background. His senses were keenly attuned to everything around him, and the scent of lilacs brushed against his nostrils. It was an aroma as familiar to him as the air he breathed. It was her scent. The breeze against his cheek changed direction as Patience rode up beside him. He turned his head slightly to make out the shape of Remus's head.

"She doesn't mean to treat you like a child, Julian. She just worries about you." The sympathy in Patience's voice irritated him.

"I dinnae need or want anyone's sympathy."

"I wasn't feeling sorry for you, you arrogant bastard. I was feeling sorry for Muireall," she snapped with disgust. "From what little she's said, you've been acting like a bear someone keeps poking. And if your behavior since my arrival is any example, I would agree."

"Your presence wasn't requested by me," he bit out fiercely, unhappy that he deserved her chastisement.

"No, Muireall did, and I can see why. She's trying desperately to help you, and you've repaid her by acting like a complete and utter ass."

The sharp words shot a bolt of remorse streaking through him. She was right, and he didn't like admitting it. Julian simply grunted and urged Romulus into a trot. For the briefest of moments, he thought himself mad for riding a horse when he couldn't see. But Romulus' stride was steady, and the animal responded to the slightest pressure of his knee into the stallion's side. Still, his lack of vision made it impossible to be sure of his direction. It left him feeling powerless—a feeling he didn't like at all. The stallion moved forward at a faster pace, and Patience was alongside him in the next second.

"Shall I take the lead so Romulus can follow?" She asked in a voice devoid of emotion.

He didn't like the idea of following anyone, but it was the sensible thing to do. Just because he might know the way in his mind, it was foolhardy to think he could get to the falls without getting lost.

Julian gave a sharp nod, and a second later, the dark shape of Patience and Remus' moved out in front of him. Even though he could feel the warmth of the sun, the breeze against his cheek had a sting to it. Winter was not quite ready to let go of Crianlarich yet. But the crisp smell of the wind aroused a sense of freedom he'd not experienced in a long time.

He might not have welcomed Patience's presence in the castle, but he couldn't deny that in the space of a day, she'd returned some of his independence to him. He frowned at the thought just as Romulus's leisurely stride became jerky as the horse cantered down a short but steep incline. Julian uttered a low oath.

As good as it felt to be back in the saddle, he'd just been given a silent warning as to how easily he could be thrown. Anger sped through him. He had no idea why God had chosen to punish him like this, but he wanted his vision back. He wanted to see where he was going. He wanted to read a book for himself, not have Muireall read to him. Most of all, he wanted to see his wife's face. He wanted to look into her soft brown eyes that had always reminded him of a doe's eyes.

A grimace tugged at his cheek. Why should he believe her reason for being here was anything more than duty? She'd said she came because she wanted to. It didn't mean she was here because she loved him. Julian clenched his jaw. He'd told her that her presence was unnecessary. It was a lie.

One of several he'd told her, but this time it had been to keep from revealing how much he loved her. The idea of giving her power over him again wasn't a risk he was willing to take. Especially when her presence at Crianlarich filled him with more pleasure than he wanted to admit.

Romulus hit another uneven section of ground, and Julian forced himself to concentrate on staying on his horse. In the past, he'd given Romulus his head, and the two of them had raced across the beautiful, stark moors. Today the animal seemed to sense something different about its rider, and the horse seemed quite content to slow down to a much slower pace.

"I'm glad you decided to slow to a walk," Patience said as she drew alongside him. "Remus' appears to be growing tired."

"Dinnae patronize me, Patience."

"I'm not. When was the last time someone exercised these animals?" There was a rebuke in her voice that set him on edge.

"I have nae been capable of riding in some time."

"And yet you're riding now."

Julian didn't answer her. She was right, but he wasn't about to agree with her. The only reason he was on horseback now was because she was his guide. Anger surged through him. He didn't want to be obligated to her. It made him appear weak, and he refused to allow his handicap to define him. In the next breath, he acknowledged he'd been doing just that since the accident. Patience was treating him like the man he'd been before the accident simply by not allowing him to wallow in his self-pity.

"Thanks to you," he grumbled. Silence met his expression of gratitude, and he wondered if she'd not heard him. "If you expect me to—"

"You took me by surprise," she interrupted in a quiet voice. "I'm happy you've found me helpful."

Silence drifted between them, and he allowed himself to breathe in the crisp Highland air. A sense of peace settled over him. Julian closed his eyes and allowed his senses to take in his surroundings. Heather grew nearby, for he could smell it. In the distance, Julian heard the chirp of a black-throated thrush. An image of the bird flew into his mind as he reminded himself that Patience's hair was the same soft brown as the black-throat's feathers. They rode in silence for a long time, both lost in their thoughts. It was a comfortable silence, and he took pleasure in being outdoors with Patience near him no matter how she felt about him.

Ahead of them, Julian heard the water crashing over rocks. *Eas Falloch*. What had possessed him to suggest they ride to the Hidden Falls? A devil, perhaps? A means of pointing out that she meant nothing to him? It was a ludicrous notion. She meant the world to him, but he was no longer capable of being a husband. Even if she'd returned for some other reason than duty, he would always be a liability unless his sight returned. The sound of the falls grew louder, and the amount of water he could hear crashing over the rocks made him realize the snow was melting, which was a sign spring was on its way.

"There is a great deal of water coming off the falls," Patience raised her voice slightly to be heard over the growing noise of the rushing water.

"The snow in the north is melting. Where are we?" His question was met by a brief note of silence.

"Just below the whirlpool." The pause in her reply was no more than a heartbeat, but he heard it nonetheless. "The glade is beyond that."

"We should water the horses."

"Yes, of course." There was a breathless note in her voice that puzzled him.

Was she disturbed that they'd returned to the falls? The moment hope slipped its way into his thoughts, he grimaced. He needed to remember she'd not returned to Crianlarich because she still loved him. No doubt, the only thing troubling her about their visit to the falls was that it was an uncomfortable reminder of the past.

To his satisfaction, Julian dismounted in a much more elegant manner than he had mounting Romulus. One hand gliding over the stallion's sleek coat, he ducked under Romulus's head and stretched out his hand in search of Remus's cheekpiece.

"What are you doing?" Patience asked with a confused note in her voice.

"Helping you off this horse."

"I don't need…" Her voice trailed off as his hand found the soft wool of her riding habit.

Julian's hand moved up over her leg, and Patience made a small noise as his hands caught her by the waist. With ease, he lifted her out of the saddle and enjoyed the way she slid down the front of him. The feel of her in his arms made him want to hold her close for as long as he could.

Aware of how dangerous it was to have her pressed against him, he quickly released her and turned back to Romulus. His fingers found the animal's reins, and he urged the horse forward, allowing the animal to lead him to the edge of the fast-moving stream. Patience joined him, and they stood in silence as the horses drank. When the animals had had their fill, Julian allowed Romulus to serve as his guide as they moved away from the narrow river.

"Do we stay for a while, or do we go home?" Her use of the word home in her question startled him. She'd never referred to the castle as if it were her home as well as his.

"Since the horses haven't been exercised in a while, we should let them rest some," he said with a nod to her earlier observations. The horses hadn't exerted themselves much on their way to the falls, but in truth, he wasn't ready to return to the castle. "As I recall, there are several large, flat rocks at the edge of the glade."

"The glade then," she murmured. The faintest hint of emotion vibrated in her voice, but it was impossible for Julian to decipher it.

With Patience and Remus leading the way, Julian kept one hand on Romulus's mane as they headed toward the small glade a short distance away. In a matter of minutes, they reached the small clearing. Julian pulled his cane from the rifle sling, intent on making his way to the rocks without her hand. Despite his resolve to find his own way, he was forced to let Patience verbally guide his steps. As he sat down on one of the rocks that bordered the edge of the river, Patience tethered the horses to a nearby tree.

She joined him a moment later and sat down on the cold granite a little more than an arm's length away from him. The sound of water filled the air around them as they sat in silence. His eyes closed, he tilted his head slightly so the sun could warm his face. The air he breathed in was fresh and smelled of the cool mist that drifted off the falls.

Even though he couldn't see the water streaming over the rocks into the pool below, he remembered how it had looked the last time he'd been here with Patience. He'd made love to her in the glade directly behind them. They'd almost been caught by a guest that had been staying with his neighbor Ewan MacLaren. He could still see the flush of color she'd had in her cheeks as she'd adjusted her silky brown hair the moment they heard the jingle of horse tack.

"Did you come here often as a child?" The quiet question brought him back into the present. He turned his head toward her, the familiar shadowy outline of her against the pale light filling his view.

"Aye. My mother loved the falls. My father would bring us here for picnics," he said with a nod. "I think it might have been one of her most favorite places tae be."

"I can see why," Patience said quietly. "It's beautiful here. Peaceful."

"My mother thought so too." Julian didn't know why, but it surprised him that she would use words he remembered his mother saying whenever they came to the falls.

"I imagine she worried about you going too close to the edge of the stream." The amusement in her voice made him smile.

"Many times," he said with a chuckle. "I'm surprised she didn't tie me down. My father would always tell her to leave me be, that I had a good head on my shoulders."

"You miss him," she said without any emotion.

"Aye," he nodded. "He possessed many faults, but deep down, he had a good heart. Losing my mother changed him."

The memory of Aiden sitting in the nursery made him flinch. He'd praised his father too soon. Patience would not find his father's lies those of a good-hearted man. He needed to tell her about the boy, but he wasn't sure whether she'd

155

believe Aiden was his brother after all that had happened between them. His father's lies only added to the problem. It would make it harder to convince her the child wasn't his. He frowned at the thought.

"Are you feeling all right?"

"Why wouldn't I be," he bit out as guilt swept through him.

"Muireall said you've been having headaches, and you look as though you're in pain."

"It's nothing. It will go away soon enough," Julian lied as all the signs of a bad migraine began to flourish in the back of his head.

Silence drifted between them again, and Julian tried to relax in an attempt to stop his headache from worsening. It quickly became a battle he knew he was losing. Beside him, he heard Patience utter a small sound of annoyance.

"You might actually be even more stubborn than my brothers."

Exasperation filled her soft words as she scooted closer to him. Gently, her hands grasped his shoulders and forced him backward until the back of his head was in her lap. With a light touch, her fingers stroked his forehead in a circular pattern. It didn't alleviate the pain, but it lessened it to the point he believed he could return home without looking like a man on the verge of collapse.

The familiar resentment at his predicament twisted its way through him. Suddenly eager to leave, his hand flew up to grab her wrist and end her soothing strokes against his temple. In a split second, the feel of rough patches of scarred skin beneath his fingertips made him draw in a sharp breath. The memory of the fire flashed through his head.

His heart slammed into his chest like a freight train as he remembered the terror of watching her across the gap of flames between them that terrible night. If not for Percy, he would have plunged through the flames to reach her.

Instead, he'd been helpless to do anything except watch her struggle to live. Knowing he might have to watch her die had been the most unimaginable of horrors. He'd never felt so helpless in his life.

Now the feel of the scarred skin beneath the pads of his fingers reminded him once more of how she'd suffered that night. It made him want to gather her up into his arms and hold her close. With a sharp tug, she jerked free of his touch. Julian immediately sat upright and turned to face her. He had no way of knowing for certain, but he thought he was staring at her profile. The tension in her was almost a tangible sensation on his skin.

"You flinch where there is nae need, *mo leannan*." The endearment rolled off his lips with ease.

"Don't," she said in an icy voice. "I don't need your pity."

"I'm *nae offering you pity*, *Patience*," he denied with an anger that startled her. "I have *never* pitied you. How could anyone do so after what you did?"

"I did nothing." The flat note in her voice did little to hide the pain behind her words.

"I dinnae call the lives of nine children and two women, nothing," he said in a quiet, gentle voice as he reached out to touch Patience's shoulder. She shrugged off his touch.

"I wish to return to the castle." Her voice was icier than a the wind that blew across the moors in the dead of winter. "I'll fetch the horses."

In a flurry of movement, she rose to her feet and hurried off, leaving him alone. Julian fumbled around for his cane until he found it on the ground next to the rock. Slowly, he stood up and listened for the jangling sound of the horses. Two large shadows moved against the ghostly background of his vision. Swishing his cane back and forth in front of him, he moved toward the animals. He'd taken no more than three steps when his foot plunged into a shallow dip in the ground, and he landed on his face.

"*Fuck*," he exclaimed. His fall renewed the throbbing that Patience's touch had almost eliminated. Julian struggled to his feet as Patience's sweet perfume filled his nostrils. His heightened senses told him she was within arm's reach, but she didn't touch him.

"Are you hurt?" she asked quietly.

"Nae," he snapped, angry he'd displayed how much he needed someone to help him navigate his way.

"Good," she said with irritation that equaled his. "Perhaps it will teach you the pitfalls of not asking for help."

"I dinnae need a lecture from you, Patience MacTavish."

"Don't you?" She sniffed with irritation.

"Nae," he growled. Julian quickly reached out toward her dark curves against the pale gray background that was his vision. As he tugged her into his chest, her gasp of surprise brought a grim smile to his lips.

"Before you seek to reprimand me, Patience, look to your own unwillingness to leave the dead behind and rejoin the living."

"We're not talking about me," she said hoarsely as she strained away from him.

"Perhaps talking is nae what's required, lass."

A dark need surged through him as he curled his hand around the back of her neck and captured her mouth with his. With a demanding nip on her lower lip, he forced her to open her mouth to him. The moment her tongue danced with his, the pent-up desire inside him exploded. Images flashed through his head of other moments when her passionate response had driven him to possess her completely. Moments when she'd been beneath him, and he'd worshipped her body with his. The memory and taste of her made his cock harden until it swelled tight in his breeches.

There was the warm, spicy taste of cloves on her tongue that hinted at the fiery passion he knew dwelled deep within her. The taste ignited a fierce hunger inside him that drummed its way through his limbs with the force of a charging bull. It drove him to deepen their kiss until she was clinging to him as she had done so many times in the past. Hot and passionate, she responded to him with a familiar abandon he remembered well. She'd always been an eager student in the art of pleasure.

When her hand slid down the front of his chest to find his cock, he drew in a sharp breath as her palm rubbed over his sensitive erection. The primitive sensation the touch aroused in him pushed him to the edge of insanity. God Almighty, he was ready to come right now. Did she have any idea what she was doing to him? The question pushed its way through the desire holding him in its grip. He shuddered. How could she not know? He was hard as a hammer. Did she know his response was driven by an emotion he didn't want to feel for her? Worse, was she responding to him simply out of guilt? The thought sickened him. Fingers biting hard into her shoulders, he heard Patience gasp from discomfort as he pushed her away from him.

"We're going back tae the castle."

"Julian, I—"

"*Now*, Patience," he growled.

Damnation, what had he been thinking to kiss her? First last night and then now? He should have ushered her right out the front door of Crianlarich Castle yesterday when she'd arrived. Julian tentatively dragged his foot through the grass surrounding him in search of his cane. The stick was offered to him in silence, and he roughly took it from her. In seconds, Julian heard her leading the horses to where he stood. Aware she would need assistance in mounting, he viciously stored his cane in the gun holder on his saddle. With the walking stick secured, he glided his hand along Romulus's neck and made his way around the animal.

"I can mount Remus without—"

"Quiet, woman," he snarled.

The leather of Patience's saddle was smooth and soft beneath Julian's fingers as he sought to determine the height and location of the tack. With a turn of his head, Patience's dark curves filled his limited vision. The heat of her engulfed him as he gripped her waist and lifted her upward.

She was lighter than he remembered. As he set her in the saddle, he could have sworn her hands lingered on his shoulders before she straightened upright. A moment later, he was on Romulus's back. As he settled in his seat, his anger grew as he knew he had to rely on Patience to guide him home.

"Lead now, Patience, or I'll let Romulus find his own way," he bit out angrily.

She murmured a small noise of agreement, and he followed her shadow, which stood out against the familiar hazy gray background of his eyesight. As they rode away from the falls, Julian tried to ignore the throbbing that had returned to his head. Even though their pace was a gentle trot, the jarring impact of Romulus's stride became continuous, resounding blows to his head. With each stride the stallion took, it became more difficult to remain upright in his saddle.

Slowly, his shoulders slumped downward as his fingers latched tightly onto Romulus's thick mane. Patience remained in front of him as she'd done for much of the ride to the falls. Julian was grateful for that. He had no need of sympathy on her part. More importantly, it ensured she didn't come to his rescue as an angel of mercy.

The ride back to the castle seemed to last forever, and he was close to giving in to the pain when Romulus's hooves hit gravel. The sound filled him with relief. Slowly he dismounted, his fingers wrapped tightly in the stallion's mane in order to remain standing. To steady himself, he pressed his head against the soft leather of the saddle. Beside him, Patience's perfume gently brushed across his senses.

"I'm beginning to think you have a death wish, Mr. MacTavish," his wife said fiercely. "You could have fallen off the damn horse."

"If you use that vocabulary around Muireall, she'll think I condone it in her," he muttered as his stomach began to churn.

With a rough push away from the stallion's back, he staggered away from her and the horse. Patience uttered a cry of surprise, but he ignored it. A moment later, he threw up whatever was left of his dinner the night before. Bent at the waist, he panted loudly as he fought to regain control of his body. He didn't like anyone seeing him sick like this, especially Patience when they were estranged. Her hand touched his shoulder lightly.

"You still have your headache, don't you?"

Unable to nod without making his head throb, he simply grunted. Her touch almost tender, her fingers stroked across his temple before she gently urged him to straighten, and she wrapped her arm around his waist. Another body on his opposite side provided similar support, and he recognized Lorne's silent strength. As his wife and estate manager helped him up the stairs to his bedroom, Julian's feet seemed encased in lead boots. Jaw clenched, he forced himself to try and ignore the pain in his head. The task was a hopeless one, and when they reached his room, Julian gratefully sank down onto his bed.

"Lorne, I need lavender water and rags for compresses." The soft, clear cadence of Patience's voice drifted through his haze of pain, followed by Lorne's quiet reply. The door closed behind his estate manager, and Patience returned to his side.

"I'm sorry, Julian, but you need to sit up. You'll not rest easy until you're undressed."

The soft steel in her voice said she refused to let him argue with her. When had his wife become as strong-willed as the Scotswomen he'd grown up with? His father had been wrong about Patience in so many ways. He growled in pain as she slid one arm beneath his shoulders to raise him up and remove his jacket.

He groaned as she eased him out of his coat, and as if understanding any movement was painful for him, Patience moved all the more quickly to help him undress. With his waistcoat and shirt off, Patience helped ease him back into the feather pillows. Somewhere in the deep recesses of his mind where the pain didn't reach, he remembered other times when Patience's hands had lovingly undressed him.

Her touch was gentle now, but he knew how hot her touch could be. God, he wished he didn't feel so fucking miserable. He'd have her undressed in minutes so he could bury himself inside her. Eyes closed, he didn't move as Patience continued to undress him. The touch of her fingers made him wish he didn't have a migraine. He wished they were simply a husband and wife making love.

Sleep must have dragged him out of the conscious realm as the next thing he knew, he was naked beneath the sheets. A cool compress lay on his forehead, and the soft scent of lavender water wafted beneath his nose. His hand reached up to touch Patience's fingers as she gently removed the compress and replaced it with a new one.

"You dinnae need to do this, Patience," he whispered hoarsely. "It will pass."

"Why didn't you tell me you were too unwell to ride?" Guilt echoed in her voice. "I could have gone for help."

"It would nae have made a difference. The only way for me to come back to the castle would have been to ride." Julian could almost sense the guilt emanating from her, and he sighed. "And dinnae be thinking you should nae have thought tae challenge me tae ride. I enjoyed it. It was good tae be outdoors again."

Her hand clasped his as he closed his eyes. There was a serenity about her taking care of him that gave him a sense of peace. His head still pounded like a freight train, but that Patience was with him made the pain easier to bear. Patience released his hand, and he immediately felt the loss of her comforting heat. A moment later, her soft breast pressed into his shoulder as she raised him up slightly.

"Mrs. Lester fixed you some chamomile tea," she murmured. "It will help you sleep, and that's the best thing for you right now."

"Aye," he whispered as he drank the tea she'd pressed to his lips. When he was settled back against the pillows, sleep swept toward him, but not before he expressed his gratitude. "Thank you, *mo leannan.*"

He thought he heard Patience utter a soft sound, but it was impossible to be sure as sleep dragged him back down once more.

Chapter 11

Patience slowly opened the door that connected her room with Julian's. He'd yet to learn she was in the room next to his, and she was no longer sure what he would make of the fact. Twice yesterday, he'd called her *mo leannan*—sweetheart.

It could simply be a term of endearment he used without thinking, but it had made her hope Julian still had feelings for her buried just beneath his caustic manner. He was a proud man. Even if he still loved her, she'd sent him away under the pretext she thought him a liar. That alone would injure his fierce pride.

As she peeked around the door, she saw Julian was still fast asleep. She breathed a soft sigh of relief. She wasn't sure she was ready to face his reaction when he discovered she was in the room next to his. Quietly, Patience stepped into Julian's bedroom and closed the door linking their rooms. Julian had suffered in stoic silence for most of yesterday, with the exception of short, harsh snarls whenever he did speak.

The man abhorred anything resembling confinement. That he'd remained in bed yesterday indicated how bad he'd felt. Last night, she'd added a few drops of laudanum to his chamomile tea, hoping it would provide him with some well-needed rest. It had done precisely what she'd hoped as she'd checked in on him twice last night, and he'd not stirred either time.

Patience crossed the room and sat down on the edge of the mattress. She took Julian's hand in hers and studied him as he slept. Julian had never looked so vulnerable to her. She knew the loss of his eyesight was far more devastating for him than he was willing to let others see. He'd never found it easy to ask for help. Julian's independence was something he valued highly. His sister, despite the deep love she had for her brother, had most likely made things all the more difficult for him.

Muireall's objection yesterday to Julian riding to the falls was an example of her sister-in-law's love and concern for her brother. The girl's reaction had made Patience regret challenging Julian to go riding with her. It had been impulsive and foolhardy on her part to suggest he was afraid to ride. But his gruff expression of gratitude for giving him the pleasure of being outdoors again convinced her that taunting him had been the right thing to do.

Instinctively, she knew it had been much more than being outdoors that Julian was grateful for. He hadn't said so, but she was certain her efforts had made him more comfortable she'd given him a small measure of his independence back. But would Julian believe love had been her motivation in making him realize his lack of vision only hampered him in certain things? It didn't change who he was, how he loved, or who loved him. Patience bent her head and kissed his fingers, then left the room. When she entered the dining room a few moments later, Muireall's head jerked up to meet Patience's gaze with a look of worry on her sweet features.

"How is he?"

"He's still asleep, but I'm sure he'll be fine," Patience said with a smile of reassurance. "How often has he had these headaches?"

"Fairly often since the accident, but never one so bad as yesterday. But then Julian's nae gone riding since the accident either," Muireall said with a faint note of accusation in her voice.

Patience experienced a twinge of guilt as she met her sister-in-law's gaze. Perhaps Muireall was right. It was quite possible the ride to *Eas Falloch* might have been too taxing for Julian. But she knew the ride had also been good for him if only to make him feel free and independent again. She took a seat across from Muireall and placed her napkin in her lap. Patience directed a steady look at her sister-in-law.

"Riding did not give Julian a headache, Muireall."

Patience reached for a piece of toast in the basket sitting close to her plate. She added a thin layer of black currant jam to the crisp bread and bit into the toast. The delicate mix of gooseberry and raspberry on her tongue was delicious, and she debated adding more jam to her toast. She would have to remember to compliment Mrs. Lester on the delectable preserves. She looked at her sister-in-law again.

"I know how much you love Julian and want to protect him, Muireall," she said quietly. "But he needs to believe he's capable of doing things one wouldn't expect a blind person to do, such as riding."

"But it was dangerous. Julian could have been thrown or worse."

"It was no more dangerous yesterday than it was when he could see. The only difference was he needed someone to go with him as a guide." The explanation made Muireall frown in contemplation.

"'Tis true." Her sister-in-law nodded slowly. "But I was afraid for him."

"Do you think I wasn't worried about him too?" Patience said as she dropped her gaze to her plate and her mind flitted back to the memory of Julian sprawled on the ground. "When he stumbled and fell just—"

"*Why did you nae tell me this before,*" Muireall exclaimed. Patience shook her head.

"The man fell because he was being stubborn and refused to ask for help," she said between clenched teeth at her sister-in-law's unspoken condemnation. "The ride isn't what caused his headache, and even if had, it shouldn't change the way we treat him from now on."

"But I—"

"We cannot mollycoddle him," Patience said sternly before softening her voice. "That is the *last* thing he needs. From what little I've seen, he's been feeling quite sorry for himself, which means you have borne the brunt of his frustration."

"You cannae expect me nae tae help him, Patience."

"Of course not," she said gently. "But you must not do things for Julian unless he asks. If we don't let him try to do things for himself, then his spirit will be broken, and neither of us wants that."

"No, I would never want Julian tae feel as though he had nothing tae live for," Muireall said with dismay furrowing her brow. "But riding? It seems..."

"It might be worrisome for us, and although he'd never admit it, I'm sure Julian must have felt a bit of apprehension himself. But he had no trouble riding yesterday morning at all. He enjoyed himself, Muireall. I'm convinced of it."

A thoughtful look settled on her sister-in-law's sweet features. It was one she'd seen on Julian's face more times than she could count. In silence, she watched Muireall adjust to the idea that her brother could do a great many things for himself. After a long moment, Muireall nodded her head.

"I understand. I'm simply nae accustomed to Julian nae needing my help."

"It's not a question of him not needing your help, dearest. We simply need to help him understand he's independent and capable of doing most things on his own.

But he also has to come to the realization that it's quite all right to ask for help when necessary."

Muireall nodded her head in understanding, and Patience applied more jam to another piece of toast. If she wasn't careful, Mrs. Lester's preserves would be detrimental to her figure, but the black currant jam was incredibly delicious. The rustle of skirts announced Mrs. Drummond, and Patience looked toward the door as the housekeeper entered the room.

"Good morning, my lady, Miss Muireall." The woman smiled at both of them before focusing her attention on Patience. "Might I ask how the Crianlarich is feeling, my lady?"

"He's still sleeping, but I believe he'll be fine when he awakens." At Patience's reply, the housekeeper's worried frown was replaced with relief.

"That is indeed good to hear, my lady," Mrs. Drummond said with a bob of her head before she changed the subject. "If I may, my lady, Nurse asked me to see if you would be coming to see Master Aiden—"

"Thank you, Mrs. Drummond, that will be all," Muireall quickly interrupted the woman in the same authoritative manner Julian often displayed. "I'll see to it that Lady Patience finds her way to the nursery after breakfast."

Bewildered by the brief exchange, Patience stared at first the housekeeper and then Muireall as she tried to make heads or tails out of the puzzling conversation. Who was Aiden, and why would Mrs. Drummond expect her to visit him in the nursery? Patience looked at her sister-in-law, whose expression was one of worry and apprehension, while Mrs. Drummond appeared thoroughly confused.

"Aiden?" Patience cautiously asked, and the housekeeper nodded her head as she smiled at Patience.

"The wee bairn is a bonnie lad, my lady. He looks just like the Crianlarich did when he was a little one. And the bonnie lad has your temperament, my lady. He's such a—"

"*Thank you*, Mrs. Drummond. I *said* that will be all," Muireall interrupted the woman again.

This time her voice was almost icy. It was a tone of voice she'd never heard her sister-in-law use with anyone before. The sharp note in Muireall's voice was designed to point out the conversation had ended.

"Of course, Miss Muireall." The housekeeper flinched as her cheeks became flushed with embarrassment, and with a quick bob of her head, the woman left the room.

Patience's gaze focused on Muireall, who was studying her with an uneasy look on her face. An icy draft blew across her skin as her surprise vanished, and she absorbed Mrs. Drummond's words. Julian had a child. He'd told her he'd been faithful, and she'd been a fool to believe him. Her chest ached as if someone had ripped her heart out. Horror followed on the heels of the sickening pain pounding its way through her. He had a son. A child, the housekeeper, believed was hers and Julian's.

Dear God, Julian had told everyone she was the child's mother. The realization sent an icy chill sweeping over her skin, and Patience shivered. Why had he done such a thing? Did he really expect her to claim a son that wasn't hers? A child he'd had with another woman. The thought made her twist the napkin in her lap into a tight knot. She swallowed hard to suppress the bile rising in her throat.

"Who is Aiden?" Patience asked in a stilted voice.

"Tis nae my story tae tell." Muireall's reply made Patience's stomach churn.

"I've heard those words before," she said bitterly. Sprang to her feet and flung her napkin onto the table.

"Patience, if I—"

169

"*Don't, Muireall.* The fact that Julian didn't mention he had a son the day I arrived at Crianlarich indicates how important he feels it is to explain anything to me," she bit out in a frigid voice. A small twinge of regret nipped at her as a pained look crossed the girl's face.

She didn't wait for Muireall to argue with her. Spinning around on her heel, she walked out of the dining room, her entire body knotted with pain. *Fool. You were a fool to be taken in again, Patience MacTavish.* He'd lied. He'd fathered a child with another woman. An image of Una holding a baby popped into her head, and she uttered a soft cry of grief.

Patience swayed on her feet from the pain of Julian's betrayal and reached out to cling to the newel post of the stairs. Una had been telling the truth after all. Nausea swirled in her stomach, and she dropped her head in an effort to quiet the nasty sensation.

After a moment, the sickness ebbed away, and still in a state of shock, Patience slowly climbed the stairs. When she reached the second floor, she turned toward her room then stopped. Numb with pain, something perverse inside her made her turn around. Although she tried to fight the urge, Patience's feet carried her in the direction of the nursery.

When she'd visited Crianlarich after she and Julian were married, he'd shown her the nursery. She still remembered the deep rumble of his voice against her neck as he'd teasingly asked if she wanted to work on filling the nursery at that moment. Her heart skipped a beat as she recalled the passion that had followed.

The hopes and dreams she had then had been nothing and were nothing but ashes now. It was as if they'd ever even existed. As she entered the nursery, a matronly woman emerged from a room off the main suite. Her expression warm and cheerful, the nurse greeted her with a broad smile.

"Good morning, my lady. I've been hoping ye might come tae see Master Aiden," the woman said in a pleasant voice. "Let me fetch the young master for ye. He's just had his bath."

The nurse quickly disappeared back into the room she'd come from and returned almost immediately with a happy-looking baby. As the nurse handed the boy to her, Patience tried not to flinch. The baby came willingly and looked up at her with eyes that were just like his father's with the same full, sooty eyelashes. He was beautiful. He was everything she'd longed for in a child from the first moment Julian had possessed her body and soul.

But she would never be able to give Julian a son, and the pain of it lashed at her heart. That everyone believed Aiden was her son only emphasized the bitter truth of her barren state. Worse, how could Julian have been so cruel to tell others she was the babe's mother? Patience fought back tears at the acute pain scraping away at her insides. The baby reached up to touch her face and grinned at her.

She'd always loved children, and before she realized what she was doing, she sank down into the well-worn wood seat of the rocking chair at the window. Patience didn't know whether to laugh at the baby's happy jabbering and smiles or to cry because she was holding Julian's child by another woman.

Julian and Una's child. She grew still at the thought. As the aunt to almost a dozen children, she could tell Aiden was somewhere between nine and ten months old. The realization made her stiffen in consternation.

Una couldn't be the child's mother.

Relief spiraled through her. If Una had been Aiden's mother, the woman could never have been able to bring Patience's world crashing down around her that terrible day. Either the woman's girth would have revealed she was with child, or she would have been lying-in to regain her strength and nurse her baby.

Hope suddenly unfurled deep inside her as she quickly calculated dates. It was more than possible Aiden had been conceived a short time before she and Julian had met. Men had dalliances all the time. It was more than possible Julian and she had been married before he'd even known he'd sired a son. She could easily forgive him such an indiscretion. But where was Aiden's mother? Had she died in childbirth or had she simply given the child to Julian?

It would be just like her husband to do the honorable thing and bring his son home to raise him. The memory of Julian not coming home the night before her marriage fell apart made her draw in a quick breath. He'd refused to tell her that night where he'd been or whom he was with. His only defense had been it wasn't his secret to tell. Was that what Muireall had meant a short while ago?

Patience bounced the baby on her knee, and she smiled as he giggled and stretched out his hand toward her face. She bounced him again, and this time the baby squealed in delight. Suddenly, the nursery door flew open, and Muireall charged into the room.

"Nurse, have you seen Lady Pa—" The girl stopped and stared in amazement at Patience holding the baby. Suddenly aware of how easily she'd fallen under the spell of the child, she quickly stood up and handed the baby to Muireall. She didn't want to feel anything for the child. It was too painful.

"I've seen all I need to see," she whispered.

"Patience, you must go see Julian, *now*. He wants to explain," Muireall said with a look of panic on her face.

"I don't wish to see him," she said in a brittle voice. It was too soon. She needed to clear her head and regain control of her emotions. The last thing she wanted was to break down into tears when she confronted Julian. "Not now. I need time to think. I can't bear to hear any more lies."

"Please, Patience. I dinnae like to beg, but I am begging you now," Muireall pleaded fervently. "Listen to what Julian has to say. My brother will nae lie to you."

Muireall shifted the baby to set him on her hip and reached out to grab Patience's hand in a tight grasp. The girl's belief in her half-brother didn't surprise her, but the conviction in the girl's voice was persuasive enough for Patience to consider the heartfelt plea.

What Muireall didn't understand was how much it hurt that Julian had allowed everyone to believe the child was theirs. He knew how much it distressed her that she couldn't give him a son. The thought of seeing Julian sent panic streaking through her. Patience met Muireall's gaze then shook her head.

"I have no wish to hear what he has to say."

"Are ye afraid to let him explain, Patience?" Muireall snapped with anger. The challenge in her sister-in-law's voice made Patience stiffen, and she narrowed her gaze at the girl.

"No, I'm not afraid."

"I dinnae believe ye, Patience. Ye dinnae want tae listen. Ye only want tae run away." The passionate condemnation thickened the young woman's brogue, and Patience winced. For a long moment, she didn't say anything. She simply stared at Muireall until she acquiesced to her sister-in-law's plea with a brusque nod.

"Very well, I shall speak to him," she said in a voice that indicated she was agreeing under duress. "But I intend to return to London as soon as Sebastian can arrange for a private rail car."

"Please dinnae say that, Patience. Everything Julian will tell ye is the truth. I know it is, but he made me swear nae to tell anyone. But he needs to be the one who explains everything. Nae me," Muireall said fervently.

Patience studied her sister-in-law for a moment longer then left the nursery. Muireall was convinced she would believe Julian's explanation. What her sister-in-law didn't know was how Julian had lied to her in the past. Although they were small lies, they'd set a precedent. How was she supposed to believe him now? And yet Muireall had insisted that things were not as they seemed and that Julian would tell her the truth.

He'd once accused her of not trusting him. The thought made her bite down on her lip. Love required trust, and if she didn't trust him, how could she possibly love him? Pain, fear, anger, and hope buffeted her as she walked toward Julian's rooms as if she were a man walking to his death. When she'd decided to come back to Crianlarich Castle, she'd promised herself not only to believe Julian but to leave the past behind.

But when she'd made that decision, she'd not bargained for this current state of affairs. The past was difficult to put behind her when there was a child in the Crianlarich nursery. A child that wasn't hers. And the terrible lie he'd told everyone that she was the boy's mother only emphasized her failure as a wife.

Patience had never known her husband to be cruel, which made the fabrication all the more grievous. Julian knew how much sorrow her barren state caused her. Now she was struggling with the knowledge that he had a son. A son another woman had given him—not his wife.

The burnt flesh on her body was painfully taut as tension tightened every one of her muscles. But the physical pain couldn't compare to the agonizing way her heart was bleeding so profusely inside her breast. Would Julian proclaim his innocence with the same fiery zeal he'd done the night he'd returned home?

In defending himself all those months ago, Julian had repeatedly said he loved her. How could he have been so adamant about his love for her if it wasn't true? Why would he have married her if he didn't love her? She'd brought nothing of real value to their marriage in the way of power or social status, neither of which Julian coveted.

Not even money could have been a reason. Despite Sebastian's generosity, her dowry had not been an immense fortune, and Julian had refused to take it. Instead, he'd placed her dowry in her name rather than absorbing it into his finances. She'd never been so confused in her life, and she no longer knew what to think or believe. Not even her gift had given her a path to follow.

In the past, her visions had always given her some clue as to what they meant. Although her gift rarely served as a compass for her own affairs, it had always been a reliable gauge where others were concerned. But the visions she'd had before that horrible night at Westbrook Farms had been vague, incomplete, and misleading. Everything she'd seen, the fire, Julian's accident, and Una holding a baby had been snippets of larger life-changing events.

None of those visions had given her the chance to stop those tragedies let alone protect her heart. She'd not even had the slightest warning about Aiden. The thought made her draw in another breath of surprise. Had she lost her gift? The question terrified her. If she'd lost the *an dara sealladh*, a part of her would go missing. She'd already lost a part of herself during the fire. The idea of losing another piece of herself filled her with dread.

Patience stopped in front of Julian's room, and the chaotic emotions thrashing inside her made her tremble as she stared at the dark wood door. Determined to end this farce once and for all, her knuckles rapped a strong, staccato beat on the door. At Julian's command to enter, she steeled herself to bury her pain and insulate her heart from further heartbreak. She failed the moment she saw him. She knew no matter what passed between them, she loved him and always would.

He was fully dressed, and she was certain he'd dressed himself as his clothes were slightly askew. She swallowed hard at how handsome he looked, even in an unkempt state. The stoic look on his rugged features revealed nothing as to what he was thinking. As she stared at him in silence, the urge to rage at him swept through her, but she forced herself to remain calm and composed.

"You asked to see me," she said quietly. It pleased her that she managed to keep her voice quiet, composed, and serene.

"Aiden is my father's son."

The abrupt, unexpected confession made her stare at him in shock. Of all the explanations he could have given her, this was not even in the realm of what she'd imagined. For a moment, she simply stared at him as if he'd suddenly sprouted another head. Her mind struggled to make sense of his outrageous declaration. If what he said was true, why hadn't Muireall said the child wasn't her half-brother? Did they both think her a fool? Anger broke through her amazement.

"Your lies have become even more imaginative than ever before, Julian," she snapped. He stiffened at her scathing rejection.

"The child is my father's and Caitriona's."

"*Caitriona,*" she gasped as she stared at him in astonishment. Again, he'd managed to throw her off balance.

"She was in labor the night I dinnae come home." Julian paused for a moment as his jaw hardened with tension, and if not for the tic in his cheek, she would have thought his face that of a statue. "She asked me to care for the boy."

Patience struggled with the idea of Fergus MacTavish and Caitriona as lovers. Her thoughts drifted back to the dinner party with the Bensmores. Although she'd been preoccupied with watching Una flirt incessantly with Julian, Patience had a vague memory of Caitriona flirting with the

Crianlarich as well. At the time, she'd put Caitriona's familiar behavior down to the family's friendship. Now she saw it in an altogether different light.

"Why didn't your father marry Caitriona if she was carrying his child?"

"She dinnae tell him. She dinnae tell anyone, not even Una. I think my father suspected Caitriona might be with child when she disappeared, which is why he asked me to search for her. I would nae have...I would nae have remained in Scotland for so long otherwise." Julian's jaw shifted with a restrained emotion before his stance became even more rigid and prideful. The pause in his speech made her think he'd been about to express regret about lying to her.

"Why didn't Una tell anyone the reason Caitriona had left?" Patience asked quietly as she contemplated Julian's explanation.

"Una dinnae ken until Caitriona sent for her, and it was then Una sought my help," Julian said with injured pride. His dark expression made her think he was remembering her accusations of Una being his mistress. "Caitriona swore me to secrecy and gave me guardianship of the child. She dinnae want her father to know the truth."

"Then why are you breaking your word to Caitriona and telling me all of this now?"

"I am nae breaking my word," Julian snarled like an angry bear as he stared blindly at a point past her head. "Nae, if I keep to the letter of my promise. Caitriona asked me nae to tell her father about the boy and to take care of Aiden. She dinnae ask anything else of me."

Julian stood stiff and rigid like a tall oak. His voice and demeanor illustrated he believed he was stretching the boundaries of his promise to Caitriona. Patience was certain that in her husband's mind, Caitriona had entrusted her secret to him in the belief that Julian would tell no one, not even his wife, of her shame. The thought angered her that he could not have confided at least some of the truth to her.

"And now, after *all* this time, you've suddenly decided to share Caitriona's secret with me. How benevolent of you." Patience didn't bother to keep the bitterness out of her voice.

"*Bloody hell.* I'd been up all night, woman. I was nae thinking straight," he roared. "I would nae have kept anything from you that day if I'd nae been so dead tired.

"Yet you've had nine months to realize your vow to Caitriona wasn't completely binding," she snapped. "You had the chance to tell me everything when you came to Westbrook Farms the night of the fire. In fact, you've had nine months to tell me the truth."

"If you'll recall, you refused tae believe me that night at Westbrook Farms, and then you sent me away from you and Melton House after the fire."

"With good reason, it seems," she snapped. "It's obvious you feel compelled to share this sordid tale because you need an explanation as to why you lied and made everyone think I'm Aiden's mother."

"I *dinnae lie*," he growled. His response was a dangerous rumble of anger. "My father is the one who chose to say Aiden was his grandchild. I dinnae discover the truth about what my father had done until after—until I returned to Crianlarich."

His words held a fervent ring of truth to them. Julian stood tall and proud in front of her in a defiant stance that dared her to question his explanation, yet he didn't plead with her to believe him. Deep inside she knew he was being honest with her, but he'd given her no explanation as to why he'd helped to perpetuate his father's lies.

"And yet you didn't refute the lie when you returned home. You continued to let everyone believe your father's lies." This time it was impossible to keep the bitterness out of her voice.

"Our marriage was over. I had nae reason to believe you would ever return to Crianlarich." Julian's icy words skated across her skin to sink deep into her pores until she longed for the warmth of a blanket. "I had planned to tell the boy the truth when he was old enough. I thought it best nae to have the lad branded a bastard simply because my father dinnae marry his lover."

Over. The word echoed in Patience's head like a death sentence. He'd actually said their marriage was over. A chunk of ice in her breast pumped cold blood through her veins. She'd lost everything. All because she'd refused to believe him—trust him. Patience winced and took a step toward him, then immediately stopped.

She was certain he would reject any apology she offered. His demeanor was that of a proud Highlander from the distant past who'd been accused of a crime by a British tyrant. Patience flinched at the thought. She had accused him of betraying her, and the knowledge was a physical blow to her stomach.

Nausea rolled over her. She was responsible for setting her marriage on the path to destruction, not Julian. And now, she might have lost the chance to win his heart back. Patience was abruptly startled out of her thoughts as Julian released a low growl of something that bordered on the edge of disgust.

"My father wronged you with his lies, Patience, but I cannae take them back," he said in a rough voice.

"And if I'd not come to Crianlarich, would you have told me what your father had done?"

A long pause followed her soft question as Julian fumbled in his efforts to retrieve the cane resting against the front of his bed. The tense silence of the room was broken by the tap of his stick against the floor as he moved toward her. Julian brushed past her, and despite her anger, her senses drank in the warm, spicy scent of him. Patience watched as his hand wrapped around the brass doorknob, and he jerked the door open.

"I've told you everything, Patience. Now pack your things and get out of my house."

The low, icy command scraped across her senses like a razor. She stared at Julian's harsh, unyielding features with a feeling of hopelessness. He said their marriage was over, and now he had emphasized that statement by showing her the door. Patience's heart sank for a moment before her Rockwood blood slid hot and fierce in her veins. Julian might say their marriage was over, but she wasn't willing to walk away from him until she was certain she couldn't reach his heart.

"I believe you, Julian." The cold expression on his face didn't change as he remained where he was. "Did you hear me, Julian?"

"I heard you," he said in a cold, heartless voice.

"And you have nothing to say to me?" she asked as her body tensed at his inflexible expression.

"What you think nae longer matters to me, Patience. Now get out and dinnae come back."

The indifference in his voice made her heart skip a beat. His voice was so detached and unfeeling. It was almost as if he were impervious to her. No, he couldn't be. If he were, how could he have kissed her so passionately the day she'd arrived at Crianlarich? Then there was the quiet camaraderie they'd had at the falls and the way he'd kissed her in the glade.

No, she'd hurt his pride all those months ago, and after the fire, she'd cast him aside. There had to be a way to reach him. Frantically, she tried to think of something that would help break through the barriers between them. The solution came to her in one delicious breath of anticipation. Seduction.

She would seduce her proud, beautiful Highlander. Intimacy had a way of breaking through every emotional barrier there was. It was the most base of emotions, and she had to believe Julian would reveal his true feelings in the heat of passion. Patience pushed aside her fears as determination bloomed inside her. A Rockwood never went down without a fight, and she refused to be the first one in her family to walk away from a challenge.

Slowly, she approached the door and touched the strong fingers gripping the doorknob. Julian's reaction was immediate, and he jerked away from her to shuffle two steps backward. As she closed the door, Julian turned away as if thinking she'd left the room. The soft rustle of her skirts as she faced him made his back ramrod straight with what she thought was surprise.

The moment he turned around, she realized her mistake and trembled at the fury she saw on his face. She'd taken on a challenge that would have intimidated even Angus Stewart himself. Patience's mouth went dry as she stepped backward until her back was against the door. She stared at him as he pinned his sightless eyes on her as if he could see her. Gathering her courage, she swallowed hard.

"I have no intention of going anywhere," she said with a quiet, unshakable resolve. "I'm still your wife, which makes this *my home* as well."

"Dinnae make me say or do something I shall regret, Patience." His voice was dark with an emotion she'd never heard before. It made her think of a wounded animal that had been cornered.

"There's nothing you can do to me, Julian MacTavish that hasn't already been done."

The dismissive note in her voice made him release a low, primitive sound that sent her heart skidding out of control in trepidation. Perhaps she'd made a mistake in taunting him. As if he could see her without any problem, he closed the small distance between them.

Instinct pushed her spine deeper into the door and away from him as she recognized the predatory nature of his stance. His heat pressing into hers, Julian bent his head until his mouth lightly touched the burnt flesh of her ear. Without thinking, she jerked her head away from his lips and instantly regretted the move.

Cold amusement crossed his sharp, angular features as his body pinned her to the door. Despite her best intentions, a tremor shook through her at the suppressed violence pulsating off him and into her body. This wasn't the man she'd married. This wasn't even the man who'd made love to her in the past. This was an untamed warrior Scotsman—a man unwilling to give any quarter. As she stared up at him, her heart skidded out of control. He was magnificent, and she was determined to make him hers again.

"Are you afraid, my lady?" he asked with a biting sarcasm that infuriated her.

"Of you? *Never*," she said fiercely as she chose to fight fire with fire. Her hand cupped the back of his strong neck, and she tugged his head downward to kiss him hard. Julian stiffened against her for a brief moment before his body roughly pressed her deeper into the wood door behind her. It was a display of domination, and a small thrill raced through her. He immediately took control of the kiss, his mouth crushing hers beneath his.

The raw heat of him engulfed her like a hot summer day just before a thunderstorm. Inside her breast, her heart pounded a familiar rhythm of white-hot passion. He'd always had the ability to excite her, but the wild emotion heating her blood now was unlike anything she'd ever experienced between them. It was a wild, primitive throbbing that made her body ache to feel his skin against hers.

His tongue thrust its way into her mouth and tangled with hers in a fiery dance of passion. Mint teased her taste buds as her fingers scrunched up the warm wool of his work kilt to touch a rock-hard thigh. A large hand tugged at her bodice, and the soft pop of buttons being torn free of her gown echoed in her ears. As his hand roughly yanked her bodice open, she trembled with excitement. It was an undisciplined act that said he was out of control.

A sultry warmth swirled in the pit of her stomach. It spread its way through her veins until her entire body ached with a familiar need. Patience's fingers brushed across his inner thigh to grasp his thick, hard length. The low growl echoing out of him sent her heart skidding out of control. Her hand tightened and slid upward to the tip of him, where she found a small drop of male heat. She smeared it over the top of his erection. He was hard as steel, yet his skin was velvety smooth against the pads of her fingers.

Another note of dark desire rumbled in his chest as he tugged her gown down to her waist. The moment his mouth caressed the top of her breasts, she drew in a sharp breath that became a small moan when she exhaled. Need swept through her with the ferocity of a wild wind that threatened to carry her over a cliff of mindless passion. Desperate to feel his skin against hers, she released her hold on him to push his jacket off his broad shoulders.

It fell to the floor as his hands assisted hers in removing his vest and shirt. The tips of her fingers trailed a slow path across his skin then paused over the beat of his heart. Hard and rapid, it pounded a fierce pace beneath his skin. The pulse of it reverberated through her fingertips and into her body. A strong, masculine hand wrapped around the nape of her neck as he forced her head back to capture her mouth with his in a hard kiss. It seared her lips with the sinfully hot taste of his desire.

Without hesitation, she surrendered to the silent demand of his lips. As Julian branded her with his mouth, his hands pushed her gown off her hips until it fell to the floor. Every part of her burned with need, and in a quick movement, she freed herself from his embrace to circle around him and pressed herself into his back.

A low, dark sound of protest erupted out of him, and she smiled as she pressed one kiss after another against the hard muscles of his back. He was the sharp edge of everything male against her lips. Spice and the soft scent of leather teased her senses as she savored the hot taste of him. She could happily spend the rest of her life caressing his body like this. Love and desire swept through her to heighten the raw passion streaking through her blood.

Her hands glided over his shoulders and moved downward until she reached the buckle of his kilt. Before she could undo the metal clasp, long masculine fingers pushed hers aside. In seconds, he'd made short work of the rest of his clothing until he was completely naked. The moment he turned to face her, she drew in a sharp breath. Had he always been this beautiful, or was she simply appreciating him more because she'd not been in his arms for so long?

Julian's sightless gaze was focused on a point above her head, and she reached out to clasp his hand in hers. She took a step backward toward the bed, gently pulling him with her. A frown of frustration began to replace the desire darkening his features. Alarmed his affliction might stem the tide of his desire, she quickly stepped forward to pull his head down and kiss him hard. In response to the heated caress, his hands gripped her waist to pull her into his unyielding embrace once more.

The hard, thick length of him pressed against her thigh, and desire coiled in her stomach. It unfurled and spread through her until her body clung to his. The moment she deliberately shifted her hips, so his erection was pressed into the apex of her thighs, he released a low growl of desire. Once more, she escaped his grasp and pulled him with her the last few steps to the bed.

They tumbled down onto the mattress, and her lips clung to his as she undid the tapes of her combination garment. His hands brushed hers out of the way as he finished the task for her and tugged the corset from her body. Despite his lack of vision, his touch was as confident and sure as if he could see her. A large hand reached for the bodice of her chemise, and the garment screamed a soft protest as the fabric ripped beneath the strength of his hands to fall off her. Startled, she gasped loudly, and a rush of excitement streaked through her at the primal act. He worked quickly until her shoes and stockings were all that was left.

Fire blazed its way up across her skin as he took his time easing her stocking downward. The moment his hands touched the destroyed tissue on her leg, she stiffened. Unable to prevent it, she jerked away from his touch. It was a reaction of sheer self-preservation. An odd expression crossed his face, and his hand grew still against her leg. In the haze of desire, she thought it was a look of despair. But the emotion vanished too quickly to tell as his touch drove everything out of her mind.

Julian quickly removed the stocking from her scarred limb, and his fingers didn't linger as he removed the other stocking. When her legs were bare, he ran one hand up her unmarked leg. The moment he lowered his head, she drew in a sharp breath, which became a quiet moan as he branded her with a gentle nip of the flesh of her inner thigh.

The primitively possessive action caused her breath to come in small pants as his teeth abraded her skin, and his mouth worked its way to the apex of her thigh. A strong hand caressed her stomach before he pushed her back into the mattress. In one heated stroke, his mouth caressed her sex, and she arched upward with a soft cry of pleasure. His tongue licked and stroked her until, with a hard shudder, she climaxed. He continued to caress her with his mouth as she trembled against him.

Slowly her tremors abated, and he slid his hard body up over hers to take one nipple into his mouth. A small cry of need escaped her at the primal urges stirring in her. She wanted him—needed him inside her. She tried to shift her body beneath his in a silent demand, but he used the weight of his body to pin her down. In all the times he'd made love to her, she'd never experienced such an intense, primal need for him to make her his. Unfulfilled desire spilled through her at the way his body was controlling hers. It had been her idea to seduce him, but he'd taken control of her body the same way he had her heart from the moment they met.

"Oh God, please, Julian…I need you," she whispered as she tried to move beneath him. In the next breath, his body moved against hers, and he thrust into her hard and fast. As he filled her, she cried out in joyful surprise. Heat and pleasure engulfed her until everything disappeared, and the only thing in her world was him and his touch.

Chapter 12

The moment Julian thrust into her, his body was complete again. White-hot velvet wrapped around his cock, as her body tightened in an attempt to hold him in place. He had no difficulty retreating, and a soft moan passed her lips. A quiet whimper escaped her as he retreated, then slid into her again as he resolved to delay the ultimate pleasure his body was shouting for.

Small spasms vibrated around his cock indicating her body was demanding satisfaction as well. But he refused to lose control of his senses just yet. He was determined to savor these few moments with her. He could not afford to succumb to his wife's tempting mouth and body again. The need to bury himself deep inside her made him slip his arms beneath her legs and tilt her body upward. With the soft cheeks of her bottom pressed against his thighs, he filled her completely in one swift stroke.

With each thrust into her sweet, hot core, his body cried out with unrestrained pleasure. God help him. She was as tight now as she'd been the first time he'd made love to her. His cock stretched and hardened as he drove himself into her over and over again. With each moan that blew past her lips, his body craved her with a renewed strength.

The silky heat of her cream against his cock mixed with the soft, musky scent of her desire. It clouded his thoughts until she was the air he breathed. Her body tightened around him, and he realized she was on the verge of a climax. But he wasn't ready to part with her so quickly. Not now. It was too soon. He slid out of her until he was just at the edge of her sex.

"*No*, oh God no, Julian." Her voice was filled with desperation as she writhed beneath him and her hands clutched at his hips. "Don't stop… oh, please."

Every part of him was taut with desire, and the need pulsating in her voice made his blood roar. His breathing ragged, he bowed his head and drew in the essence of her with all of his senses. She was nothing but a shadowy form to his eyes, but there was so much more to her than what his eyes had told him in the past. He took his time as he leaned forward and kissed her. Their lips met in a fiery meld of passion, and he thrust his tongue into the warmth of her sweet mouth.

The hint of tart gooseberries melted its way across his tongue. Her hands slipped between them to touch him, and he quickly grasped her wrists and pinned her to the bed. With a small cry, she tried to tug free of his grasp. Attuned to every part of her, Julian sensed a wave of panic rising inside her as his fingers gripped her scarred wrist. Quickly, he released his hold on her and softened their kiss as his fingers entwined with hers.

The moment his fingers were no longer pressed into her burnt flesh, she relaxed. It was a fleeting observation as the taste of her pushed him close to the edge of a place only she would ever be able to take him. He lifted his head and plunged back into her again. His reward was her small scream of delight.

Although it was impossible to see her face, the quiet pants of excitement escaping her brought back the memory of moments when he'd watched her come apart in his arms. Slowly, he retreated from her then drove back into her once more, taking pleasure in her small cries of ecstasy.

With each thrust, he increased the speed of his strokes, his body in harmony with everything about her. She was a part of him, and the sudden spasms clutching his cock made him draw in a sharp breath of anticipation. Furiously, he thrust his body into hers with deep, powerful strokes. Beneath him, she thrust her hips upward in a sharp movement then froze against him as her hot velvety core grabbed him tight.

He breathed her into his senses, and she exploded over him with an intensity that made him pump his body harder and faster into her. She continued to writhe beneath him, her scream of pleasure music to his ears. Intense pleasure rolled over him as his body caught the wave of passion. He rode along the edge of it until a shout poured out of his throat, and he throbbed inside her.

For a long moment, he remained joined with her as the last raw-edged emotions ebbed away from his heart and body. The ragged breathing parting her lips matched his own as her climax continued to tug at his body. The reality of what had just happened made his heart sink. What had he done?

The question was rhetorical. He'd made love to his wife. There was no sin in that. No, it wasn't a sin, but it illustrated how easily his passion for her could bring him to his knees. That was a dangerous thing. It gave her the power to destroy him all over again. He refused to endure a repeat of that hellish existence.

The fact she'd come to Crianlarich to be his caregiver, whether out of duty or pity, was painful enough. A gentle hand caressed his cheek, and he batted it away in a rough gesture. The soft sound she made was indecipherable, but the sudden tension flowing through her body made his harden in response.

With a swift move, he retreated from her and left the bed. The pent-up need for her over the past months had made him lose sight of the fact as to why she'd come to Crianlarich. If she'd come back because she loved him, she would have said so. She would have told him she'd made a mistake not to believe him. But she hadn't.

Still, she'd been the one to instigate their moment of passion. Did it mean she felt something more for him than simply a sense of responsibility as his wife? Even if she still had feelings for him, what sort of husband would he make as a blind man? More importantly, he would never really be certain that love had made her return to Crianlarich. How could he when even after the fire, she accused him of being unfaithful with one simple word?

"Julian?"

Even with her voice, she had the ability to twist his insides. Any other man would be willing to accept what she'd given him moments ago without hesitation. He wasn't one of them.

"Get dressed," he said between clenched teeth.

Julian turned away from the bed and tried to remember where he'd left his clothes. Infuriated by his inability to see, he stood still. The last thing he wanted was the humiliation of winding up on the floor in front of his wife.

"Julian, please, we need to talk."

The air whispered softly beside him as she moved to stand in front of him. As she pressed her body into his, he froze. God help him. Just the feel of her against his skin made him want to drag her back to his bed.

"There's nothing to say, my lady. You've done your wifely duties and quite enthusiastically, I might add."

His words slashed through the air like one of the Claymores hanging in the main hall. The sharp gasp of horror escaping her said the brutality of his comment had achieved his intended effect. Yet, it pained him to be cruel. Suddenly, her finger poked painfully into his chest, and he grunted at the hard jab.

"One could say the same of you, you bastard," she snapped. "Don't you dare stand there and tell me you felt nothing a moment ago."

Hope barreled through Julian. He savagely destroyed it. He was tired of praying for something that would never happen. All he wanted now was for Patience to leave Crianlarich. Her presence at the castle threatened his peace of mind. At any minute he was apt to reveal he'd never stop loving her, and that would be the end of him. Compassion for his blindness was difficult enough to deal with. For her to pity him for loving her—he refused to let that happen.

"I'll nae deny feeling lust, lass," he said with soft deliberation. "I have always enjoyed our romps in the bedchamber."

He didn't have to see her face to feel the violence in her sharp retreat from him. Guilt plowed through him at the small sound she made. It was the noise a hare made when it was at the mercy of a predator. Although he'd deliberately pushed her away with his words, every part of him wanted to close the expanse growing between them.

The dangerous thought died a quick death as he crushed it. The silence hanging in the air between them was hard as steel. It clanged against his senses and threatened to break his steadfast desire to push her as far away from him as he could.

"I always knew you were a stubborn man, Julian MacTavish, but I never thought you to be a cruel one."

"Would you prefer I lied to you, Patience?" he said with restrained bitterness. "Can you nae agree that when we have shared a bed, it has been quite satisfying?"

"Yes," she bit out in a strained voice. "But those weren't just moments of pleasure. They were...we cared for each other back then."

"Aye, but I dinnae see things now as I did in the past." A long silence suspended the gap between them, and his muscles were twisted in painful knots.

"Are you saying you never loved me?"

The whisper echoed with a note of agony that made him hesitate. Damn fate for taking away his ability to see her face. If he could see her face right now, he'd know for certain how she felt. She'd never been able to hide her feelings behind a blank expression, but her voice was different since she'd arrived at Crianlarich. He'd not been able to determine what she was really thinking simply based on the inflections in her voice. It didn't matter, and he hardened his heart.

"Love is for the foolish, lass. It is fleeting at best."

The sharp inhalation of air she drew in would have been inaudible to someone whose auditory senses weren't sharpened like his. The sound made him long to take the words back.

"Blindness has revealed that you *are* your father's son, Julian," she said with contempt.

The accusation stung like a blow from a whip. The love he'd felt for his father had not blinded him to the man's faults. Now Patience's declaration that he possessed his father's trait of being callous and unsympathetic was a bludgeon against his body. Julian's mouth tightened as he realized he deserved her scorn. But at least it would ensure her departure. He glared in the direction of her voice.

"Then it should nae be difficult for you to leave Crianlarich for a second time," he bit out through clenched teeth, thinking he'd resolved his problem.

"I won't give you that satisfaction."

The outrage and stubbornness in her voice made his heart sink, and he suppressed a growl of frustration. She'd always been one to dig in her heels when it came to something she did or didn't want to do.

"Do as you please, my lady," he said through clenched teeth. "But dinnae come in here again. I have nae use for a wife who thinks tae act as my mistress as well as my nursemaid."

A breeze stirred the air around him as she moved past him, and her body was a fire brushing across his skin. The sound of clothes thrashing in the air filled his ears as she snatched her belongings up off the bedroom floor. He turned his head toward the furious rustling of her dress.

Despite only seeing the gray silhouette of her body, he didn't miss the way she snapped upright in a sharp movement. In the next instant, he watched her shadow stalk away from him toward the door. Stunned that she might actually think to walk through the corridors wearing nothing, he opened his mouth then quickly closed it. The door she was heading toward didn't lead out into the corridor. She was headed to the bedroom that adjoined his—the mistress of the castle's room.

"Where the hell do you think you're going?" he snarled. Julian stumbled forward, trying to close the distance between him and her shadow. He saw the dark outline of her body move abruptly as she whirled to face him.

"I'm going to my room," she said with an icy anger he'd never heard in her voice before. As he continued to haltingly close the distance between them, he tried to process the fact that she'd been sleeping in the room next to him since her arrival at Crianlarich. Her shadow remained frozen against the pale gray background of his vision.

"Why would you choose the bedroom that belongs tae the mistress of the house?" he growled with anger, uncaring whether he frightened her not. "Did you think it would make it easier for you tae see to my needs?"

"I took the room because your sister insisted and because, for all intents and purposes, I *am* the mistress of this house, you arrogant jackass." Patience turned away from him once more, and he followed.

"You cannae sleep there, Patience," he growled fiercely.

Julian reached out to keep her from leaving the room. Rough, scaly skin rubbed against the pads of his fingers. The scarred skin distracted him for a moment as raw anguish for what she'd suffered crashed through him. Before he could say a word, she broke free of his grasp with a violent tug.

"Do *not* touch me." Block ice cut from Crianlarich's frozen loch in the dead of winter could have warmed the air between them better than her voice.

"Why should I nae touch you, Patience?" He tried to focus his sightless gaze where her face should be. "As my wife, it is my right tae touch you whenever and however I wish."

"Whenever and however—" she exclaimed with all the fire of the Stewart clan. "You can go straight to hell, Julian MacTavish. The law may give you the right to take what you want of me, but you will not find me a willing participant."

"But were you nae willing tae let me touch you just a few moments ago?" he murmured as he stepped forward and her clothes brushed across his chest.

"That was different… I was…" The faint hint of lilacs drifted beneath his nose. He'd always loved the way she smelled. The confusion in her voice puzzled him as he sensed her anger had dissipated. The sudden tension pulsating in her beat its way into his own body.

"You were what, Patience?"

"I was trying… I wanted… I wanted to make it like it was before everything went wrong between us."

The statement made him stiffen. He closed his eyes for a brief moment then turned away from her. His clothes— where did he leave his clothes? He visualized where he'd left them and cautiously moved forward. Grateful he knew every inch of his bedroom, his feet brushed against his shirt. He bent over and retrieved it, then pushed his arms into the sleeves. As he buttoned the linen garment, he cleared his throat.

"Why would you want things to be as they were, Patience? You made your opinion of me quite clear months ago." Julian heard the bitterness echoing in his quiet words.

"I was wrong," she said softly. An undefined emotion ran like a fast Highland brook beneath her words. "I should have believed you—trusted you."

Stunned by her confession, Julian's fingers fumbled as he buckled his kilt. It was the second time since her return that she'd said she'd been wrong not to believe him. He turned toward her.

"Do you nae think it's a bit late for that, Patience," he said in a tight voice. After all this time, she'd chosen *this* moment to admit she judged him wrongly. He wasn't sure what to make of her change of heart.

"No, I don't think it's ever too late," she said softly yet in a firm voice that exemplified her stubborn Rockwood nature. "I told you a long time ago that we married too quickly. We didn't take the time to get to know each other first."

"Are you proposing we do that now?" Tension made his jaw ache. "It does nae make sense to do so when we are to be divorced."

The soft rustle of her gown broke the stillness in the room. Julian froze as he breathed in her sweet scent the instant she stopped in front of him. Although she didn't make a sound, the fragility vibrating off her puzzled him.

"We are both different people now, Julian. But we cared for each other once." Her voice was a piece of silk sliding across his senses. "Can't we just try to find the people we once were inside the people we are now?"

Patience's hand grasped his. The touch sent an electric shock up his arm. Of all the women he'd ever known, she was the only one who could bring him to his knees whenever she asked for something. This time it was different. In the back of his head, a warning as loud as the screech from a badly played bagpipe filtered its way to the front of his brain.

He'd be a fool to agree to her proposition. But deep inside, he was willing to be that fool if it meant having just a few hours more with her before she walked out of his life forever. His tongue was thick in his mouth as he debated how to agree to her proposal without revealing he was a drowning man eager to accept her offer of a life preserver.

"Please, Julian." If he'd not already made up his mind, her fervent, sweet plea would have easily convinced him.

"As you wish," he said with a stoicism that blessedly hid the strength of the emotions racing through him.

"Thank you," she said.

The note of relief in her voice took him by surprise. Was it possible she'd been worried he'd say no? Had she forgotten he'd never been able to say no to her? An awkward silence drifted between them until she leaned into him and kissed his cheek. The unexpected caress was a tender one that astonished him.

"Shall we go for a walk after Mrs. Lester sends up some breakfast for you?" The sweet note of her voice was almost that of a loving wife. Desperately, he tried to stifle the happiness threatening to rob him of all his senses. God almighty, what would he do when she left him? He chose to ignore the question.

"If you like."

Julian nodded as he allowed himself to relish the contentment slowly winding its way through him. He would deal with the hell he'd be cast into once she was gone. Until then, he would savor the time he had with her.

The sun warmed Julian's face as he walked through the thick grass with Patience's arm linked with his. They walked for some distance in awkward, yet at the same time, pleasant silence. A small laugh escaped her.

"I'm feeling as gauche as a debutante at her first ball." Her voice was a breathless sound that reminded him of the night he'd met her.

"As I recall, you were equally flustered the night we met."

"I was not," she exclaimed. The moment Julian arched his eyebrows, Patience laughed. "All right, flustered. But not without cause, you terrified me."

"What the devil did I do that made you afraid of me?" he growled, irritated by the thought he'd made her uncomfortable at their first meeting.

"I think terrifying is the wrong word," she said ruefully. "Perhaps intimidating is a better choice. Every woman in the room was glaring at me from the moment Ewan MacLaren introduced us."

"I dinnae notice," he said with a shrug. Julian wasn't about to admit she was the only thing he could concentrate on that night.

"Of course, you wouldn't." There was a smile in her voice that made him visualize the way her mouth always quirked upward when she was amused. "You've always been oblivious as to how women look at you or *me* when I'm with you."

"I mean, I dinnae notice because all I could see was you."

"Oh." Her response was little more than a gasp, and a smile tugged his mouth. "Did I nae ever tell you why I asked Ewan tae introduce us?"

"No," she murmured.

"It was because of your laugh."

"My laugh?" she said with surprise.

"Aye, that and your appetite. I have never cared for women who dinnae allow themselves tae enjoy a meal."

"I think I prefer the first reason over the second." The musical sound of her laugh was as warm as the sun on his face. He grinned.

"Perhaps I should have said your appetite was the first thing about you I found pleasing then your laugh."

"I would still prefer my laugh as the main reason you had Ewan introduce us."

"I was worried he might nae have," he muttered with a scowl as he remembered the other man's reluctance to present him to Patience.

"Why would he do that?"

"He said he had been considering courting you himself."

"Good Lord," she gasped.

"Then you would nae have accepted his suit?"

"Ewan?" Her body shook slightly, and he realized she was shaking her head vigorously. "No. I like him a great deal, but I never considered him as a possible suitor. Besides, he's even more intimidating than you."

"I dinnae like the way you keep using the word intimidating," he grumbled in disgust.

"Don't you dare try to deny it, Julian MacTavish."

"I dinnae intimidate people."

Annoyed, he came to an abrupt stop. Patience stumbled as he stopped moving, and she clung to him to avoid falling. He tried not to enjoy the pleasant sensation of her pressed into his side. He failed.

"Oh? Then explain why you didn't ask but arrogantly stated you would take me riding the next day."

"Dinnae make me sound like a tyrant," he snapped.

"I'm not trying to. But you do like to get your own way. That's something entirely different." There was a note of amusement in her voice, and he grimaced.

"I wanted you tae myself," he muttered defensively. "Name something else where you found me intimidating."

"The day you proposed," she said quietly. "You refused to listen to my objections that it was too soon to marry."

"If you dinnae want to marry me, why did you?" he asked in a terse voice tone. Did Patience really believe he'd coerced her into marrying him?

"I married you because I fell in love with you."

Her reply referred to the past, not the present, and his heart sank. Patience didn't speak for a long moment. Despite her request they get to know one another better, he didn't have the courage to ask her how she felt now. She suddenly heaved a sigh.

"It was also hard for me to believe you could love me as much as I loved you."

"You dinnae make any sense, Patience. Why would you think such a thing?"

"Because every other man in the past who'd courted me, for whatever reason, never stayed."

"They were fools," he bit out. A cold chill sprinted through his veins at the thought he might have lost her to another man.

"No, they simply didn't want an eccentric wife," she said. "Especially a wife incapable of…"

"Incapable of what?" Julian frowned at the note of sorrow in her voice.

"Nothing," she said quietly.

Her dispassionate response almost hid her grief, but he heard it nonetheless. The sudden memory of her blaming herself for her brother's death shortly after waking up at Melton House filled his head. Did she really think she was to blame for Devin and Caleb? He came to an abrupt halt, and she stumbled against him once more, a small cry of surprise escaping her.

"Dinnae say it's nothing," he bit out through clenched teeth. "You dinnae finish that remark because you think that unless you interpret the *an dara sealladh* correctly, you are to blame when bad things happen."

"Don't be ridiculous," she snapped, but he heard the guilt layered beneath her words

"You forget I was there when Caleb and Devin died," he snarled. "I saw your face when they fell, and I heard you blame yourself after the fire."

"Very well," she said in a harsh voice. "I *am* to blame. I had the same vision three different times, and I failed to understand what it meant. If I had, maybe I could have saved them—saved you and your father."

"*Christ Almighty, Patience.* Even if you could have known there would be a fire or the carriage accident, you could nae have known when or where the events would take place. You have always said your visions are nae always clear. You cannae blame yourself."

Silence greeted his fierce censure, and he desperately wished he could see her face. She pulled away from him, but Julian immediately reached out for her. His fingers slipped on the smooth silk of her sleeve until his hand caught her wrist and held her fast. Beneath his fingers, a hard layer of scar tissue made him wince. The moment he did so, she stiffened and tugged hard against his firm hold. Julian let her go, his brain trying to comprehend the pain she'd suffered. It was impossible to do so.

For the first time, it occurred to him that her rejection of him after the fire might not have been her belief he'd been unfaithful, but something altogether different. What if it hadn't been the discord between them but her fear he would find her hideous after being burned so badly? She'd not only refused to see him after the fire, but the rest of the Rockwood clan had found themselves barred from her rooms. The only exceptions for the first three months were the doctor and Aunt Matilda.

If Patience had thought herself a monster then, he could only imagine what she might think his reaction would be. Aunt Matilda had said the scars were not as bad as Patience thought. But if he was right, it indicated how little Patience knew him. The only thing her scars would ever stir in him was the fact that he couldn't have carried the burden of the pain she'd suffered.

Her scars would never make him love her any less. They could only make him love her all the more for her courage. How was it he'd never taken the time to explain to Patience what it was about her that he loved? From the first moment, he'd heard her laughter, it had been her heart—her soul— that had called to him. It had taken just one look into her brown eyes, and he'd been lost.

"I wish I'd died that night, too," her whisper was almost audible, but it jerked him out of his thoughts as if she'd slapped him. Anger swelled over him like a powerful wave. His hands grasped her shoulders as he growled at his inability to see her face.

"I told ye once before ye are never tae say such a thing again in my presence, Patience MacTavish," he growled with a fury he could barely contain. "Nae ever. Do you understand?"

When she didn't answer, he shook her hard.

"*Answer me*, Patience. Do ye understand?"

"Yes." There were tears in her voice, and instinct made him pull her close.

"It was nae your fault, Patience. It was a tragedy, one ye cannae take the blame for, lass. It was terrible enough for your family to lose Caleb and Devin. Would ye be so selfish as to wish one more death for all of us to grieve for?"

Patience shuddered against him. Julian's arms tightened around her as he remembered the look of defeat on her face after the two men had fallen into the flames. He'd been certain she'd resigned herself to death at that moment in time as well. The thought had filled him with a horror unlike anything he'd ever known, and he'd made her angry enough to leap through the fire into his arms.

Now, after all she'd been through, to hear her say she wished he'd just stood by and watched her die made him realize the extent of her anguish. It wasn't simply the physical agony she'd suffered for so long after the fire. He knew she was convinced her scars made her a monster. But those scars represented more than just her mistaken notion she was a monstrous creature to be pitied. They were a constant reminder of the horrors of that night. Patience slowly pushed her way out of his arms and stepped back from him.

"I think we should go back to the house," she said in a composed voice. "It's almost teatime, and you ate little at lunch."

"Dinnae try to change the subject."

"I'm not. I'm simply refusing to discuss the past anymore."

"For how long?" he demanded in a harsh voice. "You cannae let this fester inside you, Patience. It is nae healthy."

"Let me be, Julian. I have no desire to discuss the matter any further." The obstinate tone in her voice made him frown. He'd backed her into a corner, and if he pushed her too hard, he would live to regret it.

"As you wish," he said with a shrug as he fought to hide his frustration. Patience slid her arm through his again but didn't press into him as she had earlier. It indicated the invisible gap between them had widened, and he didn't know if it were possible to bridge the divide.

Chapter 13

"Kings bishop four to kings three. Checkmate."

The clink of marble against marble echoed its way upward to the library's tall ceiling as Muireall planted her chess piece on the board. In his mind's eye, all the chess pieces and their placement were vividly etched in his head.

Julian growled softly at how Muireall had capitalized on the error he'd made a few moves back. His sister's gleeful laugh made him scowl in her direction.

"You dinnae need to gloat, Muireall. It is nae ladylike," he grumbled.

Beside him, he could hear the faint coughing noise Patience made as she choked back laughter. He turned his head toward the sound. Although he could not see her face, he knew she was struggling to hide her amusement. The instant he scowled at her, she laughed as hard as his sister.

"I dinnae understand what you find so amusing," he said with irritation.

"I'm sorry, Julian," Muireall said with distinct amusement.

"You dinnae sound like it." He shook his head in disgust.

"If it makes you feel better, you were close to winning." This time there was a note of regret in Muireall's voice, and he grimaced. Before he could say anything, Patience's hand touched his forearm in a silent gesture of chastisement.

"Don't you dare feel guilty for winning, Muireall MacTavish," Patience chided. "You won fair and square. Your brother had the advantage until just a few moments ago. He's just annoyed you took advantage of his mistake."

"A mistake caused by my wife," Julian growled.

"*Me?*" Patience's voice was filled with surprise and amused disbelief.

"Aye, the honey-sweet scent of your hair distracted me," he said as he bit back a grin. Patience grew still beside him, and Muireall gave an unladylike snort of laughter.

"Your face is red, Patience."

Julian grinned openly as the air stirred beside him the moment Patience lifted her hands to her face. When he sensed her retreating from him, he quickly caught her hand. The horrific scars from her burns were on the opposite side of her body, and she didn't try to jerk free of his grasp. Deliberately he traced a small circle in the small hollow of her wrist with his thumb. Julian heard her rapid breathing, and he carried her hand upward to kiss her fingertips.

"On second thought, I should have said it was your perfume that distracted me. Lilacs smell delightful on your skin, my lady."

The tremor that rippled through her vibrated into his fingers. He smiled as satisfaction surged through him. Over the past three weeks, Patience had ensured that everything between them was as circumspect as possible. It was obvious she was determined to have the courtship they hadn't had before they were married. This was the first time she'd allowed him to touch her since the day he'd made love to her.

Other than to accept the offer of his arm or when their fingers touched when she handed something, she'd avoided physical contact with him as much as possible. Somehow he didn't think she was worried about him coercing her back into his bed—something he was beginning to crave like a man without drink. More than likely, her distant manner was rooted in her fear he would bring up the past.

"You are an unrepentant rogue, Julian MacTavish," his wife said with a breathless laugh.

"I shall nae deny that." He chuckled in an unapologetic manner. "But I find it easy to do so where you're concerned."

"Stop teasing her, Julian," his sister said with a laugh. "Her cheeks are bright red now."

"Are they?" Julian grinned, and then he frowned. He wanted to see his wife's face when he complimented her. Patience had always blushed so sweetly. No longer amused, Julian released Patience's hand. The grandfather clock in the main hall announced the half-hour in a sonorous chime.

"It's time you were in bed, Muireall."

"I am nae longer a child, Julian," his sister said crisply. "I will be seventeen next week."

"Aye, that you will," he said with a nod as Muireall reminded him how quickly she was growing up. "But it's still late. Patience and I should retire as well since we are riding in the morning."

"Why not come with us, Muireall?" Patience's invitation made Julian's mouth tighten as he fought to appear amenable to the idea of his sister accompanying them on their morning ride.

"I cannae. I promised Mrs. Lester that I would review the dinner menu for my birthday party next week," Muireall said with obvious regret before her tone lightened. "But the day after tomorrow, I would like to go. Will you ride then, Julian?"

"Of course," he said with a smile.

Satisfaction swept through him at the thought he would have Patience to himself in the morning. It would be their first ride since the day he'd suffered his migraine. Ever since Patience had agreed to their outing, Julian had been looking forward to having her alone without the prospect of someone interrupting them. Suddenly, he realized his wife had gone unusually still.

"I didn't realize we were having guests next week," Patience said softly.

"We dinnae have to invite anyone," Muireall said hastily, and although she did an excellent job hiding her disappointment, Julian still heard it in his sister's voice.

"Of course not, dearest," Patience said quickly. "I was simply surprised."

"You dinnae mind," Muireall asked hesitantly.

"Not at all." Charged emotions vibrated off of Patience that he could feel as easily as if she were touching him. Her silk gown rustled softly as he saw her shadow lean toward Muireall. "We must make your birthday a wonderful one."

His wife was far more skillful than Muireall in hiding her misgivings beneath a well-modulated tone of voice. But Julian could feel the raw tension humming through the air between them. She'd had a shock, and she would need time to adjust to the idea of visitors. He frowned.

It was the first time since the accident that he didn't find himself objecting to the prospect of guests at Crianlarich. The thought surprised him. Patience had given enough of his self-esteem and independence back to him that the idea of visitors to Crianlarich no longer troubled him. He smiled.

"I think you've procrastinated enough for one evening, Muireall MacTavish. Bed, young lady." Laughter filled the air as Muireall's chair scraped against the stone floor in a loud screech. A second later, his sister was at his side, and she bent to kiss his cheek.

"Good night, Julian," she said.

Muireall's hand squeezed his shoulder before she moved around him to say good night to Patience. He turned his head and saw the shadows of the two women merge as his sister hugged his wife. A few seconds later, Muireall left the room. The silence that remained was dense with unspoken emotion. Patience's apprehension was a palpable sensation throbbing off of her.

Julian pushed his chair back from the table and turned his head to where Patience sat. He frowned in puzzlement as he saw the sharp outline of Patience's soft curves against the fuzzy, pale gray background that was his vision. The clarity of her shadow seemed crisper than usual.

He dismissed the thought as he knew Mrs. Drummond had taken to increasing the lighting in the room in the evening hours to help him see the outline of furniture in the room more easily. Julian grimaced as he tried to think of a way to broach the subject of Muireall's party. Almost as if she could read his thoughts, a small sound escaped her.

"I don't know if Muireall has mentioned it, but I've been visiting the nursery every day since you explained who Aiden was."

Stunned, Julian's jaw sagged at her comment, leaving him unable to speak. The sound of her laughter made him recover from his amazement.

"What amuses you, woman," he said with a grunt of annoyance, knowing full well she was laughing at his reaction.

"I never thought I'd see the day when my husband would find himself without words." The fact she'd referred to him as her husband sent hope barreling through him.

"I am nae speechless, Mistress Crianlarich."

"No?" The word vibrated with amused disbelief.

"No," he said with an emphatic shake of his head. "But I will nae deny being astonished at your interest in the child."

"He's not responsible for the circumstances of his birth."

Something poignant threaded its way through Patience's soft reply, and he winced. When Caitriona had left Aiden in his care, he'd hoped Patience would want to raise the boy as her own. But then things had gone from bad to worse with their marriage and Patience's lack of trust. That she'd even returned to Crianlarich at all was a small miracle in and of itself.

"Did you know Aiden has a birthmark on his leg, just like you?"

"No," he said with an indifferent shrug. "It does nae surprise me, though. My father once told me most of the MacTavish men bear the mark, including himself."

"*What!*" She gasped in horror and astonishment. "*why didn't you tell me this before now?* Why didn't you tell me that day—"

"Would you have believed me?" His indignation echoed harshly in his question.

Stiff with anger, he leaned forward a small fraction as he waited for her reply. When she remained silent, frustration barreled through him at his inability to see her face and he flung himself backward into the chair. The silence in the room was a palpable sensation. Tension and shock radiated off her, but he couldn't tell him what she was thinking.

The sudden memory of her harsh accusations the evening he'd returned home after Caitriona had died giving birth to Aiden sent pain, disappointment, and anger barreling through him. Julian had lived in hell ever since then. To think his lies that day might have been forgiven if Patience had known about the MacTavish mark created a tight, invisible band around his chest. Angry at the events that had driven them apart, Julian focused his attention on her dark silhouette

"Answer me, Patience." At his harsh command, she made a small sound that echoed in the air like the cry of a wounded animal.

"I don't know, Julian. I know I would have thought twice about Una's lies if I'd known, but I can't change the past," she whispered in a voice filled with sorrow and regret. She leaned forward to touch his arm as if pleading with him to understand. "I can only say I was *wrong* not to believe you, and I bitterly regret doing so."

Pain hovered beneath her words, and it aroused the need to pull her into his arms and comfort her, but he didn't move. It was enough for the moment to know she had as many regrets as he did. They sat in silence for a moment, each of them lost in their thoughts. Ever since their conversation that day in the garden, they had avoided any mention of the past.

Instead, they'd done as Patience had asked. The two of them had spent their time together getting to know each other better. Laughter and warmth had filled the hours spent in her company over the past few weeks. With each breath Julian took his love for her had deepened until it bound him to her with a strength that could destroy him.

Now the past had returned to illustrate just how deep Una's and his father's words and deeds had driven the wedge between him and Patience. Julian had failed her from the first moment he'd brought her to Crianlarich Castle. When she'd expressed her fears, he had brushed them aside, but two people had seen what Julian had not. Una and his father had exploited Patience's self-doubt until that fateful moment when his own lies had placed the last brick in the wall between them.

Julian turned his gaze toward the soft curves of Patience's shadow, which was emphasized by the numerous candles Mrs. Drummond had lit earlier in the evening. How could his father not have seen how happy Patience made him and welcomed her as a daughter with open arms?

Perhaps Fergus MacTavish had viewed it as betrayal on Julian's part for not marrying the bride the Crianlarich had chosen for him. But Julian had married a woman he loved more than life itself. A sudden gasp escaped Patience, and he quickly straightened in his chair thinking something had frightened her.

"What's wrong," he demanded in a stern voice that dared her to lie to him.

"Nothing."

"It dinnae sound like nothing, Patience MacTavish."

"I was simply think about your father…" Her voice trailed off without finishing her thought.

"What about my father?"

"I just wondered if he might have…" Her voice trailed off to a halt before she huffed a sound of annoyed disbelief. "It's not important."

"Wondered if he might what, Patience?" As he asked the question, a whisper of something unthinkable tried to push its way out of the back of his mind.

"Nothing," she breathed "It's ridiculous to even have thought it."

"Tell me." At the stern command, he saw her shadow jump in surprise.

"It's just that I wondered…I thought…perhaps your father might have mentioned the birthmark…to Una." As Patience's words faded in silence, Julian frowned.

"Why would my father tell Una about the MacTavish birth—*bloody hell*," he snarled as anger tightened every one of his muscles. "Una shared my father's bed."

"It would explain how she knew about the birthmark," Patience murmured.

"The mon wasn't satisfied with ruining one of his best friend's daughters, he had tae ruin them both."

"While your father was less than kind to me, I never thought him a man without honor. I find it difficult to believe he seduced either Catriona or Una." Patience leaned forward and caught his hand in hers and squeezed it. "While I know little about Catriona, I *do know* Una's strong desire to be Mistress of Crianlarich might have made her seduce your father in the hope of becoming his wife."

"Dinnae make excuses for him," Julian growled.

"I'm not, but we both know your father led Una to believe she would live here one day as Mistress of Crianlarich," she said with a sigh. "Una just thought it would be as your wife."

"Aye," he said quietly. "But I dinnae want her, I chose an Englishwoman with all the fire and stubbornness of a true Stewart."

"I'll take that as a compliment," she said in a breathless voice.

"It was meant as one," he chuckled. "I've often thought you more a Stewart than a Rockwood."

"Why do I think that's more a commentary on my worst traits than on my family bloodline?" The words were filled with ironic amusement.

"I think I shall retire for the evening before I find myself in hot water." With a laugh, he rose to his feet. Following his lead, Patience rose from her chair as well.

"Would you like me to walk with you?" she asked quietly. As she had since she'd first arrived at Crianlarich, Patience gave him the option to ask for help. She never forced it on him.

"I would nae object if you would lend me your arm," he said with a smile.

In silence, she slipped her arm through his, and together they left the library. As they climbed the stairs, Julian enjoyed the pleasure it gave him to be this close to her. In the past three weeks, she'd captured even more of his soul than ever before. When they reached the top of the stairs and turned toward their bedrooms, Patience's hand rubbed gently over his sleeve in a manner he could only describe as tender.

"I was thinking we might start taking Aiden out into the garden with us when we go on our afternoon walks."

Her quiet suggestion stunned him almost as much as her earlier declaration that she'd visited the child daily. Abruptly coming to a halt, Julian turned his head toward her. Not for the first time, he longed to see her expression. What the devil had made her suggest such a thing?

"Take him with us?"

"Yes," she said with a laugh. "He's a happy little fellow, and I think he would enjoy the time outdoors."

The lighthearted note in her voice made his lips twist in a slight smile. If she were ever to leave Crianlarich, her laughter is what he would miss most. Julian's heart sank. If she left, life would become the same bleak hell it had been before she'd arrived. But what would it do to Aiden? Where would the lad be when she left? He cleared his throat then resumed the path toward his room with Patience's arm still linked in his.

"Do you think it's wise to continue visiting the child? The lad could become quite attached to you. If you left—"

"And if I chose to stay at Crianlarich? Do you think that would be a wise choice for the two of us?" she whispered in a hesitant voice. His heart slammed into his chest at her question.

"Are ye asking tae stay, Patience?" He heard the way his brogue thickened as his mouth went dry.

"I…I would like for us to consider the possibility of a reconciliation."

Unable to reply to her proposition, he paced himself as he silently counted the feet to where his bedroom door was. She'd asked to stay. She'd offered them the chance to move out of the past and into the present. He suppressed the shout of happiness threatening to roll out of his throat.

She'd not said anything about the feelings they might have for each other. If she were asking to remain because she believe it was her duty to do so, he wanted no part of that. Before he agreed to her staying, she would need to face her demons. The memory of her reaction at the prospect of guests next week for Muireall's party filled his head.

"Are you asking tae stay because you want tae, Patience, or are you staying because you want tae hide?"

"Hide? I don't know what you're talking about." Her voice had gone from the warmth of a summer sun to the frigid chill of a gray winter's day in the space of seconds. Julian frowned as they stopped in front of his bedroom.

"Then you should think about my question," he said gently as he crossed the threshold. His back to her, he began to close his bedroom door. "Good night, Patience. I will tell Muireall tomorrow that we will have a quiet family celebration instead of a party next week."

Julian heard her draw in a quick breath as he shut the door. The moment the latch clicked into place, he walked toward his bed, counting each step in his head. Julian had barely reached the number three when the door was flung open behind him. As he'd expected, it hadn't taken Patience long to confront him. He'd known she would not take kindly to his speaking with Muireall about the party. The bedroom door slammed shut behind her as she brushed past him to stand in his way.

"I did not ask you to tell Muireall to cancel her party, Julian MacTavish." The fiery note in her voice made him wish his father could hear her now. There was no doubt as to her Stewart blood at the moment.

"I dinnae recall saying I'd ask Muireall tae call off the party for your sake, Patience," he said quietly.

"Don't you dare pretend you have any other reason for doing so."

"As you wish." He shrugged. "I shall nae lie that you are my reason for speaking with Muireall."

"Well, don't," she snapped. "You're not to say one word to your sister about her party."

"So you're nae alarmed by the prospect of guests here in the castle."

"Why on earth would I be?" Patience's exclamation was filled with more than a touch of panic that confirmed his belief she was lying.

"Because every part of you vibrated with fear, the minute Muireall mentioned the party."

"Don't be ridiculous." The sharp note in her voice emphasized her valiant efforts to deny his allegations.

"Then I'll send for Mrs. Campbell in the morning," he said, determined to force her into facing her fear and not letting it rule her. If she was to stay, it would only be if she loved him and could face the past and its effects on her. In the back of his head, he ignored a voice scoffing at his own hypocrisy.

"Mrs. Campbell?" she asked warily.

"Aye, the village seamstress. You and Muireall will need new gowns. Although, I'm sure it will cost me a pretty sixpence as it's on such short notice."

"I do *not* need a new gown."

"Since when have you ever passed up the opportunity to buy a new dress? I have paid plenty of seamstress bills where you are concerned," he snapped.

"That was different."

Julian's jaw clenched with tension. Patience was right. That was in the past. While the two of them had enjoyed getting to know each other better these past few weeks, there was a great deal they didn't know about each other. But at the moment, he was all too familiar with this particular trait of Patience's.

The Rockwoods hadn't earned their reputation simply for being reckless. They were known to be headstrong as well. Patience had inherited more than her fair share of her family's stubbornness. Just as he had the night of the fire, he would have to challenge her and make her angry enough to face whatever truth she feared. The question was whether her confession would make her come back to him, changed, but unafraid to accept herself for whom she was.

"How is it different now than it was in the past, Patience?" he asked quietly.

"Because I…because I needed clothes then."

"I dinnae understand, Patience. Are you suggesting you dinnae need a new gown for the party?"

"You are being deliberately difficult, aren't you?" she snapped, and he could imagine the fiery glare she'd be directing at him. "Most husbands would be grateful for a wife who doesn't drive them into bankruptcy with dressmaker bills."

"But you are nae most wives, are you, Patience?" he said fiercely as he stepped toward her.

The moment he sensed her within arm's reach, he caught hold of her and pulled her into his embrace. With one arm, he held her tight against him then touched her scarred face. A wounded cry welled up out of her throat. She jerked her head away from his touch before twisting in his arms in an attempt to free herself from his grasp. When she failed, she shuddered against him.

Gently, but with tender determination, Julian explored her face with his fingers. Patience trembled violently against him, and he murmured a calming noise as he touched her. Against the pads of his fingers, soft, smooth skin became scar tissue about an inch in front of her ear. The once soft lobe was now rough and scaly from the inferno she'd survived. His fingers skimmed across the burnt skin of her left cheek and down to the edge of her jawline before following the trail of damaged flesh across her neck and the curve of her shoulder.

Something wet hit the back of his hand as he stroked her cheek. The teardrop wrenched at his gut, and his heart ached as though it were being crushed beneath granite. Wanting to take some of her heartache away, he bent his head and brushed his mouth over her scarred cheek. The instant he did so, a cry of dismay broke past her lips. With a strength that surprised him, Patience twisted her way out of his arms. As she escaped his embrace, he experienced a bolt of fear that he'd pushed her too hard.

Patience put several feet between them and stared at Julian. His expression made bile rise in her throat. Pity. He pitied her. Desperately ,she fought not to make a sound as tears streamed down her face. Not since the day she'd made Percy send Julian away from Melton House had she felt this alone and vulnerable. One hand covering her mouth, she tried to stop her trembling but failed.

What had made him touch her like that? Had he thought it would make her feel better if she allowed him to her injuries? Her fingers trailed across the place where he'd kissed her cheek. She'd done everything possible to keep him from touching her scorched skin since she'd arrived at Crianlarich.

Even when they'd made love, she'd managed to keep him from touching the hard, rough scars that covered almost half her face. There had been something deliberate in his actions a few moments ago. He'd said she wasn't like other wives. Had he been referring to her scarred flesh? Although she had never been a vain beauty, Julian had always made her feel beautiful.

But she knew how ugly her scars were and how marred her face was. She knew because of the way people recoiled from her or whispered loudly about what a piteous creature she'd become. To think he was suggesting she was different because of her scars was the same as if he'd pierced her breast with a sharp blade.

"What did you mean I'm not like most wives?" she bit out in a stilted voice.

"You are nae like other women because you are my wife, and you are a Rockwood," he said quietly. "You possess your family's stubbornness and sometimes foolhardy nature, but above all, you are the most courageous person I've ever known."

Julian extended his hand toward her, and she leapt backward. Her trembling had eased somewhat, but she had no doubt that if he touched her again, she would lose complete control of her emotions. Silence hung thick and heavy between them, and Patience blinked the tears from her eyes. Julian was staring at a point past her head, and the expression on his ruggedly handsome features had become harsh and unreadable, while his posture was rigid and inflexible.

"Do you know how many times I've wished it had been me trapped in those flames and nae you, my brave lass?" His throat bobbed, and his mouth drew up taut against the low, roughly uttered statement.

Patience's heart skipped a beat as his words hung in the air between them. An image of Percy preventing Julian from leaping through the flames to reach her fluttered through her head. She closed her eyes for a moment. Julian understood her. He knew her family was a stubborn clan. Their bloodline ensured that trait. It was one of the reasons why he'd taunted her so ruthlessly after Caleb and Devin had fallen into the inferno.

He'd known that if he made her angry enough, she would jump across that terrifying gap of flames. Without his taunts, she would have died that night. No, not his derisive words. It had been his threat of coming after her that had saved her. She would have done anything to keep him safe. Something she'd failed to do where Caleb or Devin were concerned. Not even her gift had been enough to save them. A draining weariness sank into her pores, burrowing deep into her soul.

"I'm tired, Julian," she said hoarsely as she turned away from him. "I'll say good night."

"You cannae run forever, Patience."

A wave of panic assaulted her. It rolled over her with an unexpected strength that left her with the sensation of drowning. Why did he feel the need to plague her with the past? All she wanted to do was forget. Deep down, a voice mocked her. She would never forget.

"I'm not running from anything," she bit out. "Unlike you, I simply don't feel the need to discuss the past."

"It's time you did discuss it, Patience," he said firmly. "You've hidden from the world for long enough."

"I am *not* hiding from the world," she exclaimed angrily.

"Your family disagrees with you." Julian glared at a point above her head. "Do you nae remember all the times Percy and the others urged you to come out of that damn room of yours at Melton House?"

"I wasn't well—"

"Tell me why you sent me away, Patience."

The harsh command made Patience's heart stop before it resumed beating at the speed of a runaway train. How could she respond to that? Was she supposed to lie or tell him the truth? Tell him that she believed he'd always been faithful to her? Should she tell him everything?

"I want an answer, Patience. Why did you send me away?"

This time his voice echoed with the ferocity of the ancient warriors he descended from. It dislodged a small brick from the wall she'd built between her and the past. Like a piece of a dam, the wall began to crack at its weakest point. Desperately, she fought to push her pain and fear back into the void. As she studied his face, her heart jumped painfully in her chest. She didn't have the courage to tell him the complete truth. The idea of confessing how terrified she'd been when he'd seen the extent of her scars appalled her. How could she begin to explain her fear that he would look at her and find her revolting like so many others? He frowned angrily.

"*Tell me*," he ordered, and his voice ripped away the wall holding her emotions at bay. Pain, regret, fear, and grief flooded her senses.

"Because I didn't want your pity," she cried out as her emotions erupted viciously inside her.

"My pity?" An odd expression darkened Julian's features.

"*Yes*, pity," she cried out with a fury that shadowed the pain spreading its way through her. "I knew before I even looked in the mirror what a hideous creature I was. How could you feel *anything* but pity for me?"

"Do you deem me of such low character that I would have only pity for my wife, Patience MacTavish? The woman I loved?" His voice was a clap of thunder in the room. She gasped at his reaction to her words. In the back of her mind, she noted he'd spoken in the past tense, and it intensified the sensation of pain from the brittle glass-like shards slicing into her.

"*No*, that's not what I meant." She took a step toward him then stopped as disgust slashed across his face.

"Dinnae mock me, my lady," he snarled. "What else could you have meant?"

"The woman I was died in that fire. The creature I've become is reviled," she said coldly. "I couldn't bear having you look at me with...with disgust."

"If I were concerned solely with my wife's appearance, I would nae have spent two weeks at her bedside or waited *six months* for her to send for me, which she never did." His voice was icy with contempt as a thunderous cloud of dark anger settled on his face. "You are a hypocrite, my lady. You would nae allow me the chance to prove myself to you, and yet the minute you learned of my affliction, you raced back to Crianlarich. For what—to act as my nurse? Would you have come here if I could see?"

Patience stared at him in horror. Was that why she'd come back to Crianlarich? Was it simply because she knew Julian wouldn't be able to see the terrible scars on her body? He'd asked a fair question, and in the back of her head, she didn't like her answer.

"*Answer me, damn you*," he roared, and the violence in his command made her flinch.

"No," she whispered.

"*Nae what?*" he snarled.

"No, I wouldn't have come back to Crianlarich," she said clearly as her heart pounded painfully in her chest.

"I think that's the first honest thing you've ever said to me."

"That's not true," she gasped.

"Get out, Patience," he said in a voice devoid of emotion. Although he was pale, his face was an implacable mask of scorn.

"Please, Julian, I didn't—"

"*Now*, Patience." The emphatic command dared her to disobey. Frozen where she stood, Patience realized her attempt to make Julian fall in love with her again was dying a painful death.

"Julian, please. Let me—"

"Get out, Patience," he roared.

The fury in his voice made her recoil from him. Her heart breaking, she turned and slowly walked away, leaving him standing in the center of the room. A few seconds later, she closed the door between their rooms. Tears streaming down her cheeks, Patience undressed slowly in the dark. She'd made a terrible mistake sending him away.

For six months, he'd been at Melton House every day asking to see her. She'd been so wrapped up in her own pain she'd failed to see that only a man in love would have been so relentless in his determination to see her. She wiped tears off her face. She'd misjudged him terribly. The silent admission left her feeling as though someone had cut her heart out of her chest and left her bleeding.

She'd been such a fool, and now everything she'd done to win Julian's heart back since she'd returned to Crianlarich had gone down in flames. All her efforts had fallen by the wayside with her complete lack of understanding as to the kind of man her husband was.

As she slipped beneath the bedcovers, she tried to form a plan for correcting the terrible damage she'd done tonight. For a long time, her chaotic thoughts made her toss and turn restlessly. When her eyes finally drifted closed, it was with the knowledge that she'd failed to come up with a way to make Julian understand how wrong she'd been.

Chapter 14

C oughing violently, Patience scrambled out of bed. The floor beneath her bare feet was hot, and she raced to her bedroom door. Thick smoke filled the corridor, and fear held her frozen where she stood. Her mouth moved as she tried to cry out a warning. When the sound finally rolled out of her, it was a piercing cry.

"*Fire*," she screamed. "*Fire*."

Panic and terror propelled her forward. The screams of her sisters echoed in the hall, followed by shouts of alarm from her brothers. Caleb. She raced to the door next to hers, pounding on it before flinging it open.

"*Caleb*," she cried out. "*The house is on fire*. We have to get the children out."

A loud oath sounded in the room. Satisfied her brother was awake, she ran back out into the hall. Behind her, she heard her brother call her name. Patience ignored his command to stop. Her feet pounded against the increasingly hot floor as she raced toward the nursery. As she reached the rooms where the children slept, she threw the door open, barely noting the noise it made as it hit the wall.

"Nanny Smythe," she cried out. The nurse emerged from one of the rooms with her nightcap askew, a look of amazement on her face. Patience headed toward Braxton's bedroom. "Get Greer and the others up out of bed. The house is on fire. We need to get the children out now."

Not waiting for a response, she hurried into the darkened bedroom. A small fire burned in the hearth, and she could barely see for all the surrounding smoke. Fear caused tears to roll down her cheeks. She had to get the children out. When they were safe, she could save Caleb and Devin.

Quickly, she hurried to the crib and gently picked Braxton up in her arms. He uttered a soft cry, and she stroked his forehead soothingly. Nanny Smythe was still standing in the middle of the playroom when Patience emerged from Braxton's room. She glared at the woman with raw fury.

"Didn't you hear me," she cried out. "Look at all the smoke. The house is on fire."

"But, my lady—"

"*Get the children.* We have to get them out of the house."

"Patience." The gentle sound of Julian calling her name made her turn toward the door. Braxton was beginning to cry loudly, and she kissed his cheek.

"It's all right, my darling. Julian's here. He'll help us."

"Give the boy to the nurse, *mo leannan,*" Julian said softly and with calm reassurance.

"But she has to save the other children. Aunt Matilda's room is just down the hall. We have to get her—oh, God, Caleb. She quickly handed Braxton to the nurse and darted past Julian to run out into the corridor. The smoke was even thicker now, and she cried out in terror as a wall of flames shot out of the wall beside her. Staggering to one side, she raised her arm in an attempt to keep the fire away from her face. It was a vain attempt as the flames bit deep into her skin.

Agony speared its way through her, and she screamed as a piece of the wall fell down on her. Despite the pain, she stumbled to her feet. She had to reach Caleb and Devin. She couldn't let them die a second time. Patience took two steps forward then blinked as the smoke swirled away into nothing. The flames shooting out of the walls vanished along with the searing pain on her face and arm.

Dazed, she stared down at her arm, which was covered by the sleeve of her nightgown. A tremor rocked her body, and she wrapped her arms around her waist to keep it from engulfing her. Eyes closed, she saw Caleb's handsome face as he'd hugged her tight against him just before his death. She hadn't saved him. She hadn't saved Devin. Her gift had failed her the one time it had really mattered. A sob escaped her as tears streamed down her face.

"Oh, Patience, dinnae cry," Muireall's quiet plea made her stiffen. What was Muireall doing in her room? She opened her eyes and saw the castle's small staff looking at her with concern.

"Muireall?" Confused, she shook her head as she met her sister-in-law's troubled gaze. "How did I get into the hall?"

"Patience." Julian's quiet voice echoed behind her, and she turned around. Concern was furrowed deep in his brow, and his mouth twisted slightly as if he were in pain. How had he gotten to the nursery? Where was his cane? He stretched his hand outward, his sightless gaze directed at a point down the hall. With a quiet sob, she took two quick steps forward into his arms and buried her face into his chest.

"It will be all right, *mo leannan.*"

The quiet words made her tremble as he held her tightly in his arms. Over the top of her head, she heard Julian issuing orders. A second later, he swept her up into his arms. Cradled against him, she gasped in surprised dismay.

"Julian, put me down, you—"

"Muireall will be my eyes," he said gruffly. "You're trembling so badly I dinnae think you can walk back tae your room."

"But—"

"Dinnae argue with me, Patience." When she didn't protest any further, he nodded sharply. "Muireall, show me the way to my room."

Patience was too drained to object, and she pressed her face into his shoulder, taking comfort in the powerful strength of his arms.

In less than a minute, they were in Julian's room, where he carried her to the bed. Muireall helped Julian nestle Patience under the covers. When his sister was gone, Julian circled the bed to slide beneath the blankets and pulled her into his embrace. Craving the need for physical comfort, Patience snuggled into his side. Julian didn't say anything. He simply held her close with his chin resting against the top of her head. Exhausted, she closed her eyes feeling safe in the comfort of his arms.

The soft rumble in her ear penetrated Patience's sleep, and she stirred sleepily. As her eyes fluttered open, she frowned. Where was she? Her gaze swept toward the window where the sunlight brushed the edge of the navy brocade fabric of the curtains. Julian's room. How had she ended up in her husband's bed when the last thing he'd said was to order her out of his room? She closed her eyes and tried to think what might have happened last night. Suddenly the memory of smoke and panic filled her head. She winced as she remembered sounding the alarm about a fire that didn't exist. Julian had come for her and carried her back to his room.

Patience tilted her head slightly upward to study his face for a moment. She'd always loved watching him sleep. There was a gentleness to his face when he slept. It was at times like these that she could see the boy he'd once been.

Tentatively she reached out to touch the dark shadow on his face. Rough and bristly against her fingertips, she remembered how he'd once threatened to grow a beard and whiskers when she expressed disgust at the trend among men. She pulled her hand away from him and gently reached for his arm to slide out from his embrace. The second she moved, his arm tightened around her.

"Stay, lass." His command held a hint of a plea as well, and she remained where she was. The silence between them was soft and comforting. She thought he was dozing until his fingers pressed gently into her arm.

"I am to blame for last night." It wasn't an open apology, but she took it for the apology it was meant to be. When she remained silent, he cleared his throat. "What do you remember?"

"Most of it," she murmured. "I must have frightened Aiden very much."

"The lad will nae remember it."

"I'm sure the rest of the household thinks I belong in an asylum."

"Nae. Muireall used to sleepwalk as a child. They are familiar with the signs. Have you done this before?"

"Once or twice, it was troubling for everyone, but Harlan had already warned the family something like this might happen.

"Harlan?" The word was a low growl in his chest. "Do you nae mean Dr. Branson?"

"Yes, Dr. Branson. But he's my friend as much as he is my doctor," she said with a sense of gratitude for everything Harlan had done for her. "He's been my healer, counselor, and friend."

Julian didn't respond for a moment, and there was a tension about him that made her look up at his face. His expression was harsh and unyielding. Almost as if he was aware of her eyes on him, his lips became a straight line.

"And have you discussed the past with him?" The question was chilly in tone, and she winced. Was it possible he was hurt by the fact she'd discussed the events of that terrible night with Harlan, but not him?

"Yes, it was part of my treatment. Dr. Branson insisted on it," she replied, referring to Harland by his title in an effort to ease Julian's obvious displeasure when it came to her friendship with the doctor.

"Yet you dinnae wish to discuss the past with me," Julian said with restrained anger. Patience sat up, and he didn't try to hold her in place.

"Talking to Har—Dr. Branson is different. He wasn't there that night. When I talk to him, it's as if I'm simply telling him about a story I've read and how it makes me feel." She sighed when his hard expression didn't change. Closing her eyes, she tried to keep the tears from flowing. "It hurts—no—terrifies me to talk about it, Julian. I couldn't do anything to save them. What do I have my gift for if I can't help the people I love? It just hurts too much to think about it all."

Unwilling to continue the conversation, she started to slide out of bed, but Julian's hand reached out for her. His firm grasp rested on her shoulder before sliding down to her scarred hand.

"It does nae do any good to keep it bottled up inside you, *mo leannan*." The endearment rolled off his lips easily, and her heart skipped a beat. His mouth twisted slightly as though he was debating a problem. "And if you cannae trust me with your pain, I dinnae think you can trust me with your happiness."

"They're not the same thing, Julian," she exclaimed.

"Are they nae?" He shook his head and rolled away from her to sit up on the edge of the bed. "You must trust me completely if we are to reconcile, Patience. I will nae accept anything less."

It was a quiet, firm ultimatum that chilled Patience until her skin was covered in goosebumps. There was such a finality to his statement. Deep inside, she knew he was right. Loving him meant she had to trust him with her deepest, darkest secret. A secret so terrible that not until this moment had she'd actually even dared to think it.

She'd survived, and she was glad. She was relieved she wasn't the one who'd died in the fire.

Patience drew in a sharp breath at the terrible thought then quickly scrambled off the bed. The admittance shook her down to the depths of her soul, and guilt assailed her with a gale force. How could she possibly tell Julian the truth? How could she even consider making such a horrible confession to him? It was a vile thing to be grateful she'd survived while Caleb and Devin had died such terrible deaths.

"Then there's nothing more to say," she said softly as she fought back tears. "I'll return to London as soon as arrangements can be made."

"As you wish," he said in a flat, emotionless voice. "Have the divorce papers sent to me when they are ready for my signature."

Patience jerked at his words. She didn't want a divorce. She never had. She'd lost him. She'd failed—not because she didn't love him, but because she didn't have the courage to trust him anymore than she could trust herself.

Julian's back was ramrod straight, and Patience wanted to leap forward across the bed to pressed her body into his back. She longed to embrace him and confess the deepest part of her soul. Most of all, she wanted the courage to tell him what was in her heart. Patience did none of those things and turned away and headed toward the connecting door between their rooms.

"Will you nae at least stay for Muireall's party?" he asked quietly. The thought of facing people she didn't know terrified her, and she hesitated in her response.

"She will be disappointed if you are nae here."

"Yes, I'll stay for the party," she replied softly. Her response apparently surprised Julian as he jerked slightly but continued to keep his back to her.

"Thank you."

It was a soft dismissal that forced her to resume her course. A moment later, she moved through the connecting door and closed it behind her. It was like shutting everything out of her life that was good, leaving only a devastating heartbreak that would haunt her for the rest of her days.

The moment Patience closed the door behind her, Julian released a low noise of pain. Christ Jesus, he'd backed himself into a corner, and in doing so, he'd driven her away. He'd misjudged the depth of her fear. It went far deeper than his own need not to be the subject of pity. He understood that much of her pain. But there was more to Patience's suffering than her desire not to be treated with pity.

It was even deeper than her belief that her scars made her a creature to shy away from. Julian knew better. He'd touched her face, and what Aunt Matilda had said was correct. Patience's scars were severe, but not to the extent she believed. Somehow he knew she was hiding a far more crippling wound beneath her scars. One he knew she would have to accept of her own accord. The realization hacked its way through him like a claymore would his flesh.

Bleakly, he went about the business of dressing for another day. One of the last few days he could enjoy hearing Patience's laughter or breathing in her sweet scent. It was unlikely she would even give him the opportunity to touch her again. The thought filled him with the state of gloom he'd not experienced since the accident. Julian reached for his cane next to his bed and made his way down to breakfast.

Patience's presence had given him the confidence to move about the castle as freely as when he'd had his sight. She'd insisted he learn to be as self-sufficient as possible. He'd done precisely that, and he enjoyed his renewed sense of freedom. The quiet clink of silverware on china greeted him as he paused in the dining room doorway.

"*Julian*, I thought you were to ride with Patience this morning."

"Our plans changed."

"I dinnae understand," Muireall said with an air of puzzlement. "Patience refused breakfast as she said she was going for her morning ride."

"She went alone?" He knew it was a ridiculous question.

"Aye," Muireall said with a hint of worry. "Should she nae have done so?"

Julian's gut knotted with fear. He knew Patience had been distraught when they'd parted company, which could easily make her careless. The Crianlarich estate was rife with treacherous terrain, and as skilled a horsewoman as his wife was, there was always the chance of something going wrong.

"I'm sure she'll be all right. If she doesn't return in an hour, I'll send Lorne out to look for her."

The morose feeling plaguing him deepened as he sat down. Like Mrs. Lester and Patience, his sister knew the precise placement of food on his plate and quickly fixed him something to eat. Almost half an hour later, he'd barely touched his meal. Hands braced against the edge of the table, he shoved himself out of his chair. The hunger he was experiencing had nothing to do with food and everything to do with his wife.

"Send Lorne into the library. I want him to read the Times to me," Julian bit out tersely as he retrieved his cane from where it rested against the table leg.

"But Patience always reads the Times to you in the morning."

"I said send for Lorne. *Now*, Muireall," he barked.

"All right, but you dinnae have to bite my head off."

The sulky note in his sister's voice made him grimace, but before he could apologize, she was gone. Angry that he'd taken his foul mood out on his sister, he muttered an oath. With his cane guiding him, Julian made his way to the library. He only had to wait a few minutes before his estate manager arrived. The man didn't ask why after almost three weeks, Patience wasn't reading to him.

As Lorne read the paper, Julian tried to focus his attention on the business and political news items. It was proving to be a difficult task when all he could do was compare Lorne's dry reading of the paper to his wife's melodious voice. Lorne had almost finished with sharing the news of the day when the sound of Patience's laughter mixed with male voices filtered its way from the main hall into the library. Frowning, he reached for his cane and stood up. No sooner had he done so than Patience entered the library followed by two more people.

"Julian, look who's come to visit," she exclaimed. Beneath her excitement, there was the sound of panic in her voice. "Percy decided to surprise us."

"Percy, this is an unexpected pleasure." The tall, dark shape of his brother-in-law loomed against the gray background of his vision. An ally to help convince Patience, she had to face her fears. A smile of delight on his face, Julian extended his hand in greeting.

"It's good to see you too, Julian," his brother-in-law said pleasantly as the two of them shook hands. "We arrived late yesterday and chose to stay at the Crianlarich Inn before riding over this morning. We met Patience on her way home."

"We?" Julian's senses were immediately on high alert as he remembered the odd note in Patience's voice.

"Yes, Dr. Branson was interested in Patience's progress. I invited him to come with me to see my wayward sister, who has been negligent in writing to the family." Percy's reply made Julian go rigid. The good doctor had come to check on his patient.

"It's a pleasure to see you again, Mr. MacTavish. I do hope you'll forgive—"

"Crianlarich," he said coldly at the doctor's cheerful greeting.

"I beg your pardon?"

"I am now the Laird of Crianlarich. You may address me as Crianlarich." An uncomfortable silence followed his harsh words, and the man in front of him cleared his throat.

"Forgive me, Crianlarich, I should have remembered you assumed your title only just recently. My condolences on your loss."

"Thank you," he bit out as his antagonism for the other man began to get the best of him. He didn't like being caught by surprise. Worse, he didn't want the man anywhere near Patience.

"Julian," His wife's voice floated across his senses. It was like a tendril of mist, tangible yet intangible.

"I invited Percy and... Dr. Branson to stay with us until Muireall's party next week."

The words were like a lash across his back. Not only had she invited the doctor into his home—a home she'd already given up—but she'd invited the man to stay at Crianlarich until her own departure. Pain snagged its way through him. Livid that she had so much power over his happiness, he turned his head in her direction.

"Muireall will be delighted to hear the news. She need nae fret about Molly Campbell or Una Bensmore being without partners for her party."

At his remark, he heard Patience's quiet gasp. Triumph surged through him. At least he would not look like a lovesick sheepherder during the time she and the good doctor were in his home.

"I trust Patience will see to your comfort, gentlemen. Lorne, I believe you mentioned there was estate business and correspondence that needed my attention."

"Aye, Crianlarich," Lorne said quietly. Julian was certain he heard a note of concern in his old friend's voice. He nodded with a satisfaction he didn't feel.

"Gentlemen, Patience," he said abruptly. Julian's voice echoed loudly in the awkward, uncomfortable silence. He didn't care that he was rude. Patience and her doctor were fortunate he didn't bring the wrath of God down on their heads. The shadows in his vision parted like waves in the sea as he used his cane to find his way out of the library.

With every step that widened the gap between him and Patience, Julian had to fight the growing urge to charge back to her side. Patience was his. She didn't belong to Branson. She was the Crianlarich's woman. When he reached the main hall, he paused for a moment. Quiet whispers in the library told him Patience and her brother were arguing vehemently. A quiet, even-toned voice interrupted the siblings, and Julian released a snort of disgust. The doctor was far too deeply involved in the affairs of the Rockwood family. With another growl of dark emotion, he made his way back to Lorne's office.

For the next several hours, Julian ruthlessly immersed himself in running the Crianlarich estate. He'd allowed things to languish since his father's death, and it was time he took a deeper interest in the estate's business prospects and its tenants. When Muireall came to tell him lunch was ready, he ordered her to have lunch sent to the office. His sister protested, but his estate manager quietly supported Julian's order. It was late afternoon when Lorne released a sigh of disgust.

"Enough, Julian," he snapped. "We cannae accomplish in one afternoon something we've nae attended to in several months. It will take time tae resolve everything. We dinnae to address everything all once, which is why I've held them back for so long."

"You should've pushed me tae do something sooner."

"*Push you,*" Lorne snorted with disgusted amusement. "The only person capable of getting your stubborn arse to do something is the Crianlarich's wife."

"Guard your words carefully, Lorne," he said with a vicious snarl.

"Dinnae patronize me, Julian MacTavish. You might be the Crianlarich now, but I can still beat your hide just like I did when we were lads. Only now I can do it blindfolded and with one hand tied behind my back."

Lorne's anger took Julian by surprise before the words of his childhood friend settled in his brain. Had the man just suggested Julian's blindness wouldn't be the reason for losing a fight? Certainty swept through him. For a moment, he didn't respond. His friend's words clarified it wasn't his blindness that defined who he was to himself or to others. Even more amazing was the fact that Lorne's words amused him. Suddenly, he snorted with laughter. Lorne chuckled as well. In seconds, the two men were laughing loudly. As their amusement died away, Julian rubbed his head. Even despite the brevity of the moment, he had the beginnings of a headache.

"You're right, Lorne. It cannae be accomplished in one day," he said quietly. "Attend tae the matters we discussed today, then we'll tackle more at the end of the week."

"As you wish, Crianlarich," his estate manager said respectfully.

Julian nodded as he rose to his feet and headed toward the office door. His hand on the doorknob, he paused.

"Thank you, Lorne. You helped me understand what Patience has been telling me all along. I am nae a blind man, just a man who sees differently."

"You're welcome," Lorne said before he cleared his throat. "She loves you, Julian. You cannae see her face as she looks at you, but I can. The Crianlarich's woman loves only one man, and that's you."

"Aye," he said wearily as he rubbed his jaw. "But she does nae love me enough, Lorne."

With those last words, Julian left his friend's office and headed toward his room. Lorne's observation reflected a conclusion he'd come to this morning. Patience would not have suggested a reconciliation if she didn't care for him. He simply asked more of her than she was willing to give. The throbbing in his head was still at a low threshold, but he knew lying down would help avoid another migraine. The last thing he wanted was being at the mercy of Patience's tender care. It would be his personal version of hell. The thought made him grunt. He was already in hell, and the pain of it would only intensify when Patience left.

Worse, when she left, it would be on the arm of another man. His head throbbed at the thought, and he grimaced. He'd not done much to help the situation by mentioning Una. Lying about the woman's attendance at Muireall's party had been beneath him, but it had been impossible not to strike out in the face of Branson's presence. The thought of appearing weak to the enemy was not something he could stomach.

Julian entered his room, closed the door behind him, and rested his cane at the foot of the bed. He turned toward the window. The tall, narrow-shaped panes of glass revealed a bright, ye dingy gray patch of color framed by dark drapes. Wishing he could see the scenery from the window, he took several steps forward.

In all the time he'd lived in the castle, he'd never seen the view from the Crianlarich's room. As a child, his father's room had been off-limits. The old Crianlarich had been possessive of his status and belongings. The quiet sound of the door to Patience's room opening made him stiffen. God help him. What did she want with him now? He didn't move as he waited for her to speak.

"Una Bensmore and her father are downstairs," she said in a strained voice. "They're demanding to see Aiden."

Patience's announcement made him go rigid. Bloody hell. Had Patience been forced to speak with the woman? He turned to face her.

"What did she say to you?" he growled softly, ready to make Una's head roll at the slightest provocation.

"I didn't speak to her…I was at the top of the stairs when they arrived a few moments ago. Mr. Bensmore demanded that Mrs. Drummond bring Aiden downstairs." Although her voice was composed, he could hear the trepidation and the residual pain the woman had caused them both.

Anger tightened his muscles. Una had obviously told her father Aiden was Caitriona's child. But why had she waited so long to do so? As always, Una's timing was impeccable. The woman always managed to pick the worst possible moment to cause trouble. Julian nodded his head, ignoring the pain the gesture caused him.

"I'll deal with it."

"You won't let them take Aiden away…will you?" The tentative question made him slowly turn toward her.

"Does it matter? You will nae be here to care." The moment he said the harsh, unfeeling words, he regretted them, but it was too late to take them back.

"He's far too sweet for you to give him to that woman, Julian," she snapped. "Una Bensmore will destroy that child either with indulgence or contempt."

Julian didn't answer her. Instead, he retrieved his cane and headed for the door. Fingers wrapped around the doorknob, he opened the door and paused.

"You dinnae have a say in the matter anymore, Patience. You gave up that right the minute you chose to go back to London and your Dr. Branson." Not waiting for her reply, he continued out into the hallway to make his way downstairs for the battle that would ensue. It wasn't something he welcomed at the moment. The sooner he could retreat to his bed, the better. But he was damned if he'd let Bensmore come into his home and make demands. Secondly, he refused to let the man take his brother from Crianlarich Castle.

Chapter 15

Patience flinched at the sound of angry voices coming out of the drawing room as she slowly crossed the hall floor. Mr. Bensmore roared out a fiery denouncement at a quiet response from Julian. She desperately wanted to enter the salon to support him, but her feet dragged at the prospect. Una Bensmore was in that room, and she had as much desire to face the woman as she did a snake. Julian said something she couldn't hear, and it seemed to increase Bensmore's ire. Patience came to a stop just outside the drawing room to listen to the argument.

"Una has told me everything, Crianlarich," Caitriona's father said with a mix of anger and anguish.

"Exactly what is it Una has told you?"

"She says Caitriona's son dinnae die, and that you refused to let her bring the child home where he belongs."

"And when did she share this news with you?"

"Last night," Bensmore snarled. "The lass came sobbing to me, saying she could nae bear tae keep the truth from me any longer."

"Forgive me, but I find that difficult to believe," Julian said with cool skepticism. "Una has rarely done anything that dinnae serve her own interests first."

"*Tis nae true,*" Una exclaimed angrily. Julian uttered a noise of contempt.

"I speak the truth. You care about your own needs and comforts ahead of anyone else," Julian replied in a harsh voice that dared her to challenge him a second time. "Which makes me wonder why you chose this moment in time to tell your father about the boy."

"I thought I could honor Caitriona's wishes, but the thought of her wee bairn growing up here without a mother's love was breaking my heart."

Una's defiant words made Patience bite down on her lip. The woman was right. When she left Crianlarich, the only woman to serve as Aiden's surrogate mother would be Muireall. Julian's sister was young and didn't deserve such a burden, no matter how willing the girl might be to care for her young brother. Guilt swept through Patience. She had only to bare her heart to Julian, and she wouldn't have to leave Crianlarich. It was a terrifying thought when she hardly had the courage to admit the truth to herself.

"Your sudden change of heart for the child's welfare is touching," Julian sneered. "You had nae desire to take the boy almost a year ago. So again, I express my curiosity as to why you have developed this sudden need to act as the child's guardian?"

"Because my father deserves to know his grandson." An indecipherable emotion ran through the haughty note in Una's voice, and Patience frowned. The woman was hiding something. She was certain of it. Without warning, an image of Una sobbing uncontrollably as the woman sat in a moving carriage filled Patience's head.

Just as abruptly, the vision ended leaving Patience bewildered. What would make the woman cry with such heartbreaking intensity? Una Bensmore was not the type of woman who would surrender to weakness of any kind. As she contemplated the vision, Patience suddenly jerked in amazement.

She still possessed the *an dara sealladh*. The fire hadn't taken everything from her. She closed her eyes as she welcomed the relief the knowledge gave her. Although her gift of sight had failed to help her save Caleb and Devin, it was a part of her. Without it, she wouldn't be Patience Rockwood MacTavish. She didn't ponder the revelation for long as her attention was drawn back to the small drama being played out in the salon.

"And yet Caitriona left the boy in my care, nae yours."

"She was dying," Una said belligerently. "She dinnae know what she was doing."

"Your sister knew precisely what she was doing," Julian bit out with an icy fury that would have made most people think twice before responding.

"I cannae believe my Caitriona would nae let her sister bring the boy home to me." Bensmore's fierce objection indicated the man intended to dig his heels in where Aiden was concerned.

"Caitriona wished to protect you from her shame, and I gave my word to ensure her request was honored. If I had it to do over, I would nae have agreed to such an oath." The regret in Julian's words was met with a brief silence before Bensmore heaved a sigh.

"I dinnae doubt my Caitriona would nae want to burden me so," Bensmore said quietly. "She was a thoughtful child, but I want to take my grandson home with me."

"That I cannae agree to." Julian's soft reply was firm and emphatic.

"Ye will nae keep me from the boy, Crianlarich."

"I have nae said I would prevent you from seeing the child," Julian replied calmly, but with irritation. "All I have said is that the boy will remain at Crianlarich under my care as Caitriona requested."

"Caitriona might have been misguided in her thinking as to whom should care for the child. But I dinnae think she would want ye to keep the boy if I am willing to take him." Bensmore persisted in his attempt to convince Julian to give Aiden into his care.

"Caitriona is nae here to speak for herself, so I must abide by her request."

"Was it her wish that ye lie and claim the boy was yours?" The anger in Bensmore's voice was softened by the dull edge of grief. "The whole countryside believes the boy is yours and your woman's."

"That was my father's doing. When I discovered his lie, the damage had already been done. Despite my father's deception, I felt it in the best interest of the child to leave things as they were."

"The best interest of the child?" Una's laugh was sharp with derision. "Do ye nae mean ye stole my sister's wee bairn to raise as yer own because yer wife cannae give ye an heir?"

"Your daughter forgets she is talking to the Laird of Crianlarich, Bensmore." The words were as cold as they were menacing, and Patience took a small step forward until she was standing just inside the salon. Bensmore and Una stood with their backs to her as they faced Julian, who was staring blindly at a point over their head. Bensmore gestured angrily at his daughter in a silent command for the woman to apologize. After a long moment, Una uttered a churlish apology. The man glared at his youngest child before turning back to Julian.

"My apologies, Crianlarich," the older man said in a placating manner. "I have indulged her too much over the years."

"Aye, which is another reason why I will nae give the boy to you. You may visit him here, but he will remain in my care. I'll nae have you, *or your daughter*, ruin the child."

"I'll nae do anything to harm my nephew," Una bit out her answer in a restrained manner, obviously angered by Julian's comment. From where Patience stood, she saw

Bensmore nod in agreement although Julian couldn't see the man's silent confirmation of Una's words.

"The lass speaks the truth. She will love the boy as if he's her own. Una says ye and your wife are estranged. It cannae be good for the boy living here without a woman's touch."

"My personal affairs are none of your business, Bensmore. It has nae bearing on the matter at hand. Aiden will remain at Crianlarich Castle."

"But ye dinnae deny the situation with your wife. 'Tis said in the village that ye will divorce the Mistress of Crianlarich. If ye do so, you'll need a new wife." There was a sly note to the man's voice that made Patience flinch.

"I suppose you have someone in mind for the role *if* that were ever to happen?" Julian's mouth thinned with anger as Patience drew in a quick breath. Was it possible he'd been bluffing about agreeing to a divorce? Did he still intend to refuse to grant her one? The thought made her heart swell with hope.

"Your father promised us that Una would be Mistress of Crianlarich."

Bensmore's words made Patience stiffen. Why would Fergus MacTavish make such a promise? Her mind raced as she tried to understand what her father-in-law had been thinking at the time he'd made such a promise. Images flooded her head at the thought, and Patience caught her breath in surprise. Her gaze quickly scanned the other woman's figure.

Una still possessed the lithe figure she'd had the day the woman had driven a wedge between Julian and Patience, but the woman's curves were softer—more pronounced now. Patience pressed her hand against the base of her throat as she remembered her vision of Una holding a baby. Una was carrying Fergus MacTavish's child. The woman had shared the old Crianlarich's bed, just like her sister.

"My father filled Una's head with visions of being the grand lady of the manor. Even if I dinnae love my wife, I would have nae interest in granting Una such a boon," Julian said with an icy anger Patience knew well.

At Julian's declaration, Patience drew in a sharp breath of amazement. Had he just said he loved her? Disbelief held her immobile for a moment as she struggled to believe she wasn't dreaming. Slowly, a warm layer of joy wrapped around her as she accepted the fact that she'd heard her husband correctly.

Her heart stopped beating for a long pause before it resumed beating at a frantic pace. Joy swept through her as she accepted what she'd heard as truth. He loved her. But why hadn't he told her over the past few weeks? The answer was as blinding as it was simple. He was uncertain of her. She'd rejected him—called him a liar. His pride would never let him reveal his heart to her a second time unless he was sure of her.

"Ye should nae be caring for the boy. The wee bairn is our blood, nae yours," Una said fiercely.

"You had nae desire to take the boy almost a year ago. So I ask you again, why this sudden need to act as his guardian?" Julian's voice was as harsh as a cold winter storm.

"I made a mistake. I thought when ye divorced..." Una's voice trailed off as if she realized she'd said more than she intended.

"And you thought I would marry again? Marry you?" Julian's contempt was almost a tangible force, and Una jerked as if he'd hit her. The woman quickly straightened her back and held her head high.

"Ye need an heir, and I can bear ye fine sons," Una declared with confidence. "I could be of use to you, Julian. I would make ye a good wife."

"I have nae need of your help or anything else. I already have a wife," Julian said with disgust.

"But she does nae plan to stay at Crianlarich, does she?" Una sneered. "Her brother has come to fetch the Mistress of Crianlarich and take her back to England. What will ye do when she leaves ye? Ye will need an heir. If ye divorce the Englishwoman, I will give ye the son ye need."

While Percy hadn't come to take her home, Patience understood how the woman could have easily jumped to the conclusion. Even though the Crianlarich staff was a small one. It was naïve to think servants didn't gossip. Una would have known there was still discord between Patience and Julian. Her gaze settled on Julian's face, which was no more readable than a marble statue.

Patience noted his color had become a shade lighter at Una's words. The strain the conversation was having on him was evident by the tight, pinched corners of his mouth and the thinness of his lips. Patience stiffened with dismay. He wasn't just angry. He was in pain.

When she'd entered his bedroom a short time ago, she'd been too distraught at Una's presence in the house to even grasp the fact that Julian had looked ill. Now she knew better. He had another headache, and the stress of his argument with Bensmore and his daughter was taking its toll.

"Well, Crianlarich? Do ye deny that ye will soon have need of a wife to give ye an heir?"

Una's calculating tone ignited a fire of indignation inside Patience. The strength of it reminded her that she was a Rockwood worthy of the maternal Scottish blood that flowed in her veins. Armed with a confidence she'd not experienced in a very long time, Patience moved deeper into the room.

"I don't know that I'll give my husband an heir, but I do know we shall raise Aiden together," Patience said firmly as both Bensmore and his daughter jerked in surprise and whirled to face her. "And he will become every bit the wonderful man my husband is."

Patience kept her eyes focused on Julian as she walked toward him. She didn't bother to glance at Una and her father as she walked past them to halt at her husband's side. All that mattered was Julian and her need to tell him how much she loved him. Julian's expression was still unreadable, but his posture had become less rigid. The moment she reached him, Patience slipped her hand into his.

Immediately, he squeezed her fingers hard. Despite the slight discomfort, she reveled in the possessive nature of the silent gesture. Slowly, she turned to face Una and her father. Although she'd not seen their initial reaction to her scars, she was certain their expressions had not changed. The older Scotsman averted his gaze from hers, but Una's lack of pity surprised Patience. The other woman simply stared at her for a long moment before she smiled with malice.

"Do you find it a blessing that Julian cannae see the hideous, revolting creature he married?"

"My scars are not who I am. But they *do* reflect my willingness to protect those I love," Patience replied before Julian could rush to her defense.

The moment she spoke, Julian went rigid then squeezed her hand so tightly she uttered a small gasp of pain. The pressure on her hand instantly eased, but her husband didn't release his hold on her.

"Dinnae ever insult my wife again, Una Bensmore." Julian's voice resounded with a quiet fury, and while he made no threat, his intent was clear. Patience experienced a flash of satisfaction as Una blanched.

"I think it's time you both left," Patience said as she glanced up at Julian and saw the pain that had made his mouth so thin it was colorless. "Arrangements can be made at a later time for you to visit with Aiden."

"We will see him now," Una said belligerently. "He is our kin, and we will nae wait for the likes of ye to decide when we can see him."

"As the Mistress of Crianlarich, this is my home, and you are a guest here." Patience narrowed her gaze at the woman. "I thank you to remember that when you speak to me."

Una's mouth fell open in astonishment at Patience's reply. Satisfied she'd silenced the woman for the moment, Patience turned her head toward Bensmore, who was eyeing her with calculation.

"Mr. Bensmore, my husband is an honorable man. He gave Caitriona his oath to care for Aiden. With my help, Julian will see to it that the child grows up happy and well cared for. We welcome you to visit whenever you like."

"I cannae accept that. My grandson belongs with his own kin," Bensmore said in a voice that indicated he would not give way in his fight to take Aiden home with him.

Patience heard Julian mutter a barely audible oath at the other man's stubbornness. Certain the Scotsman would not yield his position easily, Patience realized the only way to convince the man to leave Aidan at Crianlarich was to tell him the truth.

"Aiden *is* with his own kin, Mr. Bensmore," she said quietly as she met the older man's gaze.

"I dinnae understand," Bensmore said with a look of puzzled confusion. Beside her, Julian touched her arm with his hand.

"Patience—"

"If we are to settle the matter of Aiden's care, Mr. Bensmore must know the whole truth," she said firmly as she defied Julian's warning. Patience turned her head back to the Scotsman. "Julian is a good and honorable man, sir. He was put in a terrible position when he gave his word to your daughter. But I made no such promise."

"I dinnae understand," Bensmore said with agitated anger. "Speak your mind, woman."

"I have no gentle way to say this, Mr. Bensmore, other than to be blunt. Aiden is Julian's brother."

"Dinnae insult my intelligence, woman. That's nae possible," Bensmore bellowed in angry disbelief. "That would mean the child was Fergus's son."

"I'm sorry, but you may ask your daughter. Aiden bears the mark of a MacTavish that *all* the men in the family have." As Patience looked at Una, the color drained from the Scotswoman's face. The woman glanced at her father in obvious fear, but the man was muttering to himself as he shook his head in a dazed fashion.

"Fergus would nae betray me like that—nae with my own daughter. He was my friend."

Patience didn't say anything in response to his mutterings, and Bensmore glared at her in outrage as if he could make her confess she'd been lying. When she didn't flinch beneath his furious glare, the man's expression dissolved into one of horrified resignation. Bensmore sagged slightly where he stood as disappointment, shame, and humiliation swept across his face.

The man had done nothing to deserve his friend's betrayal, and Patience's stomach lurched as she wondered how the man would react if he learned his youngest daughter had shared the Crianlarich's bed as well. And Patience was certain he would ask that question of his youngest daughter soon enough.

Una wouldn't be able to hide her pregnancy for much longer. But whether Mr. Bensmore discovered Fergus MacTavish's second betrayal was still in question. The Scotswoman touched her father's arm in a genuine gesture of comfort. A moment later, Una fixed her green-eyed gaze on Patience. The hate in the other woman's eyes sent a shiver through Patience.

"Ye have nae heart," Una exclaimed as she glared at Patience. "Ye dinnae have to tell him who the bairn's father was."

"You left me with no choice. Julian couldn't defend himself against your accusations without breaking his oath to your sister," Patience said as she tipped her chin upward in a defiant stance. "And I refuse to stand by and let you or your father accuse or make demands of my husband when he has as much right, if not more, to raise his brother and heir to Crianlarich."

"Can the Crianlarich nae speak for himself?" Bensmore snapped. "Or has his blindness reduced him to hiding behind the skirts of a woman?"

The older man's insult made Julian stiffen beside her. Patience jerked her head to look up at him. The fury slashing its way across her husband's face made her heart skip a beat of fear for the older man. Her hand clutched at Julian's forearm, but he was either oblivious to the touch or cared nothing for the sign of caution.

"I've tolerated ye and yer daughter's slurs as a sign of yer grief for Caitriona," Julian snarled as anger thickened his brogue until it was harsh with a brutal fury. The rage rolling off of him in waves was evidence of the fiery line of Scotsmen he was descended from. "But ye will show me the respect I deserve, or I'll thrash ye as easily as I could if I were nae blind, Bensmore."

"Ye cannae blame me for questioning yer reasons to tell everyone but me about my Caitriona and Fergus," the Scotsman snapped bitterly.

"I dinnae tell everyone. Only five people know the truth, and four of them are in this room." Julian's words were a thunderous boom of outrage in the room. "Muireall is the only other person who knows, and I dinnae tell her. Muireall saw Caitriona sneaking out of our father's room early one morning. I jeopardized my own marriage keeping yer daughter's secret from Patience for almost a year. So dinnae suggest I shared Caitriona's secret without due consideration or care."

Defeat cast a shadow on the older man's weathered face, and Patience's heart went out to him. The man had not only lost a daughter, but he'd also been humiliated by a man he'd considered a friend. Worse, it was quite possible there was more humiliation and shame to come, and Patience could only hope she wasn't witness to it. In the space of a few moments, Bensmore had aged at least ten years or more since Patience had divulged the painful details of Caitriona's fall from grace.

Regret swept over her that she'd been forced to be a part of humiliating the man. Her gaze flitted to Una. To her surprise, the woman was looking at Julian. There was an air of desperation and fear radiating off the other woman. As if realizing she was being watched, Una jerked her head toward Patience. There was more than just hate in the woman's gaze. There was an anguish reflected in Una's gaze that she recognized.

Una Bensmore was in love with Julian. The knowledge sent pity streaking through Patience. It explained why the woman had tried to come between her and Julian. Yet even despite her love for Julian, Una had craved being the mistress of Crianlarich more. The old Crianlarich had made promises he'd not been able to keep. Last night she'd not been completely sure about Una and Fergus MacTavish, but now she was. No doubt, Una had thought being in Fergus's bed would secure her the status she wanted.

But her desire for the title of Mistress of Crianlarich had come at a price. Like Caitriona before her, she was carrying Fergus's child. With Julian's father dead, Una's reputation hinged on securing a husband quickly. A husband she thought she might find in Julian if he were to divorce Patience. The fact Una loved Julian could only make her situation all the more painful. As she steadily met the other woman's gaze, Una grew pale again. Fear swept across the woman's face before her expression became as stony a look as Julian's. She linked her arm through her father's and gently pulled him toward the door.

"Let us go home, father. Ye need to rest," Una said softly. "We can come back to see the child in a few days."

"Aye," Bensmore rasped and nodded his head.

Julian's hand gently tightened around Patience's as the father and daughter walked out of the room. A moment later, the front door made a loud thud as the Bensmores left the castle. Beside her, Julian made a sound of relief as he pulled Patience into his arms. His head dipped down until his mouth brushed across her forehead.

"Ye have poor timing when it comes tae telling your husband ye still love him, Mrs. MacTavish." Julian's words were gruff, and there was a deeper, much more raw emotion threading through his words.

"I've been trying to tell you ever since I came home," she said quietly as she clung to him. "I don't know that I would have had the courage to do so if I'd not heard you tell Bensmore you loved me."

"I've never stopped loving you *mo ghràdh*." Julian kissed her gently, before he pressed kiss after tender kiss to her face and repeated his declaration over and over again. As he lifted his head, Patience sighed happily.

"I think I'll have to insist you make that a daily ritual, Crianlarich, and at least three times a day."

"Just three?" he teased in a light-hearted manner.

Despite her newfound happiness, the memory of Bensmore's defeated expression filled Patience's head. She rested her head against Julian's shoulder while her hand pressed against his heart.

"I wish it hadn't been necessary to tell him the truth," she whispered. "It will be hard enough for him when he learns Una's with child."

"*With child*," he exclaimed in a low, hoarse voice. After a long pause, he drew in a harsh breath. "Is it my father's?"

"Yes," she said as she looked up at him. Anger made his features stern and implacable. "But she's not very far along. I don't think your father knew if even Una did. I'm sure he would have married her. It would have given her almost everything she wanted."

"Almost?" he rasped with a slight jerk.

"She's in love with you," Patience said as she experienced pity for the woman who'd craved things she would never have. "When I told Bensmore that all the men in your family have the same birthmark, Una was terrified. But it was when she looked at me that I knew you were the man she'd really wanted."

"I never wanted her, *mo leannan*," Julian reassured her with an intensity that made her heart soar.

"I know that now, my love. I should have believed you…trusted you," she whispered as tears welled in her eyes. Would things have been different after the fire? The answer to that question was clear. Julian would never have allowed her to hide from him.

"'Tis in the past, Patience," he bit out in a strained voice, and she lifted her head off his shoulder to look at him.

"You're in pain," she gasped with self-reproach. "Forgive me, my darling. I knew you were unwell. I should have made you go upstairs the moment the Bensmores left."

"'Tis nothing more than a little headache. I will manage as long as I dinnae let you leave my side."

Despite the dismissive note in his voice, she could still hear the note of misery in his voice. Concern spiraled through her, and she reached up to lightly stroke his temples.

Her touch caused him to wince, and Patience made a soft sound of exasperation.

"*Uncomfortable, my foot.* You're going upstairs to lie down," she said firmly. As he opened his mouth to speak, Patience pressed her index finger against his lips. "No arguments."

"I was nae going to argue," he muttered in a disgruntled manner.

"Why do I have trouble believing that," she said with amusement.

"Dinnae sass me, woman," he growled. A second later, he came to an abrupt halt with a deep groan of pain then sagged against Patience.

"*Julian,*" she exclaimed in fear.

"'Tis all right, *mo ghràdh,*" he said hoarsely. "My head is just pounding like a blacksmith hammer on an anvil."

"Perhaps you should sit down while I find Percy or Harlan to help you upstairs."

"*No,*" he snarled, then grimaced as he looked in her direction as if he could see her concerned gaze. "I can manage with your help, *mo leannan.*"

"All right." Patience sighed at his hardheaded refusal to accept help. "And you have the audacity to call me stubborn."

His only reply was a soft grunt as Patience helped guide him out into the main hall. They were halfway to the staircase when Patience heard footsteps hurrying down the stairs. She looked up towards the sound to see Harlan and Percy headed toward them.

"*Damnation, Julian,*" her brother exclaimed. "You look as pale as a ghost."

"It's a migraine," Patience said softly. She glanced up at Julian to see him flinch, then pursed her lips in a silent gesture for her brother to lower his voice. Regret immediately darkened Percy's features.

"Let me help you up the stairs, Julian," Her brother said quietly as he stepped toward his brother-in-law. "Patience is strong, but if you collapse, you're apt to send the two of you tumbling down the steps."

Patience felt Julian stiffen before he released a small noise of agreement. Percy wrapped his arm around Julian's waist. When she didn't retreat from Julian's side, her brother arched his eyebrows at her.

"You better let Dr. Branson take your place, Patience. He's stronger than you." Percy's statement caused Julian to release a low growl of protest. Patience touched his hand in a silent sign of reassurance.

"He's right, Julian. Besides, Harlan can examine you once we get you into bed."

"I dinnae need a doctor." There was an odd note of antipathy in Julian's voice that made her look at him in surprise. Bewildered, she glanced at Harlan and saw his expression of puzzlement quickly change to startled misgiving. The instant the physician realized she was watching him, he assumed his usual professional countenance. Harlan smiled reassuringly at her, but she couldn't help thinking he knew something she didn't.

"I don't think you need a doctor either, Crianlarich," the doctor said with a quiet authority he'd always used when she had been a difficult patient. "But your brother-in-law is correct. Your wife could be injured if you suddenly collapsed on the stairs. I should be the one to help Mr. Rockwood assist you up the stairs."

Julian remained silent, but after a long moment, he acquiesced to Harlan's recommendation with a grunt. Slowly, he lifted his arm off Patience's shoulder, then with a gentle nudge, he pushed her away from him. Harlan quickly took her place.

"Let's get you upstairs and into bed," the doctor said quietly as he and Percy guided Julian up the stairs. "Mrs.

MacTavish, if you don't mind, would you retrieve my medicine bag from my room?"

"Of course," she said with a nod and hurried up the stairs leaving the two men to help Julian navigate the path to the second floor.

Patience quickly found Harlan's room and collected the black leather satchel. As she returned to the corridor, she saw her brother and the doctor half-carrying Julian into his room. Her heart sank. Julian hated anyone seeing him weak or helpless under any circumstances. She bit down on her bottom lip and walked quickly down the hallway with the heavy bag Dr. Branson always carried with him.

She reached Julian's room in time for her to see Percy adjusting her husband's legs onto the bed. Patience barely looked at the doctor as she handed his bag to him and went to Julian's side. It was easy to tell Julian was in a great deal of pain simply from the way his shoulders and neck were knotted with tension. Dr. Branson bent over Julian on the opposite side of the bed to take his pulse and do a cursory examination. A low growl of irritation rumbled in her husband's chest, but it didn't stop Harlan's efficient, professional manner.

Patience took Julian's hand in hers and bent her head to kiss his fingers. In response, his hand immediately clutched hers firmly. Harlan raised his head to look at Patience.

"I have some herbs in my bag that have proven effective with some of my patients who have migraines," he said quietly. "We can mix them with hot tea. I believe the taste is far from pleasant, but it should help."

"I dinnae need anything except rest," Julian snapped hoarsely.

"Don't be ridiculous, Julian," she said in a hushed voice. "If Dr. Branson thinks it will do you good, you should try it."

"I dinnae need the mon's help." Julian's short, clipped words were filled with anger and pain. Patience winced.

"Please, Julian. Please let him help you if only to ease my mind that you'll be all right."

"Mrs. MacTavish, Percy—why don't you let me have a few moments alone with the Crianlarich. Perhaps someone could fetch some tea?"

Startled by her doctor's continued formality when addressing her, Patience looked at him in surprise. A gentle smile curved Harlan's lips as he encouraged her to do as he asked with a slight nod. Julian's hand tightened on hers, and she pressed her lips to his fingertips.

"I'll return in a few minutes, my darling," she whispered as she pulled free of his grasp and left the bed. His only response was a low groan of pain. As she left the room, Percy followed her. The door to Julian's bedroom closed behind them, and she had gotten halfway down the hall before Percy's fingers bit into her arm. As he pulled her to a halt, Patience shot a glare of exasperation over her shoulder at her brother.

"I need to fetch Julian's tea."

"In a minute, I need to talk to you first."

"What can be any more important than seeing to Julian's well-being?"

"Nothing, except the fact that you seem oblivious to the fact that Julian doesn't want Dr. Branson's skills as a physician."

"What?" She shook her head slightly at the suggestion. "Why ever not?"

"Because Branson is in love with you," Percy said quietly. "And my guess is that Julian either knows or suspects the man's secret."

"Don't be absurd." Patience waved her hand in a dismissive gesture.

"Do you really think a doctor would make a house call so far away from his practice unless the patient was very special?"

"But I never…oh, dear Lord." She stumbled over her words as she tried to comprehend what her brother had told her. "You must be wrong, Percy."

"I wish I were, and I wish I'd realized it before we left London. I would have found a reason for the man to stay behind."

"But he knows I love Julian."

"That doesn't mean he can't still love you, Patience." Her brother bowed his head for a moment as he rubbed the back of his neck then looked at her again. "Branson's a good man. He won't do anything to make you uncomfortable while we're here."

A door closing made Patience and her brother jump as they jerked their heads toward the sound. Patience's heart leapt into her throat at the sight of Harlan walking toward them. He arched his eyebrows at her and smiled.

"It appears you were delayed in securing the Crianlarich's tea." The gentle chastisement made Patience wince.

"I'm sorry…Percy was…there was a matter we needed to discuss." She sent her brother a helpless look before she turned her gaze back to Harlan.

"Ah, yes." There was a world of understanding in the doctor's short reply, and Patience flinched as he studied her carefully. "Might I have a word with you in private, Patience?"

"Of course," she said with a nod. Percy hesitated, and Patience touched his arm and directed a reassuring smile at him.

"I'll leave you to it then," her brother said with a reluctant bob of his head before he turned and walked away.

Percy had taken only a few steps when Harlan called out to him in a quiet voice.

"I think we should return to London tomorrow, Percy." When Patience and Percy looked at him in amazement, the man's mouth curled upward. "So it *is* possible that the Rockwoods and their special gifts have limitations after all."

There was no judgment in the doctor's voice, but Patience flinched nonetheless. Regret darkened Harlan's face, and he quickly stepped forward to take her hand in his.

"Forgive me, Patience." The remorse in his apology made her smile, but it quickly abated as she looked into his eyes. There was the same look of pain she'd seen in Una's green-eyed gaze earlier. Something in her expression made him shutter his gaze against her probing look. Behind her, Percy cleared his throat.

"I'll go get that tea." Her brother's words broke through the suddenly tense atmosphere, and she gently pulled her hand from Harland's.

Glancing over her shoulder, Patience watched Percy walk away for a moment before she turned back to the physician. When she faced Harlan again, she caught the fleeting glimpse of pain that she'd seen only a short moment ago. His expression quickly changed to a kindly look. It was a look that had earned him her gratitude and affection. Resignation crossed his face.

"Your expression reveals you are not entirely oblivious to my feelings where you're concerned." His direct manner reminded her of all the other times during her period of healing where he'd forced her to face the truth.

"Percy told me just a moment ago, and even he only just realized it himself this morning."

"At least I was not as transparent as I feared," Harlan said with an ironic twist of his lips. "It was a bit daunting to guard my secret when it comes to the Rockwood ability to see things others cannot."

"But you know how unreliable my gift is when it comes to people I…care about."

"At least I am afforded some small part of your heart," he murmured with a grimace at her words. Patience quickly stepped forward to touch his arm.

"You *do* have a special place in my heart, Harlan," she said gently.

"Just not in the way I'd hoped," he said with a sad smile. "The Crianlarich is a fortunate man."

"I'm the fortunate one. I simply didn't see it until it was almost too late."

"Then you've conquered all your fears?"

The question made her swallow the knot that quickly formed in her throat. The memory of Julian's demand that she share her darkest secrets with him still hung over her head like Damocles' sword. When she didn't answer, the doctor released a sigh of disappointment.

"The man deserves nothing less than your complete honesty, Patience."

"I'm barely able to admit the truth to myself."

"Sharing the darkest, most human, part of ourselves is the ultimate declaration of love," Harlan said with the quiet gentleness she'd become so familiar with. "I know you love him, but do you love him enough? Can you forgive yourself for whatever your dark secret is? Give yourself the courage to share it with him?"

"But you *know* how terrible it is," she exclaimed as her heart ached with the knowledge she was glad she hadn't been the one who'd died in the fire that night.

"No, but I have my suspicions," he said quietly as he met her gaze steadily. When she looked away from him. He caught her chin with his fingers and forced her to look at him. "You're not the only one who suffered a devastating loss the night of that tragic fire, Patience. The Crianlarich lost his wife. Isn't it time you give her back to him, even if she's a changed woman?"

"Yes," Patience whispered.

"Good," Harlan said with a slight smile. "I'll add the herbs to his tea and along with a drop or two of laudanum to help him sleep. I think he'll be much better when he wakes up."

"Thank you, Harlan. You're so very dear to me." Patience caught his hands in hers and squeezed them tight.

"Just remember that no matter what the future brings, the man loves you no matter what has come between you in the past," he said quietly as he leaned forward to kiss her brow.

Patience nodded her head and hurried back down the hall to Julian's room. In the back of her mind, Harlan's last comment triggered a warning bell she didn't comprehend. She pushed the thought aside as she entered Julian's room. Nothing mattered except her husband and making certain that he understood how desperately she loved him.

Chapter 16

The quiet chime of the mantel clock broke through Julian's sleep, and his eyes fluttered open. He experienced a sense of disorientation for a moment as he saw the brilliant white light streaming through the bedroom window. The clarity of the dark, yet vividly visible, surroundings of his bedroom highlighted by the moonlight made his heart slammed into his chest. He could see. The knowledge made his gut twist with fear. Was he dreaming?

He blinked rapidly, expecting his vision to be gone again. It remained. He shot upright in his bed with a shout of jubilation rising in his chest. Just as he was about to release the yell when a soft, delicate sound filled the air. The cry died in his throat as he recognized Patience's gentle snore. It was the most beautiful sound he'd ever heard. She was here—with him. Julian turned his head to look at his wife.

A silky web of moonlight cast a soft sheen of pale color across her face. Staring down at her, Julian's insides knotted painfully as he struggled to grasp that he was actually seeing her face for the first time in almost a year. Christ Jesus, she was the most beautiful thing he'd ever seen in his entire life. His fingers itched to reach out and touch her, but he didn't. She might awaken, and he needed time to adjust to the fact his sight had returned to him. Time to come up with a way to tell her.

His mind flashed back to the few minutes Dr. Branson had spent questioning him after Patience and her brother had left the room earlier in the day. Even though his head had been splitting with pain, he'd wanted to wring the man's neck for having come to Crianlarich. The fact that the man had come all the way from London to see Patience told Julian the doctor had feelings for his wife.

The last thing he wanted was the man anywhere near Patience. It didn't matter that she'd said she loved him. Things were still too tenuous between them. He wasn't about to give her a reason to run into the arms of another man. Julian grimaced as a slight twinge of pain tugged at his forehead. Despite his antipathy for the man, the doctor had been professional in his manner.

Branson had said it was possible his persistent headaches were brought on by stress, but that more than likely, it was the body's way of restoring his sight. Julian hadn't believed the man at the time, but now—his gaze focused on Patience's sweet face once more. God, how much he loved her. Julian allowed himself the small pleasure of pushing a lock of hair off her face. The moment he did so, she shifted her head with a quiet murmur, and he drew in a sharp breath of horror as the moonlight exposed the extent of her scars. Bile rose in his throat. God help him. What she must have suffered those months after the fire. As he studied the damage to her face, his throat closed with emotion.

He'd almost lost her.

He still could.

Fear snaked through him. The moment she learned he could see again, she might run. She'd freely admitted she wouldn't have returned to Crianlarich if he hadn't been rendered blind by the accident. Julian closed his eyes before looking down at her again. She'd thought him incapable of loving her in spite of her burns, but she was wrong. Where Patience saw ugliness, he saw the beauty of a soul willing to die for those she loved. She possessed a courage he couldn't begin to fathom.

Patience sighed again, and he quickly laid back down and closed his eyes. He had no idea how to handle the current situation. She turned over and nestled her body against his, and a mixture of happiness and dread rolled over him with the force of the rushing waters tumbling over the rocks at *Eas Falloch*.

"Julian?" His name was barely a whisper on her lips, and a small smile curved his mouth.

"Yes, *mo ghràdh*." At his quiet reply, she released a sigh. It vibrated with the quiet timbre of sheer happiness. Julian wrapped his arm around her and bent his head to brush his mouth against the top of her head.

"Is your headache better?"

"Whatever that doctor of yours gave me worked wonders." Despite his efforts to keep his voice devoid of anything other than nonchalance, he knew he'd failed when she came up on her elbow. He intentionally kept his eyes closed as he sensed her staring down at him.

"He's only a friend," she said in a hesitant voice. "I could never love him."

"And why would that be, *mo leannan*?"

"Because I love you, Julian. I belong to you, heart, body, and soul."

The touch of her lips against his made his heart thunder so loudly in his ears he thought it might be the beginnings of another headache. The moment she retreated, he pulled her back. One hand curled around her neck, he kissed her and relished the hot sweetness of her lips.

With a sigh of surrender, she willingly gave him access to the delicious heat of her mouth. She tasted of cinnamon and sugar. Julian took his time savoring her as their tongues mated in a fiery dance of passion. Under the covers, he was already naked, and he could only assume she'd undressed him as he slept. She, on the other hand, wore a nightgown of soft linen. As he deepened their kiss, his hands gathered the material at her hips and tugged the garment upward.

The need to explore every inch of her made his hands fumble slightly as she moved to help him pull her nightgown over her head and toss it aside. He rolled her onto her back, capturing her mouth before feathering kisses across her unmarred cheek. She sighed softly, and he recognized it for the happiness he was feeling as well. Ever so slowly, he trailed small kisses along the line of her jaw as he worked his way to the left side of her face. The instant his mouth touched the edge of her scarred features, she stiffened beneath him.

"*Don't*," she exclaimed softly and turned her head away to prevent him from going any further. Deliberately keeping his eyes closed, he kissed the silky-smooth cheek she offered him.

"Let me love all of you, *mo ghràdh*," he whispered as his index finger gently turned her face back toward him. "You are mine, *mo leannan*. I love everything about you. What sort of man would I be if I loved only a part of you?"

"You don't understand." Her voice was barely a whisper, and he caught the scent of her salty tears.

"Dinnae cry, my darling lass."

"I can't help it. I'm... I'm a terrible...terrible person."

"Why in God's name would ye say such a thing, let alone think it, Patience?"

He struggled not to look at her, instinctively knowing that to do so would shift the pivotal nature of their conversation. She'd said her soul was his to love and keep, but she needed to trust him completely with whatever darkness was buried inside her. When she didn't answer him, he kissed her gently. He braced himself on his side with his elbow then traced an invisible line from the base of her throat to the valley of her breasts.

"Tell me, *mo ghràdh*," he whispered. "There is nae a part of you that I could nae love, good or bad."

"You don't know what you're saying," she said in a tear-filled voice.

"Trust me, *mo leannan*. You have given your heart to me. Trust me to treasure it as I know only I can." His words went unanswered, and he pressed a tender kiss to her brow. Silently, he urged her to break down all the barriers between them.

"I survived." The words were barely audible, and he wasn't even certain she'd spoken. His next thought was that he didn't think he'd heard her correctly. With a frown, he shook his head in puzzlement.

"Aye, that you did, and I cannae say it enough as to how grateful I am for that."

"That's not what I mean," she whispered, and he frowned in confusion at the self-loathing he heard in her voice. She dragged in a quick breath of air. "I mean, I'm glad it wasn't me who died that night."

"I dinnae understand, lass. Why should ye nae be glad you lived?"

"No, I mean, I'm glad I wasn't the one who fell into the flames." The words she choked out were filled with profound guilt. The sound made a tight band encircle Julian's chest as he realized what she was trying to say.

"Patience, did you want Caleb or Devin to die?"

"*No*," she cried out with a wealth of misery.

"Do you think either of them would nae have been willing to give their lives to see you safe and unharmed?"

"But I don't think I would have been able to die for them."

The words echoed through the room like a cry of a wounded animal. The anguish in Patience's voice made Julian pull her close as he fell back into the mattress. Tears wet his chest as his wife trembled violently against him. God help him. No wonder she'd not wanted to see any of her family or him after the fire. He had no doubt her guilt had been eating her up inside.

The fact that she'd shared her darkest part of her was humbling. Unable to think of anything to say at the moment, Julian remained silent. He simply held her and allowed her to release everything she'd kept locked up for so long. Slowly her tears and trembling abated until she lay still beside him. After several moments, Julian carried her hand to his lips.

"You are wrong to think you could nae have given your life for them, *mo ghràdh*," he said quietly as he kissed her palm. "You did that the moment you insisted Caleb carry Alma to safety, knowing you would be left alone."

"I couldn't have saved Alma. Only Caleb had the strength to save her, not me."

"Aye, and yet you insisted your brother go first with the child while you remained behind in your determination to see them and the other children safe. It was nae your fault, Patience, any more than it was your fault nae to understand the *an dara sealladh*." Julian kissed the palm of her hand once more then pressed it against his cheek.

"But the children don't have their fathers," she whispered with a deep anguish that declared how big a heart she possessed.

"Aye, tis a sad thing, but tis nae wrong to be glad you are alive. I am sorry Caleb and Devin died, but I give thanks every day that you lived," he said with a feeling of selfishness. "If that is wrong or self-serving of me, I cannae help it. You are the air I breathe, the heat that warms me, and my reason for living."

Her arm tightened around his waist, and she clung to him in a manner that made his heart swell with contentment that she'd trusted him. Julian's hands caressed the curve of a soft, plump hip. In the short month, she'd been at Crianlarich, Mrs. Lester had almost fully restored his wife's curvaceous figure. She'd been far too thin when she'd returned home.

Patience moved against him, and his cock stirred to life. She shifted her body until she was pressed into his side, and her fingers skimmed their way down across his chest to his stomach. As her hand moved downward, desire made him hard as iron. The instant she touched him, he uttered a low growl of pleasure. At the sound, she kissed his shoulder with a quiet murmur he thought might have been a laugh.

His body jumped as her hand wrapped around him in a firm, pleasantly snug grip. The touch pulled a louder groan from him. A small thumb rubbed over the tip of him, smearing the wet drop she found there across his skin. Once more, her body moved against his. While her hand worked his cock, her mouth caressed his shoulder, then his chest as she inched her way downward.

Anticipation grew inside him as her mouth burned his flesh. There was a tenderness to each kiss she placed on his body. It aroused his need for her until he was painfully hard. His cock jumped then stiffened more as she blew a gentle breeze across his erection. The moment she took him in the white heat of her mouth, he shouted with pleasure. Slowly, her mouth teased and tormented him until he was certain he would spill his seed prematurely. Unwilling to deny himself the satisfaction of losing himself in her body, he pulled her upward to kiss her hard. Without prompting, she settled herself on top of him.

A soft cry of delight parted her lips as she began to rock her hips against his. Eyes still closed, he thrust upward into the sultry heat of her core. With each stroke of her body against his, he silently claimed her as his own. The sharp edge of desire tugged at him until he was oblivious to everything but her. There was only the gentle scent of her desire, the silkiness of her skin against his, and the sweet sound of her moans of delight. This time he would not let her go. He would make her see the darkness was only one facet of her. She was his, and he would not give her up.

Desire and need swept over Patience with the strength of a wild wind across the moors. The emotions swirled around her and drove her to worship his hard body with her softer one. He filled and stretched her until she thought her heart would weep for the joy their lovemaking brought her. Stroke for stroke, her body adored his with everything she had to give.

Suddenly the first ripple of a climax skimmed through her. With each passing second, the ripples grew and expanded until her entire body was on fire. The intensity of it grew until it became a tumultuous crescendo of passion and each spasm deepened the pleasure binding her to him. Beneath her, Julian groaned as her body tightened and clutched at his with a fierce intensity.

The friction of their joining pulled a cry of ecstasy from her as her body raced toward a fulfillment, unlike anything they'd shared before. It was a moment of all-consuming need that bound them together for a lifetime. The moment she reached the threshold of her release, Julian urged her to ride him hard and fast. As he thrust into her at a furious pace, it heightened the force of her own pleasure.

Just when she thought it impossible for her to reach a higher peak of delight, his body took hers higher until she cried out and shattered over him. As she clutched at his body with the strength of her climax, Julian grasped her hips, and with one last thrust, he buried himself deep inside her and throbbed with the ultimate of possessions.

Ever so slowly, her body descended from the pinnacle he'd carried her to. Her eyes opened, and she stared down at his beautiful, chiseled features. Her Highlander was the most beautiful man she'd ever seen, and she was his—she was the Highlander's woman. The moonlight caressed his noble features, and she stared down into his coffee-colored eyes. She frowned. Something was different. It was as if he could actually—her heart plummeted to her stomach as bile rose in her throat.

Dear God, he could see her. In one violent move, she recoiled and broke away from him, intent on escape. Strong hands caught her waist, and in a flash of movement, Julian pinned her beneath him. She met his gaze for a moment, then closed her eyes, unwilling to see the pity in his gaze. Stiff and motionless against him, her heart exploded in a fiery blaze that died just as quickly, leaving her with nothing but a charred object in her breast. How could she possibly stay at Crianlarich now? Her hideous scars would repulse him. A tear slipped out from under her eyelids, and a warm mouth kissed it away.

"Do you nae realize how beautiful you are *mo ghràdh*?" he asked softly as he continued to kiss the scars on her cheek. Patience shuddered at the caress but remained motionless. How could he say she was beautiful when he could see her scars now? All she wanted to do was escape this nightmare. He'd made love to her without telling her things had changed.

"You lied to me," she said in a flat voice.

"I dinnae lie to you, lass."

"Deceived then. You made love to me knowing you could see my...you didn't give me the choice..." She didn't finish her sentence as she saw anger darken Julian's face.

"The choice to do what, Patience? Run?" he snarled. "Tis time for you to stop running from me. Did you nae tell Una that your scars dinnae define who you are?"

"That was *different*," she protested vehemently.

"How?" He glared at her, silently demanding an answer.

"You couldn't see me," she whispered. She'd forgotten how relentless the man could be when he was convinced he was right. "You only saw the woman you remembered before the fire."

"God in heaven, woman, you're the one who cannae see," he ground out harshly. "I've always been able to see you, *mo leannan.*"

"You were blind," she snapped. "How could you possibly see me?"

"There other ways to see, Patience," he said quietly as he caressed the curve of her shoulder before his hand glided down to the scarred patches of skin on her arm. "My hands saw you every time I touched your scars. They told me how you were hurting inside."

She remained frozen as his fingers lightly stroked one of the places where the fire had burned her. Unable to respond, she tried to keep breathing as his mouth caressed the inside of her wrist before his lips made their way up over the damaged skin of her arm.

"I see every inch of you simply when I breathe." There was an almost hypnotic note in his voice that slowly eased some of her tension. "Just the scent of you tells me when you're happy or when your body is ready for mine. My eyes aren't the only way I know or see you, *mo leannan.*"

"But…" her voice died as she flinched at the reality he had already seen her ravaged skin, and yet he seemed unaffected by the extent of her injuries.

"Dinnae argue with me, Patience Rockwood MacTavish," he growled. "Dinnae tell me about your scars. I dinnae see them."

"Don't be ridiculous," she snapped, angered that he could suggest her burnt skin was invisible to the human eye.

"Are you calling me a liar, Patience?" The dangerous note in his voice made her flinch. Many things could anger

Julian, but someone questioning his word was perhaps one of the worst.

"No," she said as she turned her head away from him.

Firm fingers gripped her chin, and he turned her head so her scarred face was fully displayed in the moonlight. She trembled and tried to jerk free of his grasp, but his grip was unrelenting. Slowly, Julian leaned forward and brushed the burnt flesh of her cheek with his lips.

"Where you see scars, I see a woman willing to give her life for those she loves. Where you see burnt flesh, I see the courage of a woman who chose to fight and live. I dinnae see your scars, *mo ghràdh*. I see only the heart of a woman worthy of the title, Mistress of Crianlarich."

Julian's lips deliberately caressed the rough skin of her burned cheek. His kiss was reverent, and tears flowed down her cheek as she trembled in the face of his loving devotion. Patience cupped his face in her hands and returned his kiss. Slowly lifting his head, Julian studied her intently. When she didn't say a word, a contented expression settled on his face, and his dark brown eyes gleamed with the bright edge of satisfaction in the moonlight.

"At last, my wife has learned nae to argue with me." The confidence in his voice made her eye him with resigned amusement before the image of an out-of-control blaze flitted through her head.

"You can't expect me to forget everything that's happened since…since that terrible night."

"No, *mo leannan*, you will nae forget. But I'll remind you every day and night that your scars reflect the beauty of your heart and soul." The sincerity in his voice made Patience's heart ache with love and happiness for having married a man who loved with such depth of emotion.

"I love you, Julian. I love you so much," she said softly.

Her hand curled around the nape of his strong neck, and she tugged his head down to hers. Tenderly and lovingly,

Patience kissed him with all the love filling her heart. It would take time for her to totally accept Julian's reassurance that the scars she saw in her mirror were the same scars Julian saw. But she knew his love would help her overcome that hurdle.

As their kiss deepened, Patience experienced a familiar need stirring inside her. Desire flared in her veins until her blood ran hot and thick like molten lava. Julian broke their kiss and raised his head.

"I love you, *mo ghràdh*. Dinnae ever forget that." The authoritative note in his voice emphasized he intended to ensure she had no choice in the matter. It was a command she would have no difficulty obeying. Patience smiled slightly as she shifted her hips against his growing erection.

"Then show me, my love," she whispered enticingly. Passion warmed Julian's sharp, angular features as he proceeded to do as she ordered in a way only a Highlander could.

The End

Thank you for reading The Highlander's Woman! I hope you enjoyed it. If you did, please help other people find this book by writing a review on BookBub and Amazon.

Read on for a special preview of Redemption. Percy is one of my favorite Rockwood heroes.

Redemption Preview

Prologue

June 1898

"*D̶amn it to hell*," Percy Rockwood muttered under his breath as he emerged from the well-lit New Library into the near darkness of the British Museum's main reading room. In the shadows, he made out the night watchman sprawled on the floor a short distance away.

Afraid for the man's safety, Percy crossed the carpeted floor of the large room and knelt beside the man. Fingers pressed into the side of the police officer's neck, Percy breathed a sigh of relief. Alive, but out cold. A small sound in the distance echoed in the large, oval-shaped room museum patrons used daily.

It was the same noise he'd heard while reading the latest Coptic scrolls Wallis Budge had brought back from Egypt. Although how he'd not heard Smythe crash to the floor was surprising. The officer was a burly man, and he could only surmise that the guard's assailants had eased him to the floor after subduing the guard.

Once more, the sound whispered through the air. Percy cocked his head to one side and determined the noise was coming from the Egyptian wing. Without thinking twice, he pulled a small pistol out of his coat pocket. He'd taken to carrying the weapon since he'd had his vision two weeks ago. The vivid imagery of his body lying prone in a dark place wasn't the type of omen a Rockwood who possessed the *an dara sealladh* ignored.

Over the years, he'd come to accept the fact that he'd inherited a small amount of the family's gift of sight. But the *an dara sealladh* seldom offered up as much detailed graphic information as his latest vision had. The woman's face had haunted him for the past two weeks. Her features had been hazy at best., but it had been impossible to forget her eyes. They'd been the dark color of wild violets that grew in the meadows around Melton Park.

He had no idea what the vision meant. Even now, he wondered what the connection was between the woman and the image of him lying on a dark floor. But it was the hopelessness Percy had seen in her beautiful eyes he couldn't forget. She was in trouble. He was certain of it. His tread quiet and cautious, Percy approached the wide archway leading into the Egyptian section of the museum. His back hugging the cold stone of the ceiling-high columns marked with hieroglyphics, Percy peered around the edge of the cylindrical architecture.

At the far end of the north wing, he saw a light where the pendant of Nephthys was displayed. Other than a glass-enclosed display case and the two policemen who guarded the museum night and day, there was no other protection for the precious artifact.

Anger made his jaw hardened. He'd warned Budge this might happen, and the director had agreed. Percy didn't enjoy being right, but he would love to be a fly on the wall when Budge lambasted the board for their resistance to reinforce security.

A sharp crack followed by the brittle sound of splintering glass confirmed his worst fears. Someone was stealing the pendant. Slowly, he made his way past one of the mummy displays as he headed toward the end of the exhibition hall. The low murmur of voices floated toward him, but it was impossible to hear what was being said.

Percy crept forward, sidestepping the narrow stream of moonlight that had found its way past the clouds and through the glass ceiling of the large exhibition chamber. Ahead of him, he saw a small movement in the shadowy recesses of the exhibition hall.

"Whoever you are, come out now before I shoot," he said quietly.

The sudden loud click of a pistol being cocked made Percy draw in a sharp hiss of air between his teeth. Whoever they were, they'd just called his bluff as nicely as if they were playing a cutthroat game of brag.

"Then you and I are at an impasse, sir. There are *three* of us, and just one of you. I believe the odds are considerably more in my favor than in yours."

The disembodied voice sounded different from what one might expect a thief to sound like. Perplexed, he frowned at the cultured inflections in the voice. It echoed with the intonations of someone of noble birth.

A shadow emerged from the pitch dark into the area just on the edge of the patch of moonlight. Percy narrowed his gaze at the dark figure. The fellow stood just a foot shorter than him and seemed more round than angular. A youngster, no doubt, but Percy knew better than to discount his opponent.

"If you're willing to leave the necklace you've taken, I'll not prevent you from escaping."

"Unfortunately, that's not possible." The shadow's soft voice reverberated in the darkness with a distinct note of regret. Percy scowled in the direction of the voice.

"You'll find it incredibly difficult to sell the pendant."

"Perhaps, but that's my employer's dilemma. Not mine."

Muscles taut with tension, Percy watched the dark figure take two steps toward him. Overhead, the clouds drifted farther apart, and the narrow stream of moonlight widened its path across the museum floor. The increased amount of light outlined Percy's opponent more clearly.

A black mask covered half the man's face, and although he was in process of committing a crime, there was a politeness to his manner that startled Percy. The thief projected an image of respectable gentility, despite the patches covering his coat and pants.

In his swift appraisal of the man, Percy realized the distance between them was smaller than he thought. He took a step forward, and the other man leveled his gun at him.

"Do not mistake me for a fool, sir." The sharp words made Percy stiffen. A woman—a well-bred woman. The familiarity he'd recognized in her voice earlier was rooted in his knowledge of the female sex. He'd heard the soft, womanly cadence and pitch of her voice, but had unconsciously dismissed them. He took a step closer.

"Stop." Was that a hint of fear in her command?

"I'm afraid I can't do that," he murmured with growing irritation. "I can't allow the pendant to leave the museum."

"Then you're a fool. Your life is far more valuable than a trinket, no matter how old." Her sharp words made him frown. She sounded almost worried for his safety.

In the next instant, the premonition sailed through him, and he uttered a soft oath beneath his breath. Someone was approaching him from behind. In a swift move, Percy sprang forward. Behind him, a loud pistol shot cracked the air. The bullet was more of a sting than anything else as it entered his back. The impact of it made him stumble, and as he sank to his knees, she was there to catch him.

"You are a reckless fool," she chastised him in a voice filled with agonized regret.

"It's a family trait," he rasped as pain seeped its way across his back. He raised his head to look into her eyes and went rigid.

"*Bloody hell, it's you.*" The tension in her body pulsed its way into his.

"How do you know me?" she whispered as her violet eyes widened with horror.

The dark purple hue of her eyes was even more beautiful than in his vision. His thoughts suddenly became cluttered with all manner of images. The fire at Westbrook Farms, his grieving family at the cemetery at Caleb's and Devin's funerals. Sebastian glaring at him, and Aunt Matilda with dismay darkening her warm gaze. One by one, the faces of his family drifted past his eyes. He was dying. It had never occurred to him that his vision would have such a negative outcome. Percy had expected to be knocked unconscious, not shot. Violet eyes shimmered with unshed tears of sorrow and pain as they met his.

"I'm so sorry."

"I don't understand…my vision…" he mumbled as the pain intensified. He moved slightly, and it increased the searing pain in his back. On the edge of consciousness, Percy closed his eyes and slumped deeper into her arms.

"Leave him."

The harsh, uncultured voice penetrated the cloud of pain pulling Percy under. Desperately, he fought to remain conscious. If he lived, he needed to remember the man's voice and everything he could about this miserable incident.

"Why did you shoot him?" The woman's question reverberated with fierce anger. "You could have knocked him out like you did the guard."

"Don't matter none now, does it? The bloke is dead."

"You're a bastard, Ruckley."

"So you keep saying, my poppet," the man said in a salacious manner. It made Percy long to get up and pummel the son of a bitch until the man begged for mercy. The thought evaporated as pain tugged him closer to the abyss.

"One day, I *will* kill you, Ruckley."

The anger and hopelessness in her voice was the last thing Percy heard as a yawning hole opened up. He struggled not to fall off the cliff into the darkness below. But it was the touch of a warm hand on his cheek that told him he had to live. She needed his help. It was the last thought sinking its way into his head before the black engulfed him.

Chapter 1

Melton Park,
June 1899

Y ou look lovely, Rhea. I'm glad I insisted we take an extra day to visit Madame Solange before we returned to Green Hill House two months ago," her aunt said with a smile as their carriage rolled up the long drive to Melton Park Manor.

"It was an unnecessary extravagance." Rhea softened her reply with a smile. "But thank you. At least I have an opportunity to wear it."

"It was nothing of the sort. It makes me happy to see you looking so beautiful. When I think about the day Mr. Ashford brought you and Arianna to Fremont Place…" The moment her aunt's voice faded into nothing, Rhea reached across the space between them to touch her aunt's arm in a reassuring gesture.

"It's in the past, Aunt Beatrice. All of it," she said in a firm voice as she smiled at her aunt. The older woman nodded as she squeezed Rhea's hand.

"Agreed," Beatrice Fremont said with quiet determination. "Now that Arianna is firmly settled in her role as Viscountess Sherrington, I think it's time we concern ourselves with your prospects."

Rhea ignored the comment and turned her head away to look out the carriage window. A small lake shimmered beneath the moon, while the rolling landscape made her believe daylight would reveal magnificent green pastures with wildflowers adding splashes of color.

Arianna had been fortunate to find a man willing to love her in spite of the horrific years they'd spent under Ruckley's thumb. Rhea had done her best to protect her sister while Ruckley had controlled their lives, but their past was grim enough to prevent even a commoner from marrying her sister, let alone a viscount. Despite all the odds, Arianna had found happiness, and that was all that mattered. She, on the other hand, had no intention of surrendering to a man ever again.

"You might wish to ignore me, Rhea, but I don't believe your heart is made of ice. It can't be when I see you with the children." Her aunt's words made Rhea turn her head to eye her relative with annoyance.

"I thought we'd settled this. I will *never* marry," she replied coolly.

"No matter how terrible the past, denying yourself happiness is wrong, Rhea."

"I'm quite happy with my life the way it is now," she bit out between clenched teeth before she looked back out the window and into the darkness.

Obviously, it would take a great deal of time to convince Aunt Beatrice that marriage was out of the question. Nothing would change Rhea's mind when it came to the subject. The thought of her every move being controlled again made her skin grow cold. She refused to ever go back to that type of servitude.

Marriage would be no better than what she'd experienced at Ruckley's hand. It didn't matter how many times she'd stood up to the man. Ruckley had found a way to torment and control her. His threats to Arianna and the children had always made her yield to whichever of his dictates she'd failed to circumvent.

The image of Ruckley taking coin from a man who had paid to bed her made Rhea's stomach lurch as a familiar queasiness swept over her. Fingers curled into tight fists in her lap, she fought back the nausea that always came when thinking about the past.

The soft summer night air filled her lungs as she drew in a deep breath. That life was behind her now. She and Arianna had escaped. She'd even made progress beginning to bring several of the children with them to Green Hill House. They were out of Ruckley's reach. A voice in the back of her head told her none of them would be safe until Ruckley was dead.

The small carriage rolled to a stop in front of the Earl and Countess of Melton's country manor, and moments later they entered the large house. The sound of a Scottish reel drifted out into the main foyer, and Rhea found herself tapping her foot on the marble floor as they waited in the receiving line. When she was a child, she'd always loved dancing with her mother. Thomas Bennett had disapproved of dancing, so her mother had waited for those moments when Rhea's father wasn't in the house to whirl her and Arianna around the parlor. In the receiving line in front of her, Beatrice Fremont offered the Countess of Melton a small curtsey.

"Thank you for coming, Mrs. Fremont," the countess said with a warm smile as she turned toward Rhea. "Welcome, Miss Bennett. I'm so pleased you could join us."

"Thank you for your kind invitation, my lady," Rhea said as she curtseyed. The countess nodded as she gestured toward the man at her side. "Have either of you met my husband, Lord Melton?"

As her aunt greeted the earl, fear spread an icy layer over Rhea's skin. She barely heard her aunt introduce her as she met the earl's gaze. Dear God, was it possible the earl was the man Ruckley had shot last year in the museum? Lord Melton's welcoming smile faded as puzzled amusement made him arch an eyebrow at her.

"Good evening, Miss Bennett."

The moment he spoke, she knew he wasn't the stranger she'd left to die on that cold museum floor. Aware she'd been staring, Rhea's cheeks grew hot.

"Good evening, Lord Melton. Please accept my best wishes for a happy birthday."

"Thank you," he replied with a congenial grin.

With a forced smile, she turned away from the earl and followed her aunt deeper into the ballroom.

"What's wrong, dearest?" Beatrice asked as she opened lace fan with an expert snap of her hand and waved it in front of her to create a soft breeze. "You look as though you've seen a ghost."

"It's nothing. Just a bad memory." Her reply caused a pained look to cross her aunt's features. Rhea caught Beatrice's hand in hers and shook her head with a gesture of reassurance. "The past can't find me here—not this far away from London."

"*Oh dear God*," her aunt gasped, with a distinct note of panic filling her voice. Concerned, Rhea stiffened at the apprehension on Beatrice's pale features.

"Are you all right, Aunt Beatrice?"

"I...yes. I'm...I'm quite all right."

The agitated response made Rhea frown. Before she could probe for a more definitive explanation, a gentleman in was standing in front of them. He offered a smile to Rhea before bowing in her aunt's direction.

"Good evening, ladies. Beatrice, you're as lovely as I remember."

When her aunt didn't extend her arm, the gentleman reached out to capture Beatrice's hand and carried it to his lips. His mouth lingered on Beatrice's fingers for a fraction longer than was respectable, and her aunt breathed in a sharp breath as she tugged free of his grasp.

"Lionel...I hadn't heard you'd returned from the continent." Her aunt's breathy response made Rhea glance at the woman. The pink in her aunt's cheeks made Rhea bite back a smile.

"And this must be your daughter. The likeness is uncanny." A hard glint flashed in the man's dark eyes as he smiled at Rhea, then pinned his gaze on Beatrice. All the color was gone from her aunt's face before she denied the assumption with a shake of her head.

"No, this is my niece, Rhea Bennett. Rhea, may I present Lionel Nesfield."

"A pleasure, Miss Bennett. And it's Viscount Foxworth now," he murmured as he kissed Rhea's hand before his attention returned to Beatrice, who eyed him with compassionate sorrow.

"I *am* sorry, Lionel. I hadn't heard that your father was gone."

"It happened a few months ago. I had a great deal of estate business to attend to before I could...renew old acquaintances." Something in the man's voice said Lord Foxworth was referring to Beatrice in particular. With a wicked smile he extended his hand to Rhea's aunt.

"I believe you still owe me a dance from the last time we saw each other," the viscount murmured. Beatrice hesitated slightly before she accepted his hand.

As she watched the couple begin to dance around the room, some of Rhea's tension eased. When she and Arianna had been reunited with their aunt less than a year ago, it had taken Rhea time to feel comfortable at the few soirees her aunt insisted they attend. She still found social occasions somewhat off-putting, but tonight London and the past seemed so far away. For the first time in a while she found herself enjoying the music and the room's cheerful atmosphere.

In one corner of the room, she saw two men flanking a woman of medium height. Rhea eyed the trio with curiosity. It was obvious the men were standing guard over the woman, but she couldn't discern why. Like Lord Melton, both men were dressed in formal Prince Charlie jackets and kilts. Tonight was the first time she'd ever seen any man wearing formal Scottish dress, and it was impressive.

Aunt Beatrice had mentioned the other day that the earl's family was descended from the Stewart line of Highlanders. The woman standing between the two men wore a pale yellow gown with a dark red tartan sash attached to her left shoulder. The two men exuded a commanding, protective nature as they greeted several guests who'd approach the trio. As the man to the woman's right turned his head to speak with someone, Rhea sucked in a sharp breath of horror and froze. Dear Lord, it was him.

A relief, unlike anything she'd ever known, spiraled through her. He was alive. In the next breath, she dismissed the notion. She'd already mistaken the earl for the man in the museum. The man Ruckley had shot was dead. His death was something she bore as much responsibility for as Ruckley, if not more, because the stranger might have survived if she'd stood up to Ruckley. Tonight she was allowing an over-active imagination and wishful thinking get the better of her.

She dragged in a deep gulp of air as she tried to dismiss the possibility the stranger Ruckley had shot was the man across the room. But with each subsequent breath, she became all the more convinced he was the man she'd left to die on the British Museum floor. It wasn't just his face that was so familiar. It was the way he moved. Everything about him reflected the same fluid power she'd observed in him a year ago in the museum's dark hall.

Almost as if aware he was under scrutiny, the man swung his gaze across the room. The moment their eyes met, an arrogant amusement curved his firm lips as he studied her with blatant curiosity. Rhea tried to look away from him, but there was something hypnotic in his gaze. It became difficult to breathe, and as his eyes narrowed, panic lashed out at her.

Dear Lord, had he recognized her? No. That wasn't possible. She'd been wearing a mask that night in the museum. In the back of her head, a small voice reminded her of that heart-stopping moment when he'd looked into her eyes. The haunting memory of his exclamation and the way he'd stared at her in recognition still had the ability to make her tremble. Fear crashed through her as she dragged her gaze away from the stranger. What was she going to do?

In a single heartbeat, her panic was gone, and a calm serenity wrapped around her like a warm cloak. It was the same collected composure she'd learned to maintain while she'd been at Ruckley's beck and call. It subdued her fear and panic. There was no reason this stranger might connect a street criminal with Miss Rhea Bennett, let alone think they were the same person.

Rhea retreated into a corner where it was possible to watch the guests while going unnoticed. Although her foot continued to tap in time with the music, she was content to watch Lord Foxworth spin her aunt around the dance floor for a second dance. A few moments later, Lady Melton appeared at her side and greeted her with a mischievous smile. As she gestured at the man behind her, Rhea froze.

"Miss Bennett, my brother-in-law has asked me for an introduction." Lady Melton glanced over her shoulder with a smile before looking at Rhea again. "He noticed you weren't dancing and insisted on rectifying that problem. Miss Bennett, allow me to introduce Mr. Percy Rockwood. Percy, Miss Rhea Bennett."

"A pleasure, Miss Bennett."

Rhea tried to swallow the knot swelling her throat shut, while struggling not to run. She forced a smile to her lips, and nodded her head in a polite greeting.

"Mr. Rockwood," she murmured.

"I promised my husband this next dance, Miss Bennett, but I leave you in good hands. Percy is an excellent dancer."

With an affectionate peck to her brother-in-law's cheek and a smile, the countess walked away. Silence filled the air in Lady Melton's wake, and when Percy didn't speak, Rhea turned her attention back to the dancers, all the while her mind screamed at her to flee.

"Shall we?" Rhea jumped and stared down at his strong hand. She dismissed his offer with a hard shake of her head.

"I think it best you find another partner, Mr. Rockwood. I'll only step on your toes."

"I insist," he said with a firmness that made her heart skitter out of control.

In the space of a second, he'd gone from charming rogue to a man unwilling to accept her refusal. Percy's hand wrapped around her wrist, and he led her toward the dance floor. Caught off guard, Rhea gasped at his autocratic action, but it was the electric charge streaking up her arm that prevented her from freeing herself. When they reached the dance floor, Percy pulled her into his arms. A waltz was playing, and with a skillful move, he swung her into the crowd of dancers.

Despite her trepidation, it was impossible to ignore the way her body reacted to him. It was as if every inch of her was on fire. The sensation sent tension streaking through her. A subtle woodsy aroma mixed with frankincense and another spice created an exotic, almost hedonistic, scent in her nose. It was a warm smell that coaxed her to breathe him deep into her senses.

Everything about him was raw, potent male. As her eyes met his, Rhea's heartbeat skittered out of control at the fiery anger in his dark brown gaze.

"Your eyes are quite lovely, Miss Bennett," he murmured. "In fact, they are quite unforgettable."

Rhea's heart sank as a wave of nausea rolled through her. He knew. Somehow he'd recognized her from across the room. She didn't know how, but he knew she'd been in the British Museum a year ago. Rhea stumbled only to have a steely arm lift her off her feet for a brief moment before setting her down once more to continue their dance.

"Have I said something to upset you, Miss Bennett?"

"Not at all. I did warn you that I have a tendency to step on toes," she replied breathlessly while struggling to maintain her composure.

"Yes, you did," he said with sardonic amusement. His tone said he knew she was lying. "Tell me, Miss Bennett, have you ever been to the British Museum?"

Panic sliced through her with all the force of a sword cutting its way through her flesh. The moment her body tensed and she prepared to free herself, he pulled her deeper into his embrace. Fear sped through her as she realized judgement was at hand.

Other Titles by Monica Burns

THE RECKLESS ROCKWOODS SERIES
Obsession #1
Dangerous #2
The Highlander's Woman #3
Redemption #4
The Beastly Earl #5

THE RECKLESS ROCKWOODS NOVELS
The Rogue's Offer
The Rogue's Countess

SELF-MADE MEN SERIES
His To Command #1 (Novella)
His Mistress #2

TIME TRAVEL
Forever Mine

STAND ALONE TITLES
Kismet
Mirage
Pleasure Me
A Bluestocking Christmas
Love's Portrait
Love's Revenge

THE ORDER OF THE SICARI SERIES
Assassin's Honor #1
Assassin's Heart #2
Inferno's Kiss #3

About The Author

Monica Burns is a bestselling author of spicy historical and paranormal romance. She penned her first romance at the age of nine when she selected the pseudonym she uses today. Her historical book awards include the 2011 RT BookReviews Reviewers Choice Award and the 2012 Gayle Wilson Heart of Excellence Award for Pleasure Me.

She is also the recipient of the prestigious paranormal romance award, the 2011 PRISM Best of the Best award for Assassin's Heart. From the days when she hid her stories from her sisters to her first completed full-length manuscript, she always believed in her dream despite rejections and setbacks. A workaholic wife and mother, Monica is a survivor who believes every hero and heroine deserves a HEA (Happily Ever After), especially if she's writing the story.

Find all the ways you can connect with Monica on the next page.